Carly turned toward the closet as she was speaking, and that was when Shane saw the back of her dress.

Or rather, what wasn't there. And before he knew it, he'd spoken her name in a voice that couldn't hide his desperate need.

She froze for a second, then faced him. And the invitation in her eyes was unmistakable. "I'm not really hungry," she whispered. "Except..." She caught her breath, then let it out, the faintest tremor running through her body. "For you, Shane," she finished on a rush. "Except for you."

He closed his eyes, then opened them again. And suddenly Carly was in his arms, her lips locked onto his. A rushing sound filled his ears, and he realized it was his blood coursing through his veins as his heart pounded furiously. He let Carly go only long enough to fight out of his overcoat and jacket, dropping them unheeded on the floor. Then his arms closed around her again.

Be sure to check out the previous volumes in the Man on a Mission miniseries!

Man on a Mission: These heroes, working at home and overseas, will do anything for justice, honor...and love.

* * *

Dear Reader,

When I wrote *Cody Walker's Woman*, I gave my heroine, Keira Jones, four brothers—all older, all former US Marines and all playing a role (good and bad) in shaping the woman she was.

Then I wrote *Alec's Royal Assignment* and *Liam's Witness Protection*, the stories of two of Keira's brothers. But even as I was writing Alec's and Liam's stories, in the back of my mind was Shane. The eldest. The toughest. The strongest influence on all his younger siblings.

But Shane wasn't easy to get to know—he eluded me for the longest time. It wasn't until a personal family crisis that Shane became real to me, and I knew what could make a nearly invincible man vulnerable. Then I just *had* to write his story.

After I understood Shane I realized I needed to find a tough-as-nails heroine to match him, but one with a tender, loving heart hidden beneath that tiger-shark exterior. Along came Carly Edwards, just in the nick of time. Carly wasn't easy to get to know, either, because there's nothing of Carly in me (I wish!). Once I accepted that, however, I suddenly knew who Carly was—a woman whose private pain once made the six-o'clock news...but never again.

Shane and Carly fought the odds and won, and in doing so won my heart. Isn't that what we all look for in a hero and heroine? Isn't that why we read romance?

I love hearing from my readers. Please email me at AmeliaAutin@aol.com and let me know what you think.

Amelia Autin

KILLER COUNTDOWN

Amelia Autin

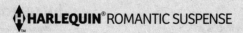

HARLEQUIN® ROMANTIC SUSPENSE

ISBN-13: 978-0-373-28146-6

Killer Countdown

Copyright © 2016 by Amelia Autin Lam

Printed in U.S.A.

Award-winning author **Amelia Autin** is an inveterate reader who can't bear to put a good book down... or part with it. She's a longtime member of Romance Writers of America, and served three years as its treasurer. Amelia resides with her PhD engineer husband in quiet Vail, Arizona, where they can see the stars at night and have a "million-dollar view" of the Rincon Mountains from their backyard.

Books by Amelia Autin

Harlequin Romantic Suspense

Man on a Mission

Cody Walker's Woman
McKinnon's Royal Mission
King's Ransom
Alec's Royal Assignment
Liam's Witness Protection
A Father's Desperate Rescue
Killer Countdown

The Coltons of Texas

Her Colton P.I.

Silhouette Intimate Moments

Gideon's Bride
Reilly's Return

Visit the Author Profile page at Harlequin.com.

For the doctors, nurses, technicians, nursing assistants and everyone at the Mayo Clinic in Phoenix, Arizona, who exemplify what medicine can and should be for patients and their families. Thank you from the bottom of my heart. For my stepson, Chris Lam, who will soon be a doctor himself and is already a great diagnostician because he asks the right questions and listens to the answers. And for Vincent...always.

Prologue

Shane Jones, junior senator from Colorado, lay in his hospital bed in the Mayo Clinic in Phoenix, Arizona, staring in disbelief at the barrage of doctors and interns assembled in his private room. He could have gone anywhere for medical testing and diagnosis—and had, with no results—but he'd chosen the Mayo Clinic Hospital when a doctor friend from his days in the Marine Corps had recommended it. No other medical professional he'd consulted had ever even *heard* of his symptoms, much less had been able to put a name to them. But the doctors here had.

"Epilepsy?" he repeated, stunned. He still couldn't seem to wrap his head around the diagnosis. "But…I don't have seizures. All I have are these little episodes where I suddenly feel chilled for no reason. That's all. It can't be epilepsy."

Dr. Rachel Mattingly, the primary neurologist on Shane's case, smiled gently. "I understand you're upset at this diagnosis. But what you call 'chilling' episodes are actually small seizures. We can't know for certain, but we can surmise the traumatic brain injury you received five years ago was the initial trigger. Scar tissue on the left side of your brain is clearly visible on your MRI, which is where you were injured in that bomb blast."

Shane touched the left side of his head, where his short brown hair was barely long enough to hide the long, white scar from where the brain surgeons had operated on him five years ago. At the time he'd just been grateful he hadn't lost a limb or suffered any substantive cognitive loss as a result of his unthinking actions that day—although his brain injury had been bad enough for the Marine Corps to honorably retire him via a medical discharge.

Losing his home in the Corps—losing *everything* for which he'd worked his whole adult life—had devastated Shane at first, but then he'd thrown himself into politics with the same dedication and fervor he'd once had for the Marine Corps. But now…if Dr. Mattingly was right, all that was at an end. Who'd ever heard of a politician with epilepsy? There might be some, but damned few. Hell, he couldn't even control the electrical impulses in his own brain. How could he expect the voters to trust him to play a role in controlling the country?

Marsh Anderson bought himself a cup of coffee from the hospital cafeteria, then brought it out to the lobby to drink it where he could watch the comings and goings of Senator Jones's staff, whom he now knew by sight.

The senator had been here for four days already, and Marsh wondered how much longer it would be.

He had no idea why the senator was here...just that he was. HIPAA laws being what they were, hospitals were damned leery about releasing *any* information on a patient, and Marsh wasn't about to draw attention to himself by asking anyway. He'd find out when Senator Jones found out. Or rather, when the man's staff found out. All he knew was that the senator was here "for observation." But why he was here wasn't relevant anyway—all Marsh really needed to know was when he was going to be released.

Soon, I hope, he thought. He was getting tired of hanging around.

He'd tracked the senator all the way from DC, waiting for his chance. But he wasn't a lunatic—Marsh had no intention of turning this into a suicide mission. He'd had plenty of time with nothing to do but think about this hit, and his plan would be foolproof before he put it into motion. Senator Jones would die...and Marsh would get clean away. Then disappear, as if he'd never existed.

Chapter 1

Nurse Cindy Watkins handed Shane a little paper cup containing one lone pill and a cup of water from the fresh pitcher she'd brought in with his medicine. "Here you go, Senator."

She waited patiently while Shane stared at the first dose of the medication he would be tied to—assuming this one worked for him without too many negative side effects—for the rest of his life. Assuming he had a rest of his life…with epilepsy.

He breathed deeply, then abruptly tipped the pill into his mouth and swallowed it with a swig of ice water. The nurse patted his arm in a motherly fashion, saying, "We understand, Senator. We really do. It's not an easy diagnosis to accept. But you're lucky—Dr. Mattingly is just about the best neurologist in the country. If she says it's epilepsy, then that's what it is."

When Shane didn't respond, she volunteered, "I think you share the general public's misunderstanding about epilepsy. But look at it this way—at least now you *know*. And it can be controlled."

"Yeah," Shane agreed drily. "At least now I know."

"Can I get you anything before I go? Do you want me to call one of your aides?" Shane shook his head. "Lunch will be here in less than an hour," she added, patting his arm again. "Why don't you try to get a little rest in the meantime? I know we didn't let you get a lot of sleep last night, what with the stress test and all."

"Yeah, maybe I will try that." Shane lay back against the pillows and closed his eyes. There was no way he could sleep; he just wanted to be alone. And if that meant pretending to be asleep...

When he was finally alone, Shane opened his eyes and stared at the wall opposite him, his thoughts in turmoil. He gave himself ten minutes to feel sorry for himself. Then he ruthlessly shut down the self-pity, the way he'd ruthlessly shut down other emotions in his life when they'd threatened to overwhelm him—put them into a little box he could lock away and not think about. Including the devastating pain caused by the death of his wife fifteen years earlier. His pregnant wife. His unborn son.

He could still remember the last time he'd seen Wendy alive—seven months pregnant and glowing. Excited about the upcoming baby shower her friends on the base were throwing for her.

And he could still remember being called to the morgue when her body had been found—he'd barely recognized her.

He hadn't cried, though. Not then, and not at her

funeral. He'd turned that grief inward, into an implacable determination to find the terrorists responsible… and he had.

He absently rubbed his fingers against the scar tissue on the left side of his skull, until a friendly voice over the loudspeaker reminded him not to scratch his head. "Sorry," he told the disembodied voice of the technician monitoring his room via the video camera mounted on the ceiling facing his hospital bed. "I forgot."

He rarely thought about how he'd gotten the scar anymore—except when he'd been on the campaign trail and some reporter asked him about it point blank. He'd done his best to put the incident at the bookstore out of his mind for two reasons: it had just about killed him to lose the life he had in the Corps…and the pregnant woman he'd saved had somehow reminded him of Wendy.

Even waking up in the hospital afterward with his mother and sister dozing at his bedside was something he tried not to think about too often, because it reminded him of things he wanted to forget. His mother had reacted the way most mothers would when their firstborn child had done his damnedest to get himself killed—she alternately cosseted and scolded. His sister, Keira, on the other hand had smiled at him in perfect understanding of his actions. "Good job, Shane," she'd whispered when their mother was out of the room. "Good job."

But he couldn't let himself dwell on what he'd done—and the unexpected aftereffects. *What's done is done*, he reminded himself. *Where do I go from here?*

Back to Washington, DC, for now. The Senate was in recess this third week of February—which was why he'd picked this time to check himself into the Mayo

Clinic on the advice of the doctors here—but it would be back in session next week. So far no news agency had discovered where he was, and he'd like to keep it that way. Not that he had any intention of keeping this diagnosis a secret from his constituency the next time he ran for reelection.

Assuming he ran for reelection.

In the meantime, the fewer people who knew about this, the better. He wasn't even going to share the news with his aides, although he'd have to think of something plausible to tell them. Not that he would outright lie, but he didn't want to put any of them in the position of having to prevaricate with the press, should they discover he'd been here in the hospital and besiege them with questions.

If any reporter asked him, he'd stonewall because it wasn't anyone's business but his own—unless and until he decided to run for reelection—and he didn't want people looking at him differently. Didn't want people making excuses for him or feeling sorry for him. The doctors had assured him the seizures could be controlled with medication, so there was no way it could impact his job—it hadn't so far and that's the way it would stay. He didn't *feel* any different, and he certainly wasn't planning to lower his expectations of himself as a result of this diagnosis.

In fact, the only change in his life was the damned twice-daily medication.

Investigative television reporter Carly Edwards stepped off the elevator on the fifth floor of the Mayo Clinic's main building, turned left, and confidently strode toward the neurology wing—5 West—as if she knew where she was going. She didn't. The hospital would say she had no business here, and in a way that was true. She wasn't a patient's relative. She wasn't visiting a loved one. But she did have business here. A source had told her Colorado's junior senator was here—Senator Shane Jones—somewhere on the fifth floor. And Carly was going to track him down if she could, get an exclusive interview, and be the first to break the story. Whatever the story was.

She saw the attendant at the outer desk, with a sign that read Desk 5 West. Before anyone could challenge her, she turned right, again as if she knew where she was going, into a corridor marked 5 West Pod A. The patient rooms—all private rooms, she knew, from the research she'd done—were arranged around the nurses' station and the various rooms behind it in a square. Some of the doors to the rooms were open, but some were closed. And Carly cursed internally when she realized the patients weren't listed outside the doors—not even their last names—the way they were in some hospitals. Which meant she had no idea if Senator Jones was in any of these twelve rooms. Had no idea if he was even in Pod A.

"May I help you?" the nurse on duty behind the desk politely asked Carly.

"I'm looking for…" She quickly amended *Senator* to *Shane* and finished, "… Shane Jones."

"That patient specified no visitors except those on a very short list—and all those names are male. Are you a relative?" the nurse asked pointedly.

Busted, Carly thought. She smiled her best smile. "Not exactly."

"If you're not a relative and you're not on the list, I'm going to have to ask you to leave."

The nurse's hand went to the phone, and Carly knew the other woman wouldn't hesitate to call Security to escort her out, if necessary. But Carly wasn't about to get this close to her prey and give up meekly. She hadn't gotten where she was in her career by being faint of heart. She glanced down at the prop she'd donned before she came here—the diamond engagement ring Jack had given her over eight years ago. She tossed her long, dark hair over her shoulder, suppressed the brief memory of Jack and the expression on his face when he'd placed it on her finger, and smiled brightly. "He didn't want me to visit him in the hospital. That's probably why my name's not on the list. But I wanted to surprise him."

"You're Senator Jones's fiancée?" the nurse asked.

Not willing to out-and-out lie, even for an exclusive, Carly didn't confirm or deny, just beamed at the nurse and let her smile work its magic. That smile had gotten her into—and out of—more dangerous places she had no business being than the Mayo Clinic.

The nurse stood up and started out from behind the desk. "Let me see if he wants to see you."

Uh-oh, Carly thought. "I wanted it to be a surprise," she demurred.

"Yes, but sometimes the patient is sleeping or just isn't in the mood for visitors." She smiled at Carly, inviting her to understand. "Since you're not on the list, maybe he didn't want you to visit for a reason—because of the way he looks with all the electrodes attached. You know how vain men are. Especially a man as handsome as the senator."

Carly's ears perked up when the nurse mentioned electrodes. *Electroshock therapy*, she quickly hypothesized. Now *that* would be an exclusive, indeed. Colorado's hero senator—a former United States marine—needing electroshock therapy for a mental illness. She suppressed the little nudge her conscience gave her that people were entitled to their privacy and reminded herself that Senator Jones was a public figure. If he were mentally ill, that could impact his job performance, and his constituents had a right to know about it. His constituents and the entire country.

"Hang on," the nurse said. "I'll tell him you're here."

Carly watched as the nurse walked into 5W-10, making a mental note of the senator's room number, then turned to make a run for it. She wasn't Senator Jones's fiancée—he didn't have one, as far as she knew—and when he told the nurse he wasn't engaged, the nurse would probably call Security. Carly would need to do some fancy explaining—if they caught her.

She was already heading down the corridor, nearly past the outer desk, when the nurse called her back. "Miss? Miss? You can see him now."

Carly hesitated. Was this some kind of trick? Maybe the senator had asked the nurse to bring her back to his room, but to call Security so she could be arrested for trespassing. Either that or the senator was so mentally out of it he actually imagined he had a fiancée? If that was the case, could she snow him into thinking she was? Again her conscience gave her a nudge—harder this time. But that didn't stop her feet from turning around and heading back toward room 5W-10.

Carly put her hand on the door latch, then pushed. The door swung open noiselessly, and she entered the room. And caught her breath as a set of stern brown eyes zeroed in on her face. She knew what he looked like—of course she knew. Handsome as sin, with a face carved in granite, and chocolate-brown eyes that could be warm as fudge or cold as a frozen Eskimo Pie... which they were now. Six-foot-two with broad shoulders tapering to a waist and hips that hadn't an ounce of flab anywhere. Long, long legs—*of course, you idiot, he's six-two!*—that seemed to dwarf the hospital bed on which he lay in a semireclining position.

The mesh cap covering his head—and the electrodes she could see attached to his skull beneath it—should have made him look ridiculous, but somehow they didn't. Not when his bare, muscular legs, clad only in a pair of running shorts, were right beneath her eyes— legs that were perfectly visible because the sheet that might have been covering them had been restlessly tossed to one side. Not when his impressively muscled chest, covered only by a short-sleeved button-down shirt, rose and fell with his steady breathing, drawing her attention there. She didn't know why he wasn't clad in traditional hospital garb, but he wasn't, and she couldn't help the way her gaze was riveted on his impressive physical attributes. Then the legs, the chest and the rest of his perfect body faded into obscurity as her eyes met his again, and she floundered helplessly beneath those dark orbs.

"Do you know who I am?" Carly blurted out, then felt foolish.

The gravelly voice she recognized from hearing him on the Senate floor giving impassioned speeches spoke. "Oh yeah. You're my fiancée. I didn't quite catch the name, but..." He looked her over from head to toe...

twice. His eyes lingered—obviously—on her breasts. Both times. "I have good taste."

It was crazy. Stupid. She wasn't the kind to get flustered by a man. Any man. Even one as blatantly masculine, sexy and irresistible as the senator was. Carly didn't have a shy bone in her body, unlike her younger sister, Tahra. But…she blushed under his pointed stare. The kind of thing Tahra did a lot, but Carly never did. Until now.

She resisted the urge to cross her arms across her chest, and instead moved farther into the room, closing the door behind her with a little snick as the latch clicked shut. When she looked at the senator again, she realized with a tiny shock that he was strapped into the bed. And if she didn't miss her guess, that was a lock on the strap.

Electro-shock therapy. Mental illness. Violent mental illness? she wondered. She couldn't keep the question out of the eyes she raised to his.

To her surprise, he laughed suddenly, a booming sound that reverberated around the room. "No," he told her, humor lightening the rather severe expression he usually wore. "It's not what you're thinking."

"How do you know what I'm thinking?" she asked quickly, her hand reaching for the door latch.

"The strap is for *my* protection," he told her. "To make sure I don't get out of bed without a nurse in attendance. To make sure I don't fall." He hooked a thumb over his right shoulder, and for the first time Carly saw the harness hooked to an inverted T bar. She followed the strap upward, to the mechanical device that seemed to run on tracks throughout the room, and into what she figured was a private bathroom.

"What in the world?" Carly had never seen anything like it.

"It's actually quite ingenious. And if I really needed it, it'd be a lifesaver. But since I don't—I never fall when I have an episode, never lose consciousness—it's a damned nuisance. But it's hospital policy."

"Episode? Fall? Lose consciousness?" Carly felt stupid for repeating his words, but she had no idea what he was talking about. Her first supposition—that he was mentally ill—seemed to be all wrong. He certainly came across as being all there. Except for accepting her as his fiancée…which he knew she wasn't. So why had he let her in his room? Never shy, she asked, "Why did you allow me in here?"

"Because I was sick of my own company and looking for a diversion."

"That's the only reason?"

"Well…" He drew the word out. "Anyone with the nerve to claim she was my fiancée—"

"I never actually said I was," Carly quickly pointed out. "I just didn't correct the nurse's erroneous assumption."

His smile was cynical. "As I started to say, I figured you had to be a reporter, Ms. Edwards." She jumped when he said her name. "And if you tracked me down at the Mayo Clinic, the only thing to do—the only smart thing to do—would be to tell you the truth and ask you to keep it to yourself. For now."

"How did you know who I was? I thought you said—"

"I didn't know. Not until I got a good look at you. You used to cover the Hill." His eyes conveyed it wasn't just her face he recognized, but Carly appreciated he was enough of a gentleman not to actually say her figure had betrayed her. She couldn't help the way she looked, and she'd learned early to dress to downplay it as best she could professionally. Her private life was a different story, but she'd taken enough grief in her career over her curves, which tended to make men think of her as nothing but a pretty face with a bombshell body. *Good in some ways*, she admitted to herself, because men sometimes grew careless of what they said to her. And that had led to her breaking more than one explosive story.

"But when I let you in," the senator continued, interrupting her thoughts, "I was praying you were a legitimate member of the Fourth Estate."

"The Fourth Estate? I haven't heard anyone refer to the news media by that title in forever."

One corner of his mouth curved upward in a rueful grin. "I'd rather refer to the members of the media by that term than a few others I could think of, including ambush journalists and sleazy paparazzi."

"Ouch."

"I didn't say *you* were, I just said some are." He indicated the chair set against the far wall. "Would you like to sit down? You'll pardon me if I don't rise." He touched the strap belting him into the bed. "I'd have to call the nurse, and she'd have to strap me into the harness, and frankly, I'd just as soon avoid looking any more ridiculous than I already do." He touched the mesh cap on his head.

"You don't," Carly said. "Look ridiculous, that is."

"Yeah, right." Disbelief was evident in his tone.

She laughed. "Really," she assured him before she sat in the chair, crossed her legs, reached into her capacious purse and pulled out her notebook. This was followed by her mini recorder, which she switched on.

She glanced up at the senator and asked, "May I? I like to have a record of what people say. That way they can't claim I made something up."

His expression turned serious again. "No, I don't mind. But I want you to understand up front that what I'm going to tell you isn't something I want to publicize to the world. I can't prevent you from broadcasting it. I can only state this is off-the-record for now, and rely on your journalistic discretion after you hear what I have to say. Deal?"

Carly considered this for a moment. "I can't agree not to report what I uncover, not without knowing more. If it's something that impacts your ability to carry out the duties of your office—you have to see how that would be news, Senator Jones, and I'd have no choice. It would be my responsibility to report it."

"Agreed. But this doesn't have a damned thing to do with my job as a senator. It's personal. And very private. If I were running for office…maybe it would be relevant and the voters would have the right to know. But I'm not—not yet, anyway. If I do run for reelection, or if I go public with the story, I promise you'll have an exclusive. Deal?"

"On those terms…deal." She leaned forward, her mini recorder in one hand. "So can you tell me exactly why you're here, Senator Jones?"

He drew a deep breath, then let it out slowly. "One word," he told her, and his dark brown eyes were the saddest things Carly had seen in a long time. "Epilepsy."

"Epilepsy?" Carly Edwards's brows drew together in a frown. "How is it this is the first time anyone has heard of this, Senator?"

"Because I just found out." Shane waved a hand that encompassed the room. "It wasn't until I came here that I learned—" He broke off, fighting down the sudden up-welling of emotion. *Guess I still haven't quite accepted it*, he told himself. When he finally trusted his voice, he said, "Apparently the head wound I received a few years back caused damage to my left temporal lobe. I knew that at the time and so did my surgeons. But no one knew the TBI—that's short for—"

"Traumatic brain injury," she finished. "Yes, I know." For an experienced reporter—which Shane knew she was—Carly's reaction was unexpected. She'd lost all color and her eyes had widened…in what looked like shock. Shock, and recognition.

He paused a moment, waiting for her to say something more, but when she didn't he said, "No one knew the TBI would eventually cause focal seizures. It doesn't happen in every case, but it did in mine."

"Focal seizures?" The question came automatically, but for some reason Shane felt she wasn't really focusing on his answer…and that intrigued him.

"The official term is focal seizure without dyscognitive features." He grinned suddenly. "That's a mouthful, isn't it? All it means is that it's a small, localized seizure in one hemisphere of the brain—kind of like an electrical 'short' in that area—which doesn't cause any loss of consciousness, loss of memory or anything like that. In my case it manifests itself with a symptom that can best be described as a sudden chill…accompanied by goose bumps."

She seemed at a loss for words. "Is that all? Just goose bumps?"

Shane allowed his eyes to wander from her face

down to her legs—long, lovely legs, he noted—then back up again. And he felt a twinge in his groin he hoped wasn't too obvious beneath his running shorts. "That's all. I feel cold everywhere, as if I've walked into a freezer. And the goose bumps on my arms, my legs, make it very real. For about thirty seconds. Then the symptoms go away."

"But you don't lose consciousness?"

"No, and my memory of each episode isn't affected. I can walk and talk normally while the symptoms are occurring, as well."

"That doesn't sound like epilepsy to me."

"You're thinking of what the general public knows of epilepsy—which isn't a heck of a lot. I didn't know any better, either, until the doctors here diagnosed me."

All of a sudden Carly clicked the button to turn the mini recorder off. She swallowed once—visibly—then said, "I'm sorry. You're right. This is personal and private. I don't need to hear any more to know it's not news. Not the kind of news I report on." She stood up abruptly, shoving her notebook and mini recorder into her purse. "I'm very sorry, Senator. Not just that it happened to you, but that you had to share this with me, when it's really no one's business but yours."

Without another word she walked out of the room.

Chapter 2

Shane tried to chase after Carly, but the strap locking him in the bed held firm. "Damn it," he cursed, tugging futilely at the strap. For just a second he thought about ringing for the nurse, but he knew by the time anything could be done to prevent it, Carly would be long gone. "Damn it!"

He lay back against the pillows, seething with frustration. He hadn't liked being bound to the bed from the beginning. He understood why it was hospital policy. And as he'd said to Carly, if he lost consciousness with his seizures or even lost motor control, that would be one thing, because the strap would keep him from falling out of bed. But he didn't, so he'd mentally railed against the restriction from day one. This was the first time he'd actively cursed out loud, however, and he suddenly announced to the empty room, "Sorry."

"Not to worry, Senator," answered the technician constantly monitoring him from the other room. "Believe me, we understand how frustrating it can be for our patients, especially the ones who think they don't need protection."

"Thanks."

Shane punched up his pillow, then settled his big frame more comfortably in the bed, thinking about his recent visitor. Carly Edwards. He'd never actually met her before, but he knew who she was, of course. She'd been a fixture on the nightly news as a war correspondent and then reporting from Capitol Hill on one of the major cable news networks. She'd just recently moved to another cable news channel, one that had surged into prominence recently, surpassing most television news agencies for hard-hitting news coverage. Everyone said she was the next Christiane Amanpour.

He wondered why she'd cut their interview short. Carly had the reputation for being unstoppable where a news story was concerned. Once she got her teeth into something, she refused to let go. It wasn't like her to cut an interview short, especially on an exclusive. And while he'd hoped she would agree with him this wasn't legitimate news, he'd figured he'd have to tell her everything before she decided not to broadcast what he had to say. It didn't make sense that she'd run out in the middle of an interview.

For a minute he also wondered what she'd been doing there without a camera operator, but then realized no way would they have been able to sneak the camera gear into the Mayo Clinic, past the various stations that guarded their patients' privacy. Not to mention Carly didn't have a reputation as an ambush journalist...although she *had* used subterfuge to gain access to him. By pretending to be his fiancée.

Shane smiled. Whether she'd intended it or not, Carly had been a bright note in his otherwise bleak week. His body hardened in a rush as he let himself fantasize about what it would be like if she *was* his fiancée. If he could peel that jacket off her, the one she wore that was not-quite-good-enough camouflage for a body that would tempt a monk. And Shane was no monk.

Carly was already in her car in the parking lot before she lost it. Before memories of Jack swamped her, bringing unaccustomed tears to her eyes. *God, oh God, who knew?*

She stared down at her engagement ring, the brilliant diamond shimmering through the haze of tears. When Jack had asked her to marry him more than eight years ago she'd been the happiest woman in the world. They'd been in love. Not just the crazy, Tilt-A-Whirl kind of love, but the solid, let's-make-this-last-a-lifetime kind of love, with dreams of children in the not-too-distant future and grandchildren far down the road.

In mind-numbing slow motion the memory of the car accident replayed in her mind. The drunk driver weaving head-on into their lane. Jack's desperate swerve to avoid the collision. Sliding sideways on the treacherous, ice-slick road. The sudden impact and the side air bag that failed to deploy. Jack's head making sickening contact with the window—numerous times—as his body was flung side to side.

After a year of mourning, she'd taken off Jack's engagement ring and placed it in the back of her jewelry box. Never to be worn again…until today. Until she'd used it as a prop to sneak into Senator Jones's hospital room.

Carly didn't believe in omens, good or bad. And she didn't believe in fate—life was what you made of it. But guilt overwhelmed her now, as if by wearing Jack's ring for a purpose he'd never intended, she'd somehow brought this whole sequence of events about. As if she was responsible for what had happened to Senator Jones the way she was responsible for Jack's death.

Shane picked up his cell phone and hit speed dial for his executive assistant in Washington, DC, a grandmotherly type who reminded him of his own mother—not surprising since she'd been his mother's best friend as long as he could remember. He still had difficulty calling her by her nickname, especially since she insisted on calling him Senator now instead of Shane. He was more inclined to call her Mrs. Wilson as he'd done growing up, but when she'd first gone to work for him when he was running for the House, she'd flatly told him to call her Dee-Dee, so he did…reluctantly.

When she answered the phone he said, "I want you to find out everything you can on a reporter, Carly Edwards." He listened for a minute, a frown forming. "No, nothing like that. This is personal, Dee-Dee, not professional. So only work on this if you have nothing else to do."

"Hah!" Dee-Dee responded. "As if I ever have nothing else to do."

"I'm serious."

"Oh, of course, you're serious. That makes all the difference," she said drily.

For the umpteenth time Shane wondered why he kept

Dee-Dee as his executive assistant when she never gave him the kid-glove treatment he got automatically from the rest of his staff. Even though she called him Senator, she still acted as if she remembered him with a dirty face and untucked shirttails, sneaking cookies when his mom's back was turned.

But then for the umpteenth time he remembered that was *exactly* why he kept her—she brought a touch of reality to the sometimes stultifying protocol he was usually surrounded with. She was a whiz at keeping him organized, too. And besides, she needed the job. Her husband had left her little but debts when he'd passed away years earlier…and his mother would kill him if he fired her best friend.

"Don't worry," Dee-Dee said, "I'll have a complete dossier on Ms. Edwards by the time you get back to DC. You *are* coming back tomorrow night, right? That's what you said. They're discharging you tomorrow morning?"

"That's the plan."

"Good. I know you've been keeping up on pending legislation even in the hospital—your mom didn't raise any slackers—but I've fielded calls from a half dozen senators, including the president pro-tem and both the majority and minority leaders, wanting to know how you're planning to vote on their bills when the Senate is back in session. Especially that pipeline one—the news agencies are calling you 'the swing vote.' Not just because of your own stance on the issue, but because others will follow your lead and vote their consciences, not their pocketbooks—if you weren't already aware. And since you haven't clued me in on where you stand,

Senator," she added with a touch of acerbity, "I wasn't able to answer for you."

"As if you don't know where I stand on every issue."

"Yes, but you haven't *officially* told me how you plan to vote, so my lips are sealed." That had Shane laughing silently. Dee-Dee's lips were *always* sealed…when it came to guarding him and maintaining the integrity of his office. Another reason he couldn't possibly do without her. He was just preparing to disconnect when Dee-Dee said out of the blue, "You *do* know her nickname, don't you?"

Shane was familiar with the way Dee-Dee's mind jumped back and forth between topics, so he knew she was referring to Carly Edwards. He cast around in his mind but came up blank. "No, can't say I do."

"Tiger Shark." Heavy silence. "Keep that in mind."

Marsh Anderson walked outside the Mayo Clinic lobby and a little distance away before pulling out his disposable cell phone—one he'd bought specifically for this job—and punching in a number he already knew by heart. "Just checking in," he said when the phone was answered. He listened, nodding his head in agreement even though he knew the person on the other end couldn't see him. "Not a problem," he said finally. "When will he be discharged?"

"He has plane reservations for tomorrow," came the clipped response. "Whether the clinic is ready to discharge him or not, he's flying out Saturday evening. The Senate will be back at work come Monday, and he has never missed a debate or a vote. He's not about to let that happen now—especially not with what's at stake this time around."

Marsh grunted. He knew what was at stake, even though his contact thought him nothing more than a hired gun. He *was* a hired gun…as far as that went. But he was a very smart one, and he'd figured out a hell of a lot more than the men who'd hired him realized. He called them the Agenda Men, because they had a concrete agenda and would stop at nothing to achieve their goal.

He knew just how much money was behind the effort to push one piece of legislation through. Not bribes. You couldn't call them bribes. *Campaign contributions* was the polite euphemism, and the Agenda Men were very good at it. But their money had availed them nothing where Senator Jones was concerned. He could not be swayed as other politicians were. So they had no choice but to contract Marsh's services.

Marsh admired Senator Jones for his integrity. But that didn't impact his willingness to carry out his job. One was personal. The other was business. And Marsh never put anything above business.

"So he's leaving tomorrow, but you don't know exactly what time he's leaving," Marsh said now. It wasn't a question, but the voice on the other end of the phone answered anyway.

"No. You'll just have to play it by ear."

"Okay," Marsh said. "I know what I have to do. Just make sure you do your part." Then he hung up. *My money*, he thought to himself. *You just have my money ready.*

Shane was the happiest man in the world when the clinic finally got around to discharging him Saturday, right after lunch. So happy he didn't even cavil at another hospital policy—wheeling him out to the wait-ing limousine in a wheelchair. *God forbid I trip over my own feet walking out and hurt myself on hospital property*, he thought with a touch of mordant humor.

The limo wasn't his first choice for transportation because he hadn't wanted to draw that kind of attention. But it made sense since it had to transport not only him to the airport but the four staff members accompanying him, as well—his deputy chief of staff, senior legislative assistant, legislative correspondent, and press secretary. So when Bobby Vernon, his deputy chief of staff, told him they'd arranged for a limo, he'd merely accepted it.

As his staff crowded into the elevator after him, Shane joked with Laney, the nursing assistant wheel-ing him out. He'd come to know Laney casually dur-ing his nearly week-long stay at the clinic—she'd even shown him pictures of her grandchildren. All his staff were dressed as casually as he was, in jeans and a Hen-ley, because he'd been adamant he didn't want to draw too much attention by making them look like Secret Service agents guarding a public figure. But his little group *did* draw eyes as they made their way across the multistoried lobby to the front door, and Shane mentally winced, hoping no one would recognize him. Not that he was ashamed—well, maybe just a little—but because he'd already dodged one bullet where Carly Edwards was concerned, and didn't feel up to answering ques-tions from the idly curious or from another reporter.

He'd just been rolled out the front door, where the limo was drawn up to the curb, when Carly appeared out of nowhere, across the curving drive to the right. "Senator Jones," she called out, lengthening her stride to catch him before he entered the limo. "If I could just talk to you for a minute," she began.

Shane's eyes were drawn to her, but out of the corner of his left eye he saw something glint in the early afternoon sun from the brushy knoll in the center of the horseshoe-shaped circular driveway.

"Get down," he yelled to his entourage as he leaped from the wheelchair, grabbed Laney and flattened her on the sidewalk just as rifle shots rang out, shattering the sliding glass doors behind them. Shane rolled Laney and himself toward the limo, using that as a shield against a further barrage of bullets.

Screams were coming from everywhere—from the people inside the clinic's lobby and those who had been eating lunch on the cafeteria's outside patio. Shane couldn't see a damned thing from his position on the ground, but he was praying no one had been hit. Laney was whispering something in a breathy little voice, but it took him a minute to focus on what she was saying.

"Mary, mother of God," she repeated over and over, and Shane knew it was a prayer.

Sirens could be heard in the distance now. Shane levered himself into a crouch behind the limo after making sure Laney was unharmed, except for the bad scrape on her elbow where it had made contact with the unforgiving sidewalk.

He peered over the limo's hood. A stocky figure was running in the opposite direction, through the center island's walkway, heading toward the far parking lot. Shane wanted to give chase, but knew that would be stupid. An unarmed man going up against someone with a high-powered rifle?

His staff members, who'd hit the ground when he

had, stood and swarmed around him suddenly, as if they feared he would do just that. Then more people rushed outside from the clinic's lobby—security guards and the morbidly curious. Shane quickly bent down and helped Laney to her feet, then brushed her off. He pulled a clean hanky from his jeans pocket and held it against her elbow, which was oozing blood.

"You okay?"

She nodded. "Thanks to you, Senator."

A medical emergency team rushed onto the scene, and suddenly police cars were everywhere, although—thankfully—no TV news crews were on site yet. Then Shane remembered Carly, and he shot a quick glance over to where he'd last seen her...only to realize she wasn't there. He scoured the parking lot for a sign of her. On the right he saw the back of a woman cutting across the drive, darting from one sheltered area to another. Moving in the same direction the gunman had been heading when he'd made his escape, but trying to stay under cover.

Shane cursed and took off running before the policemen could even exit their vehicles. He ignored the urgent cries of the people behind him in his goal to cut Carly off before it was too late. He sped through the circuitous sidewalk leading through the driveway's center island, grateful the cactus and bushes shielded him from the gunman's sight. He passed the statue of an American Indian woman, then a small waterfall, but he had eyes for neither. He took the stairs in three steps and was just about to exit the north side when he saw Carly. She was crouching behind a giant saguaro and a large agave plant, but peering around the one and over the other. She had something in her hand aimed at the running gunman…and she was right in his line of sight when he suddenly turned.

Shane made a flying leap and tackled Carly. The iPhone she'd been trying to use to film the sniper's escape flew across the gravel and skittered into the roadway. He rolled her beneath him as the unmistakable crack of a rifle shot broke the silence. Then a door slammed. Tires squealed. And a white pickup truck fishtailed out of the far side of the parking lot as the driver gunned the engine.

A police car gave chase a minute later, siren blaring, but Shane wasn't optimistic. Whoever had been shooting at him and then at Carly had too great a lead. The highway was only two stoplights and a few blocks away, and since it was the weekend, there wouldn't be rush-hour traffic to impede the getaway.

Shane picked himself up off the ground and helped Carly to her feet, first making sure she wasn't hurt. Then he grasped her upper arms and shook her. Hard. In a voice he hadn't used since his Marine Corps days he demanded, "What the *hell* did you think you were doing?"

Chapter 3

Carly shook Shane's hands off her arms and darted into the roadway. She retrieved her smartphone, which miraculously hadn't been run over by the pursuing police car. The case had protected it against most of the damage that could have occurred, but there was a scratch across the touchpad. She swiped and pressed, then heaved a sigh of relief. "It's not broken," she exulted under her breath. Her eyes caught Shane's. "And I got him."

"You got him?" Throttled temper made him rigid, and he towered over her like the USMC officer he'd once been. "You think that was worth risking your life for?"

"I wasn't in any real danger," she replied calmly.

"The hell you weren't!"

"The hell I was." She lifted her chin. "You think I'm stupid? I've covered two wars and three 'police actions,'" she said, referring to a military conflict in undeclared war. "I know how to keep my head down. There was no point at which I was completely exposed."

"You think a saguaro would block a high-velocity bullet?" He snorted. "It would slice through that like a hot knife through butter. Then go right through you."

Carly opened her mouth to retort, but hesitated as she acknowledged there was some truth to what Shane was saying. She *had* been a tad reckless. True, she'd never been injured covering a story. In fact, she'd never been wounded at all, no matter what happened to her. She'd fallen from the top of a jungle gym when she was ten with nothing but brush burns and bruises to show for it. The helicopter she'd ridden in during her first foray as a war correspondent had been caught in a hot LZ—a landing zone where the helicopter came under enemy gunfire—and she'd been untouched. She'd even walked away physically unscathed from the horrific car crash that had caused such devastating damage to Jack.

She'd led a charmed life physically…had she grown overconfident? "You're right," she admitted now. She drew a deep breath. "And I apologize for putting you in the position of having to rescue me." Then her natural ebullience returned, and she held up her smartphone. "But I got him."

The police had whisked them all away before the TV news cameras showed up, for which Shane was grateful. He hadn't wanted to be confronted by a reporter asking what he was doing at the Mayo Clinic or theorizing as to why he'd been an assassin's target. Those questions would be posed soon enough, but at least he'd have a little time to come up with suitably noncommittal answers.

The Phoenix police, who'd been joined by FBI agents from the city office, finally let Shane and his entourage go four hours later. Four hours during which he'd been grilled relentlessly—albeit respectfully—with questions that, for the most part, he couldn't answer. He hadn't really seen much of anything except the glint of the rifle scope and a stocky figure running away. The man was white—he knew that much. And he was pretty sure the shooter's hair was that indeterminable shade between blond and brown, although the ball cap the man had been wearing had concealed most of it. The shooter *might* have sported a close-cropped beard—but Shane couldn't swear to it because he hadn't really seen the man's face. Yes, he'd seen the getaway vehicle, but he hadn't caught the license plate number. And there were probably a million white pickup trucks out there.

He didn't even struggle over the decision to disclose what Carly had said, that she'd caught the man on camera, although she wouldn't thank him for it. Yes, she'd earned her scoop—by risking her life—but public safety trumped it. The shooter had been aiming at Shane, but anyone in the vicinity could have been gravely injured or killed. It was a miracle no one had been. Carly's camera footage was critical evidence, and whatever the police and the FBI could glean from viewing it was more important than an exclusive news report…even if it meant confiscating her iPhone.

Shane didn't see Carly again before he left for the airport, although he thought of her constantly as the limo ferried his aides and him from the police station to Phoenix's Sky Harbor International Airport through the Saturday afternoon traffic. He caught his flight by the skin of his teeth, dashing through the hallways once he got past the TSA checkpoint, his aides scurrying to keep up. "Last call for flight…" was just being announced when he arrived at the gate, and Shane heaved a sigh of relief. There were later flights to DC out of Sky Harbor, but this one was nonstop.

Carly's face rose in his mind once more as he handed his ticket to the smiling airline attendant and moved down the jet bridge before he tried to banish her from his mind. He quickly stowed his carry-on in the overhead compartment and took his seat in coach, his entourage settling in around him. Used to be members of Congress flew first-class as a matter of course, but Shane had never thought that was a proper use of taxpayer money, so he always traveled economy. And he was paying for this flight for himself and his aides out of his own pocket—no way could he justify this as anything other than a personal expense.

He chuckled softly to himself as the plane took off. *And that's another thing*, he thought. One of the Phoenix policemen questioning him this afternoon had asked why Shane didn't have a bodyguard or two keeping him safe, but the FBI agent had dismissed that question out of hand, already knowing the answer. Members of the Senate and the House of Representatives didn't have taxpayer-provided bodyguards—that was a public misconception. Only the president, vice president and presidential candidates had Secret Service bodyguards. Any bodyguard Shane had, he would have to pay for himself. And since he wasn't independently wealthy, that wasn't an expense he'd wanted to incur.

But he might have to rethink that position, at least temporarily. He had no idea why anyone would want to kill him, but there didn't need to be a reason most people would understand. He wouldn't be the first politician targeted by a crazed gunman with a perceived grievance. Not to mention the successful and unsuccessful assassination attempts on several US presidents over the years, despite the best protection the Secret Service could offer.

His own sister, Keira, had taken a bullet meant for another man who'd been targeted for elimination. And all because he'd brought down the New World Militia and its founder, David Pennington, years ago.

That thought gave him pause. Could this attempt on him have anything to do with that organization or a similar one? His public stance on terrorism—both foreign and domestic—had made him a few enemies, he had to admit. Was that the reason?

I wonder if Niall has any vacation time coming to him. The brother closest to him in age was a black-ops warrior—not really the name for it, but that's how it was referred to by the public. Niall had been a marine sniper years ago before he'd left the Corps to take up an even more dangerous calling. But that didn't really qualify him as a bodyguard. *If you need a bodyguard, Alec or Liam would be better suited to the task*, he reminded himself. Both of his younger brothers had been Diplomatic Security Service—DSS—special agents for years, although only Liam still worked as a bodyguard now. Alec was the regional security officer at the United States embassy in Zakhar.

But Alec and Liam were both married. Niall wasn't. Shane might call on Niall to help him out in this crisis, but he'd have to think long and hard before he put one of his baby brothers—*married* baby brothers, each with a baby of his own—in harm's way.

Shane laughed beneath his breath, imagining what Alec and Liam would say to that. He was so caught up in his inner musings that it barely registered when the seat-belt light was turned off and the announcement was made that portable electronic devices could now be used. It wasn't until a soft oath from his press secretary, Mike Adamson, impinged on his consciousness that he realized the man had availed himself of the airplane's Wi-Fi and was looking with dismay at something on his laptop screen.

"What?" Shane asked Mike, then nudged him to get his attention when the other man's earphones prevented him from hearing Shane's question. "What is it?" he asked after Mike removed the earphones.

"See for yourself," Mike replied, handing both the laptop and the earphones to Shane.

He clicked to restart the news video. It only took a few seconds before he was swearing internally, although he had enough restraint not to curse aloud—he'd long since learned that wasn't acceptable from a public figure in a public place.

"An assassination attempt at the Mayo Clinic in Phoenix, Arizona, was foiled today by Colorado's junior senator, retired Marine Lieutenant Colonel Shane Jones, in a scene reminiscent of his heroic rescue of a pregnant woman during a domestic terrorism incident five years ago," Carly Edwards told the TV camera, a microphone in her hand.

Then a video began playing as Carly's voice continued. "The alleged assassin escaped by running through a small park north of the clinic, to the parking lot, and from there to parts unknown via truck. The footage shown here was taken with a smartphone by this reporter, who just happened to be a bystander when the incident occurred. The Phoenix police warn that the suspect is armed and should be considered extremely dangerous—no one should attempt to approach or apprehend him. Anyone who recognizes the alleged shooter—described as a stocky white male of average height between the ages of forty-five and sixty—or the white getaway truck, is urged to call the Phoenix police or the FBI—" two phone numbers scrolled beneath the video "—or Crime Stoppers to report anonymously." Another phone number came up.

Carly appeared on the screen again. "Once more, please note the suspect is armed and extremely dangerous—do not approach. Stay tuned to this station for updates on this developing situation. Back to you, Phil."

"I thought the police would confiscate her smartphone," Mike muttered to Shane when the video clip came to an end.

Shane's smile was grim as he removed the earphones. "She's a smart lady. She probably knew they would. I'll bet you anything you want to name she emailed the video to herself or her news agency before they had the chance."

"No bet." Mike thought for a moment. "The reporters will be all over you, wanting a statement. We'd better have one ready."

"Yeah. Want to work one up?"

"No problem," Mike said. "But what are you going to tell them?"

Shane considered this. "Probably the best thing to say is the Phoenix police and the FBI have asked me not to discuss the details of the case—which is perfectly true."

"Yes, but…" Mike trailed off.

"But why was I at the Mayo Clinic in the first place?" Shane finished for him.

Mike's eyes met Shane's. "You haven't even told us. Well," he amended, "you haven't told *me*. I don't know what you told everyone else. All I know is you were there for observation. Observation of what?"

Shane glanced across the aisle at his other three aides. They seemed completely oblivious. Two were watching the in-flight movie, and the third was dozing with his head propped against the window.

"No one knows any more than you," he reassured Mike. "And I didn't tell any of you because I didn't want to put you in the position of lying to the press should any questions arise."

"Cancer?"

Shane shook his head. "Worse. At least…in the perception of the general public."

"What could be worse than cancer?"

He considered what if anything he should tell Mike and quickly reached the conclusion he'd been fooling himself thinking he could keep the diagnosis secret. He made a mental note to contact Carly regarding the promised exclusive—she'd kept her word, hadn't mentioned his illness when she'd reported on the assassination attempt, so he needed to keep his word, too. Then he said, "Epilepsy. And it's not curable."

"Epilepsy?" Mike looked blown away. "But you don't… I mean…you haven't…"

"Yeah, my symptoms aren't what most people think of when they think of it."

"Jeez." After a moment the younger man said, "What symptoms? You never said."

Shane quickly recounted what he'd told Carly. "I've been having these episodes for about six months now. The first physician I consulted had no idea what was causing them. He thought maybe I was depressed and wanted to prescribe an antidepressant." He snorted. "I knew I wasn't depressed, so I insisted on seeing a specialist. A whole slew of specialists, in fact, an endocrinologist and a neurologist among them. Nobody could put a name to what was wrong with me. I was complaining to a doctor friend from my Marine Corps days that even with all the medical advances, there's still a lot we don't know, and he suggested the Mayo Clinic."

"And that's the diagnosis they came up with? Epilepsy?" Mike shook his head. "Maybe you should get a second opinion."

Shane laughed, but the humor was lacking. "Don't need one. And you wouldn't suggest it if you read the literature they provided me with. What I have isn't all that common, but it *is* a specialized form of epilepsy—the symptoms are unmistakable. And even if they weren't, the tests they performed—"

"You mean all those electrodes?"

"Yeah. Those electrodes were for EEG tests. They were actually able to trigger two episodes with their stress tests. The nurses observed the goose bumps on my arms and legs—that's the reason they wanted me to wear running shorts and a short-sleeved shirt in bed, by the way, so they could observe the physical manifestations—and they talked to me during each episode and recorded my responses. Just as I'd told them, each incident lasted about a half a minute then went away, and I never lost consciousness. But the EEG recorded what was happening in my brain each time. Sure enough, I was having tiny seizures."

Mike didn't respond for several minutes as he digested this. "And it's not—you said it's not curable? What are you going to do?"

"It's controllable but not curable." Shane reached into his pocket and pulled out a little pill bottle, the prescription he'd had filled before he left the hospital. "Twice a day, and it's supposed to control the seizures."

"And that's what you want me to include in your statement to the press?"

Shane shook his head. "Not exactly. As I told you, first let's just say I've been asked not to talk about the attack. I promised Carly Edwards—"

Mike pointed to his laptop screen. "Tiger Shark? Her?"

"Yeah." He envisioned her in his hospital room... then in his fantasies. "I promised her an exclusive if and when I went public with this information. And I always keep my promises."

Carly settled into her first-class airplane seat on the red-eye flight to DC with a tiny sigh of satisfaction. She declined the offer of an alcoholic beverage and instead requested a bottle of water, which was quickly forthcoming. She sipped at it, then closed her eyes. As the plane took off, she let her mind replay everything that had happened over the past two days. High on the list was the scoop she'd managed, even though the police had seized her smartphone and the video she'd taken as evidence in the assassination attempt on the senator.

But even higher on the list was Senator Jones himself. Shane Jones. She could still see him confronting her this afternoon, a seething, very-pissed-off male. She was on the tall side for a woman, but he towered over her. And she would have bet her next exclusive there was not an ounce of fat anywhere on his body. A body that had sprawled protectively atop hers when the bullet had whizzed over them. At the time, she hadn't focused on anything except her fortunate escape, but now she realized how good it had felt to be held in his strong arms. Safe. Secure. And unbelievably, that embrace had reminded her she was a woman and he was a man. An incredibly sexy man.

Stop thinking about his physical attributes, she told herself, frowning a little. But then she remembered those chocolate-brown eyes, and the way they and his mobile mouth could express a wide range of emotions, as they had in his hospital room. He'd been angry with her this afternoon—and all marine—but yesterday…yesterday he'd seemed human. Approachable. A wounded warrior trying to come to terms with a diagnosis that made a mockery of his seeming invulnerability.

She ran through the facts she knew about him—the ones she'd known for a while and the ones she'd researched yesterday after she'd cut the interview short—and tried to assemble them into a picture of the man.

Knowing he was a widower whose wife and unborn child had died at the hands of terrorists, explained that incredibly protective streak in him. Not just this afternoon, but five years ago, when he'd used his body to shield a pregnant woman from harm in a domestic terrorism incident outside a bookstore. He'd escaped injury this afternoon, but not back then. That's when he'd sustained the TBI that most likely was the trigger for the seizures he was experiencing now.

Carly had still been in college when Shane's pregnant wife had been kidnapped and murdered, but it had made the news at the time. She remembered it vividly, but she hadn't known it was him. She hadn't made the connection until she'd researched everything she could about the senator.

Wendy Jones, wife of a marine lieutenant stationed at the NATO headquarters in Belgium, had been abducted in broad daylight by a terrorist organization in retaliation for the arrest and conviction of three of its members, including its founder. And then executed in cold blood.

Carly had read with keen interest the interview he'd given his hometown newspaper shortly after the US Marine Corps had retired him due to the injuries he'd sustained that day five years ago. He'd made the Corps his home for so long it almost seemed a sacrilege to even think of "hanging up his spurs," retired Lieutenant Colonel Shane Jones had explained to the reporter. "Twenty and out" had never been in his mind. He was a lifer. "Once a Marine, Always a Marine" wasn't just a slogan used by former members of the US Marine Corps to distinguish themselves from lesser mortals, it had been his mantra.

Shane had been reticent, but the reporter had skillfully elicited the information that Shane was one of those rarities, a marine who'd enlisted in the Corps as a buck private and then had rapidly risen through the ranks. Not just as a noncommissioned officer—a noncom—but as a commissioned officer. Tapped at twenty-one for the Marine Corps Enlisted Commissioning Educational Program, the Corps had sent him to Officer Candidates School and then to college. Everything he was, everything he'd accomplished professionally, he owed to the Corps, he'd been quick to point out to the reporter, and he'd had no intention of reneging on the deal.

"But all that's at an end," the reporter had stated. "So what's next for you now?"

Shane hadn't had an answer for the interviewer. But Carly had read everything she could find on the senator, and she knew that after knocking around for a couple of months, Shane had gone into politics with the same single-minded dedication he'd once had for the Corps. He was an avowed independent—despite his military background that made some think he must be a right-wing "hawk"—but even though he'd staunchly refused to allow his media consultants to use the reason for his medical discharge in the campaign, the local media had played up his heroism despite his own refusal to do so, and he'd won that election in a landslide.

A year later, when the then-senior senator from Colorado had announced his retirement, Shane had declared for the vacant seat in the Senate. He hadn't been the only one vying for that position, but his heroism during the domestic terrorism incident at the bookstore had still been recent enough to be the deciding factor in a close election.

Integrity counts, Carly mused. Then added with a touch of cynicism, *Sometimes*.

She shifted positions, tucking her pillow between her head and the wall of the plane, her thoughts growing drowsy. Drowsy…and dangerous.

She'd been drawn to Shane both physically and emotionally. Yesterday *and* today. But she knew better than to let herself get involved with someone like him. After

Jack she'd sworn off men completely, then modified her stance somewhat. She would only date those who didn't threaten her closely guarded heart.

And Senator Shane Jones was a threat—no question about that. Not only did he have the emotional depth and strength of character she admired, he'd suffered the kind of injury that had stolen Jack from her. And that she couldn't bear. She couldn't lose another man the way she'd lost Jack. She just couldn't.

Chapter 4

The ringing of the phone roused Carly from a chaotic dream, the basic elements of which lingered even after she pried her eyes open, glanced at the alarm clock and collapsed back onto the bed. She tugged her pillow over her head, ignoring the phone for once. She'd had all of three hours of sleep, and unless the building was on fire, there was no emergency that would get her out of bed.

Eventually the ringing stopped. Then her brand-new, less-than-twelve-hours-old smartphone began chirping. She hadn't had time to set up all her ringtones yet, so she had no idea who'd be calling her at the ungodly hour of—

She emerged from beneath the pillow and cracked one eye open to peer at the clock—8:34 a.m. Not so ungodly, but still…she hadn't arrived home until five-fifteen this morning. She'd dumped her carry-on suit-case in the hallway, stripped off her clothes without bothering to hang them up and tumbled naked into bed without even brushing her teeth, an oversight she was paying for now with the yucky taste in her mouth.

Her smartphone stopped for all of five seconds, then started chirping again. Whoever was on the other end was persistent, she'd give them that. She tugged on one purse strap until she managed to pull her purse off the dresser and into bed beside her, then fumbled until she found her new iPhone. "Hello?"

"Carly? It's J.C." The clipped British accent of her producer at the cable news network she'd joined last year filled her ear.

"You have ten seconds before I hang up on you," she told J.C. "So whatever it is, it had better be good. And quick."

"Senator Shane Jones is trying to reach you."

That made her sit up, then clutch the bedclothes to her chest as if J.C. could see her naked. "What?"

"Yeah, the subject of your broadcast last evening wants you to call him ASAP."

"Did he say why?"

"Wasn't the senator himself. His press secretary called the network looking for your contact info, and that got routed to me. You know what this is about?"

Carly slung her long, dark hair over one shoulder and scrubbed a hand over her eyes, her brain scrambling to focus. Was the senator just pissed because she'd reported on the assassination attempt? That didn't make sense—she wasn't the only reporter covering the story, and he had to know it. Of course, she was the only one with footage of the gunman, which raised her story head and shoulders above the rest. Still, even if he'd seen her broadcast, she hadn't said anything he could really object to, hadn't mentioned why he was there at the Mayo Clinic.

"Carly?" J.C.'s voice took on an impatient tone.

"I'm thinking," she countered quickly. *No*, she reasoned, *if he's trying to get in touch with me, there's only one explanation. He intends to go public with—* "He promised me an exclusive," she told J.C.

His voice sharpened. "When did he promise you that? You never mentioned it to me."

"I don't tell you everything." A long silence followed, during which Carly could have sworn she could hear J.C.'s thoughts.

He didn't say any of the things she figured he was thinking. All he said was, "When the senator arrived in DC last night, he released a statement through his press secretary."

"Saying?"

"Nothing more than he'd been asked by the Phoenix police and the FBI not to discuss the incident since it's still under investigation. But his press secretary refused to take any questions during the press conference, including the one every reporter there wanted to ask—what was he doing at the Mayo Clinic? Congress is in recess, and as far as anyone knew, Senator Jones was back home in Colorado." J.C. let that statement hang there for a few seconds, then asked, "Do you know why?"

Carly's heart skipped a beat. "Yes," she admitted. "But only on deep background. I can't report the story until he's willing to go on the record, and when I spoke with him two days ago he had no intention of doing that."

"Damn it, Carly," J.C. growled.

"But I think he must have changed his mind," she said before J.C. could go ballistic. "Or rather, the events yesterday must have changed his mind. Other than that, I can't imagine why he'd want to talk with me. It can't be anything to do with the assassination attempt—he's staying mum on that, isn't that what you told me?"

She didn't wait for J.C.'s agreement. "So the only thing he and I have to discuss is…what I can't tell you until he gives me the go-ahead." She tugged her notebook out of her purse along with a pen and added, "What's the phone number?"

A clean-shaven Marsh Anderson pulled his carry-on luggage from the overhead compartment and deplaned at Reagan National Airport in Washington, DC. He strode confidently through the airport, past the airline employees and TSA checkpoints, then retrieved his nondescript white Chevy truck from the long-term parking lot. As he drove to his home in Arlington, Virginia, his thoughts dwelled on the two phone calls he'd received yesterday—one from the man who'd hired him, one from the man on the inside. Neither had been at all happy with the outcome. Marsh agreed with their assessment that he'd screwed up. Not so much for missing his shot—that could happen to anyone due to circumstances beyond his control—but for allowing himself to be recorded as he made his escape.

"Damned reporters," he whispered under his breath. He'd planned everything so *carefully.* He'd waited nearly an hour in the little park across from the entrance to the Mayo Clinic, moving around a little from spot to spot so as not to draw attention to a man lying in wait. He'd assembled his AS50 sniper rifle even earlier, secreting it between a boulder and a large aloe plant—close enough to retrieve at a moment's notice, but out of sight. He'd known when the limo had pulled up in the driveway in front of the hospital, that was his signal the senator would be down shortly. He'd surreptitiously retrieved the rifle and had moved into position—a hidden vantage point he'd scouted and tested two days previously.

But everything had gone wrong from that point forward.

He'd followed his original plan regarding the disposal of the weapon he'd used and the clothing he'd worn, too, just as if he'd been successful in his assassination attempt. He'd immediately and without a qualm dumped the AS50 in a ravine in the Phoenix Mountains Preserve southwest of the Mayo Clinic—*after* he'd wiped it clean of prints, of course, and had rammed a metal rod down the barrel. That would ensure no one could match the rifling marks to any of the bullets it had fired—in case any had been recovered in usable form.

He'd also changed clothes in one of the restrooms there and had trashed what he'd been wearing in a Dumpster in Paradise Valley. Then he'd returned to his motel west of Phoenix to shave off the beard he'd grown specifically for this job.

But Marsh *hadn't* tried to book a flight out of Phoenix—he'd kept his original ticket for this morning. He was too smart to try to skip town right after the shooting because he knew law enforcement—the Phoenix police *and* the FBI—would be watching closely for that. He'd holed up in his motel room instead, watched the news, then had taken the trim attachment on his electric razor to his somewhat shaggy hair—which he'd also let grow for this job—to make sure no one would recognize him from the video that damned reporter had managed to capture.

No beard and short hair matched the picture on his driver's license, the one he'd displayed when he checked in for his flight in the early-morning hours.

Now he was home—*almost home*, he amended with a slight smile as he exited the freeway. But his smile faded as he acknowledged he had a hell of a lot of work to do once he arrived there. In addition to his contracted job on the senator—and the clock was ticking on that one, as the man who'd hired Marsh had reminded him last night—he also needed to take care of the witness, that damned reporter. The video she'd shot wasn't good enough to conclusively identify him—she'd been too far away and the camera hadn't been completely steady, although she'd tried. But in the unlikely event he was ever pulled in for questioning and forced to take part in a lineup, it was possible she could pick him out, despite his disguise that day. And that was *not* going to happen. Not if Marsh had anything to say about it.

Carly dialed the number J.C. had given her, identified herself to the press secretary then waited, yawning, for the senator himself. She was still several hours short of the seven to eight hours of sleep she needed every night, and she had to fight her body's demands that she go back to bed. There was a time when she could go night and day with only a few catnaps, but she'd been a lot younger then. She wasn't over the hill at thirty-five—not by a long shot!—but she didn't have the stamina she'd had at twenty-five, and she was smart enough to know it. She hadn't lost an ounce of drive—they didn't call her Tiger Shark behind her back for nothing—but she knew her physical limitations. Usually. Senator Jones might not believe that, not after yester—

"Shane Jones," said a voice in her ear. "Ms. Edwards?"

"Yes. You asked me to call you?"

She heard a slight sound, as if the senator had heaved a sigh, before he said, "Yes. About what we discussed two days ago? The assassination attempt has made it impossible to keep my presence at the Mayo Clinic secret. And I have no intention of lying about it. So I'm keeping my word—if you want the exclusive now, it's yours."

If she wanted it. *If* she wanted it? "Of course I want it. And given the sudden interest in you, the sooner the better. I can come to your home or office, but I'll have to bring a crew with me. Easier if you come to the television studio."

"Sounds good. What time? I'm meeting with the FBI at ten and with my entire staff at eleven, but I'm free from noon until four. I have a cocktail party I'm supposed to attend at five..." He mentioned the name of the president pro-tem of the Senate. "And I've been invited to a reception at the Zakharian embassy that starts at seven, which my executive assistant already accepted on my behalf once she knew I'd be back in time. I don't like to blow off prior engagements, but I will if—"

"That won't be necessary," Carly said quickly. "Noon to four works for me." She gave him the address of the studio. "They'll pull you in for makeup first—"

"Oh, cra—I mean crud. Is that really necessary?"

Carly smiled to herself. "It is if you want to look healthy. And I think you do, Senator, especially given what you're going to reveal. The lights wash all the color out of your face—trust me, I know—so in order to look natural, you definitely need makeup."

"Okay, I guess."

"Shouldn't take too long," she assured him. "Oh, and wear a light blue shirt, red tie. The cameras love that combination." She didn't wait for his assent before adding, "I'll have a list of questions prepared by the time you show up, and I'll review them with you while they've got you in the makeup chair."

He chuckled. "That's unusual."

Carly was surprised by the touch of anger that darted through her, and she wanted to leap to her profession's defense. But…there was some truth to his statement. "No surprises, Senator. This isn't an adversarial interview."

"Shane. If we're not going to be adversaries, just call me Shane."

"Shane," she agreed. "And my friends call me Carly."

"Thanks, Carly." Her name sounded different coming from him. Or was that sexy undertone just the way he spoke normally?

Out of the blue she remembered her chaotic dream earlier this morning. Something about Shane and her and a tropical island. But just as they'd been about to make love a platoon of US Marines had landed on the island with one of those landing craft from WWII and swarmed Shane to protect him. He'd immediately ordered the marines to protect her, not him.

But I'm not targeted for assassination, she'd protested as the marines promptly shifted at his command. *Think again,* Shane had said in that deep voice that sent shivers down her spine. *You saw him. You can identify him. He'll be coming after you—count on it.*

* * *

Shane glanced apprehensively at the array of cosmetics, brushes and spray cans on the counter before him, then at the makeup artist draping a large cotton bib over his chest and tucking a towel around his throat, pushing the edges into his shirt collar to keep it from accidentally getting smeared. "Do your worst," he said in the resigned voice of a man going to the guillotine.

The fiftysomething woman chuckled and patted his arm. "Don't worry, honey, I'm the best in the business. When I'm done, you won't look as if you're wearing makeup at all."

Shane tried to ignore whatever it was she was doing to him and focus on Carly sitting on the stool next to him. She'd obviously already been worked on—her face still looked like her but...polished. *That's it*, he thought. *She looks polished.* Her long, dark hair had been braided and coiled into gleaming perfection, her bright blue eyes were huge and thickly fringed with dark lashes, and her mouth—*holy crap, her mouth!*—curved sweetly with the barest hint of gloss to add color. He shifted in the chair, grateful for the expansive bib that hid his body's obvious reaction to the woman he'd known he wanted two days ago—from the first moment he'd met her.

"... At that point I'll ask you to describe the symptoms that caused you to contact the Mayo Clinic," Carly was saying, her eyes on her script, and he forced his attention away from his sudden fantasy of the two of them alone on a desert island. "Keep it short. And don't use any fancy words our viewers might not understand."

"Got it."

She went through the rest of the questions, none of which Shane considered anything but softballs that would allow him to hit home run after home run with his answers. Only once did he object—when she brought up how he'd received the traumatic brain injury the doctors theorized had been the trigger for the seizures.

"No, I'm not going there."

She said patiently, "You don't understand, Senator. People—"

"Shane."

"Shane," she amended. "You don't understand. People are going to want to know what happened."

"It's not up for discussion."

She pursed her lips, her eyes narrowing. "Okay. We won't go there." She crossed a line through that question in her script. But Shane was watching her closely, and he thought he saw something in the expression that fleetingly passed over her face. Something she knew, which she wasn't going to tell him.

He opened his mouth to ask Carly about it when the makeup artist said suddenly, "There, honey, you're all done." She removed the towel and whipped off the bib, then patted the knot of his tie back into place.

He looked in the mirror and realized the woman had been right—he couldn't even tell he was wearing makeup. He looked like himself...only better. And for the first time in his life he understood why women wore makeup. Not that he would ever wear it for anything other than the TV cameras—he could hear his brothers snorting with laughter and making crude jokes at that idea—but still...

"Thank you," he told the woman, catching her eyes in the mirror. "I was wrong. You didn't do your worst, you did your best."

The woman beamed back at him. "'Course I did, honey."

"How do I get this junk off afterward?"

"You leave it to Maggie," Carly said, smiling at both of them. "I'll bring you back here when we're done. Thanks, Maggie, you're a treasure."

As Carly led him toward the sound stage where the interview would be recorded, Shane tugged her sleeve to hold her back for a moment. "Before I forget, I wanted to ask you something."

"What?"

"Would it be breaking any journalistic ethics rules if I asked you to accompany me to the reception at the Zakharian embassy tonight? The invitation was for me and a guest." Carly's eyes widened, as if he'd taken her by surprise. "I hate these formal affairs, but I'd hate them a lot less if I had an intelligent woman to talk with while I was there." He laughed suddenly. "Sorry, that wasn't very smooth. The truth is, I'd really enjoy your company. Will you go with me?"

After they finished taping the interview, J.C. came out of the sound booth to shake Shane's hand. "Great job, Senator. Sorry about the diagnosis, but very glad to hear it's controllable with medication."

"Thanks." Shane didn't say any more, but Carly saw the speculative way he assessed J.C. and then her, as if he was wondering if there was anything between them.

Because he's interested in you? she wondered. *Seriously interested in you? Or just because he's curious?*

Until that point Carly had never really looked at J.C. as a woman would look at a man, but now she did. And what she saw explained why Shane might wonder about their relationship. J.C. was nearly as tall as Shane, just as physically fit and a couple years younger. He wasn't quite as handsome, but he had the kind of face—not to mention that terrific British accent—most women would be attracted to. *But not me*, she insisted. There was no spark with J.C. and never had been. She couldn't say that about Shane.

Carly's gaze caught Shane's, and she shook her head slightly, answering the question she knew he wouldn't ask outright. His dark brown eyes warmed—*there's that chocolate fudge*, she told herself—and a tiny smile played over his lips. And despite telling herself not to, she returned his smile with a tiny one of her own.

She took Shane back to Maggie for removal of what he'd referred to as "junk." Then she returned to the soundstage to confer with J.C. about the interview, which would be "spliced and diced," and put back together, along with a computer-generated reenactment of the domestic terrorism bombing at the bookstore where Shane had been injured five years ago, for broadcast that evening.

A twinge of guilt touched Carly's conscience because she hadn't told Shane about the reenactment when he'd refused to allow any questions about that incident. It had been J.C.'s idea, and she'd enthusiastically agreed this morning, thinking it would be a great visual. But now she wasn't so sure. Oh, it would still be good— but she was fairly sure Shane wouldn't like it. Even less would he like the two-minute film clip interview with the woman whose life—and whose baby's life— he'd saved.

There was something appealing about Shane's in- sistence on keeping that door closed. It said something about his character that he wouldn't use his heroism five years ago to his advantage now. But just as he hadn't been able to keep the news media from telling and re-telling the story when he'd been running for Congress and then for the Senate, he couldn't keep her network from playing the hero card during this exclusive interview. Heroes helped ratings. And though Carly was a hard-hitting investigative reporter with a strong ethical background, ratings were a fact of life.

She considered asking J.C. to ax either the reenactment or the film clip, then decided against it. The network had already spent the money on the computer graphics and to interview the woman. The only argument she could muster was that Shane wouldn't like it, and she didn't think that would carry much weight with J.C. It wouldn't have carried much weight with her, either, three days ago.

Before she'd met Shane.

That realization scared her right down to her shoes, and made her wish she'd turned down Shane's date request instead of accepting it with alarming alacrity. Because if she was looking at herself and her actions differently after only knowing Shane for two days, any more time spent in his company was a disaster waiting to happen.

Chapter 5

"Wow," Shane said when Carly opened the door of her Georgetown town house at his ring. "You look fantastic."

Carly knew from the warmth in her cheeks she was blushing under Shane's admiring stare. Again. She'd blushed in his hospital room and had chastised herself for it. But apparently it wasn't a onetime thing. Not with Shane.

"Thanks. You look pretty fantastic yourself," she said. And he did. From his close-cropped golden-brown hair right down to the spit-and-polish shine on his black dress shoes, Shane looked the epitome of a well-dressed man. His tuxedo, which she could see because his black, camel-hair overcoat was unbuttoned, fit him as if it had been sewn together with him inside it. A gleaming white handkerchief just barely peeked out of his breast pocket. And the white carnation in his lapel was the perfect touch.

He held out a small plastic box, which contained a gorgeous white gardenia wrist corsage. "You said you'd be wearing blue, so I figured white was safe," he said.

Carly managed to get the box open, and the fragrant scent wafted upward. "I love gardenias," she admitted in a low voice. She wasn't going to tell him he'd hit upon her favorite flower, one she hadn't worn since Jack... Gardenias would have been in her bridal bouquet.

She blinked away the sudden tears and stepped back. "I'm not quite ready, so why don't you come on in," she invited, although at that moment she would rather have invited a rattlesnake into her home—and she had a phobia about snakes. She glanced at the schoolhouse clock on the wall in the foyer. "Five minutes," she promised as she dashed up the stairs. "Make yourself at home. I'll be right back."

Shane watched Carly ascend the staircase, grateful for a moment alone to pull himself together. She'd looked so unbelievably lovely when she'd answered the door—her dark hair still in the sophisticated chignon she'd worn during his interview, her sapphire-blue dress shimmering as it clung discretely in all the right places—and he'd been stunned. His heartbeat had quickened and he'd hardened in a rush. *Wanting* was such a pitiful word compared to what Carly made him feel.

He stood right where he was in the foyer, unwilling to make himself at home without Carly there, but glanced at his watch. Plenty of time. He took off his overcoat and slung it over the banister railing, then his eye caught the antique mirror beside the clock and he moved toward it, making a minute adjustment to his bow tie.

That's when the sudden chill hit him.

Shane froze. Not because the chill and the goose bumps incapacitated him, but because he'd believed the doctors at the Mayo Clinic when they told him the seizures would be controlled by the medication he'd been prescribed. Yeah, he'd only been taking it for two and a half days, but still…

"Damn it," he whispered. "Damn it all to hell and back."

"Shane?"

He whirled around. He hadn't heard Carly come down the stairs, but there she stood at the foot of the staircase, her hand clutching the banister, her eyes wide in a face from which all color had fled. "It's happening, isn't it?"

A statement, not a question. And Shane knew she knew. He didn't confirm it, but he didn't deny it, either. He waited a few more seconds, and the symptoms disappeared, as always.

"I thought you said the seizures were controllable."

He nodded slowly. "But I didn't tell you the medication has to build up in my system. Two days isn't long enough. A week. Two weeks. Possibly more. The doctors weren't able to give me a set time frame."

She put a hand over her mouth for a moment, her eyes meeting his in empathy. Eventually she drew her hand away and said, "I'm so sorry, Shane."

He shook his head. "Nothing to do with you. I'm just impatient, I guess. I want it to be over *now*."

She moved until she was standing right in front of

him. He had six inches on her normally, but her heels gave her added height. Her hands cradled his face, then she touched her lips to his. "I'm so sorry," she repeated, her breath catching in her throat. Then her hands were sliding down, over his shoulders, over his chest. "I know bad things happen to good people, but it just doesn't seem fair that—"

Her left hand paused at the lump beneath the right arm of his tuxedo jacket. "What on earth...?"

Shane stepped back from Carly. "I'm strapped for a left-handed draw because I'm left-handed," he told her, his voice suddenly cool. "And yes, I have a permit for it. I can't carry a handgun into a government building, so I haven't worn it recently. But after yesterday I'm not going anywhere unarmed if I can help it."

To his surprise, Carly suddenly laughed. She tried to hold it back, but it bubbled out of her, and her eyes danced with merriment. "Oh, Shane, I should have known." She bent down, grasped the hem of her sapphire-blue gown, and tugged it upward, revealing those long, lovely legs he'd first admired in his hospital room. She kept raising the hem until she revealed something else. A gun strapped securely to her right thigh.

"Are you kidding me?" Shane could scarcely believe it. "*You're* packing?"

"I have a concealed carry permit, too, which I got a little while ago," she admitted, letting her hem slide back down her leg. "And thank goodness I did. But I've had my twenty-two for years, and I know how to use it. I told you, I've covered two wars and three 'police actions.' And DC isn't the safest city for a single woman to live in."

"Were you armed when—"

She shook her head. "I have a permit for DC, and while some states do have reciprocity, including Arizona, it's not easy transporting a gun on an airplane even if you do have a permit for it. Whenever I leave the country on assignment, though, my twenty-two goes with me."

"So you were going armed to the embassy tonight?" he asked.

"I might have to check my gun at the door," she told him. "I totally get that. But I'm not risking anyone taking another shot at you if I can prevent it."

From the shelter of his darkened truck halfway down the block, Marsh Anderson watched Senator Jones walk out of the town house, a woman on his arm. Then he did a double take when the couple passed under a street lamp right before the senator held the door open for his companion and helped her into the car he'd parked at the curb a few minutes ago.

Marsh smiled grimly. Both of his targets together—the senator *and* the reporter. He'd trailed Senator Jones here, expecting him to head for the Zakharian embassy—the insider had insisted that's where he was supposed to be from seven to ten—so he'd wondered when the senator had driven to Georgetown instead of heading for Embassy Row.

He'd almost been tempted to try installing the little surprise he had for the senator's car when Jones had entered the town house, but his caution had paid off. He would have needed more than the few minutes the senator was out of sight.

Marsh was nothing if not resourceful. He had to be. Paid assassins were only paid in full when their targets were dead. And his reputation was only as good as his last kill. Some assassins were expert marksmen. Some had a light touch with gelignite and detonating cord—common explosives. Some were even stupid enough to dabble in plutonium and similar heavy metals that were as dangerous to the killer as they were to the target.

Marsh wasn't stupid. And he had no intention of dying. So he had no plans to ever get anywhere near anything that could kill him as easily as it killed his target. But gelignite and det cord? If you knew what you were doing, which Marsh did, you could take care of two problems—a junior senator and a nosy journalist—at the same time.

Marsh started his engine and put his truck into gear as soon as the senator's car pulled away from the curb. Then quietly...from a safe distance...followed his targets.

The reception was in full swing when Shane handed his invitation—along with his Beretta M9—to one of the guards on the door at the Zakharian embassy. He glanced at Carly, who handed over her .22 without a word...and without having to pull up her skirt.

His eyes asked the question, and she whispered in his ear, "I put it in my coat pocket when we were in the car."

After they checked their coats, she placed her hand on Shane's arm and they both passed through the portable metal detector without setting off any alarms. They circulated for a couple of minutes, then joined the receiving line. At the far end stood a tall, regal-looking man in a white dress uniform with a diminutive, dark-haired woman at his side, also in white, wearing the most spectacular diamond tiara Carly had ever seen atop her raven tresses.

Her mouth dropped open for a moment, then she closed it. "That's not—you didn't tell me the King and Queen of Zakhar were going to be here."

The corners of Shane's mouth twitched into a half smile. "Don't you stay abreast of the news?"

That had been strictly true when she'd been a national correspondent—*everything* had been connected, and her job had depended on her being in the know. Always. But she'd switched to investigative journalism last year, which had freed her to concentrate on one story at a time, and she'd quickly grown to love it. "I usually do," she explained to Shane, "but not when I'm focused on another story." She didn't have to tell him what story that was.

"He was here to meet with the president—there was a state dinner on Friday to which I was invited…but had to decline for reasons you already know. She's here because she goes almost everywhere with him, although they don't travel with their son."

"I understand why, but it must be difficult for her— for *them*," she corrected quickly, "to be away from their baby."

"They don't do it often. This is the rare exception. After they leave here he'll address the United Nations tomorrow before they head home to Zakhar."

"How do you know so much about them?"

"Unlike you, I *do* keep abreast of the news." When she shot him a dagger look, he chuckled. "Okay, I'll confess. My brother Alec, who's the regional security officer at the US embassy in Zakhar, is friends with the king."

Carly blinked. "Alec Jones is your brother?"

"You know him?"

Her brain was working furiously. "No, but my sister, Tahra, works for him in Zakhar, and I covered a major story he was involved in—the human trafficking case."

"Small world."

"Then that means Liam Jones is your brother, too?"

"Right again."

Her respect for Shane grew. "You have an amazing family."

"You know Liam?"

"I interviewed his wife after the trial. She was the primary witness in that case and an incredibly brave woman. I don't know if I would have had the guts to testify in open court to what she went through."

"Yeah, Cate's pretty terrific."

"I only exchanged about ten words with your brother during that interview. What I remember most about him was how he sat quietly beside his wife, holding her hand the entire time. Her story had to have sickened him just as it did me, but he didn't flinch once. Just held her hand and squeezed it reassuringly from time to time."

"Sounds like Liam."

"Didn't he save her life twice? Once by taking a bullet meant for her?"

He chuckled. "Yeah. Liam always was a bit of a white knight."

Her tone was dry when she drawled, "It must run in the family." Shane had no snappy comeback, and Carly got the impression compliments of that nature made him uncomfortable. She filed that little tidbit away to consider later and changed the subject. "I had no idea you were related to Alec and Liam."

"I didn't know your sister worked for Alec, either."

"It *is* a small world, just as you said." She tilted her head to one side as she tried to figure the odds.

"Smaller than you think." She raised a questioning eyebrow, and he told her, "Alec's wife, Angelina, heads up the security detail for Queen Juliana," he said, slanting his head in the queen's direction. "I kid you not," he assured her. "I've never met either of the royals myself, but I figure Alec and Angelina are why I was on the guest list for the state dinner, and why I was invited to tonight's reception." He gave her a self-deprecating smile. "A junior senator from Colorado doesn't rate otherwise."

She didn't know why she did it, but she leaped to his defense. "That's not true. You haven't been in office very long, but you've made an impact. That domestic terrorism bill you cosponsored was—"

"Shot down."

"Yes, but you didn't give up," she argued. "A revised version is on the agenda for the upcoming legislative session, and—"

"Will probably be shot down again. I'm a realist, Carly," he said gently. "Stubborn about what I believe in, but realistic enough to know when I'm tilting at windmills."

That made her ask, "Then why do you keep doing it? Tilting at windmills."

"Because I can't *not* do whatever I can to make the world a safer place."

She suddenly remembered his wife and unborn son had been killed by terrorists fifteen years ago, so she didn't pursue the discussion further. *Some wounds shouldn't be touched*, she acknowledged. She cast around in her mind for another topic of conversation, and her gaze fell on Zakhar's royal couple, much closer now that she and Shane had been shuffling along in line as they spoke.

"I wish I'd known they'd be here," Carly said in a rueful undertone. "I wish you'd told me. I would have—"

"You're perfect as you are." His eyes, those beautiful brown eyes, softened. "You take my breath away."

She gazed up at Shane, suddenly caught in a trance where everything around them faded into nothingness. The quiet, sincere way he'd uttered that sentence gave it far more importance than the words themselves, and Carly's stomach quivered. Something else quivered, too. That had *never* happened to her in the middle of a conversation, not even with Jack. "Shane, I…" She couldn't continue because suddenly she couldn't breathe.

He stared back at her, and she knew he was as entranced as she was. Then he seemed to shake it off. "Come on," he urged, but his voice wasn't quite steady. "We'll lose our place in line if we don't keep moving."

Carly let Shane draw her forward, but she scarcely knew what she was doing because her thoughts were swirling so chaotically she couldn't really focus on anything but him. All she could feel was his arm beneath her hand, his body next to hers. All she could hear was his voice in her ears.

Desire curled in her belly. Desire she hadn't felt in forever. It was crazy. *Crazy.* She didn't sleep around. Especially with men like Shane. Carly had had exactly two lovers in the eight years since Jack died. Two. Six months with one, eight with the other. Both men she had known for a while and liked. Respected. But both had known going in that Carly had boundaries they were never going to cross. It wasn't just sex with them, but...

Both times Carly had ended the relationship when the men had shown signs of wanting permanence. Which was never going to happen, not with them. She hadn't broken their hearts—she'd made sure of it. And both men had ended up marrying women she knew, women who were right for them, something Carly could never have been. She still saw both men socially, still maintained casual friendships with them and their wives. There could have been awkwardness, but she'd made sure there wasn't because everyone had known her heart belonged to Jack. Still. Always.

Only...what she was feeling for Shane threatened that. Which was crazy. She'd known him three days. Three *days*. Not only that, he'd suffered a traumatic brain injury similar to Jack's. Which meant it was possible he'd end up the way Jack had, and she'd end up the way she'd been eight years ago—devastated, guilt-ridden and alone.

Not going to happen, she admonished herself, frantically trying to rebuild her protective walls, walls that somehow crumbled to dust when Shane was around.

It's just sex, she thought feverishly. *You haven't had sex in three years—that's all it is. Shane is a walking advertisement for everything good about men, and you're feeling needy. So take him to bed, let him put out the fire he started and cross him off your list.*

Carly realized with a start that they were nearing the front of the line. Bodyguards stood at the elbows of the king and queen of Zakhar, their eyes hard and watchful. And an aide also stood ahead of them, taking names and announcing them to the royals.

"Senator Shane Jones and Ms. Carly Edwards," Shane murmured when it was their turn. The aide dutifully repeated his words, then King Andre Alexei IV was shaking her hand.

"Ms. Edwards, so glad you could join us," he said with a faint smile that seemed sincere.

Carly managed a slight curtsy. "Thank you, Your Majesty."

She moved on to Queen Juliana, who clasped her hand, saying, "I've met your sister, Tahra, Ms. Edwards. A very sweet young woman." Before Carly could express her surprise that the queen knew of her family connection, Queen Juliana added, "Tahra talks about you a lot—she's very proud of her famous sister."

Carly responded suitably, but she couldn't help overhearing the exchange between Shane and the king.

"Senator Jones, I was sorry you were unable to make dinner at the White House Friday night—I specifically asked for you because I wished to make your acquaintance," the king was saying. "I am so glad you were able to be here tonight. Your family speaks highly of you, and praise from them is praise indeed."

Shane laughed softly. "I'm the oldest of five," he admitted, then added tongue in cheek, "I've brainwashed my brothers and sister into thinking I can do no wrong."

The king laughed. "Hardly that. But I would enjoy talking with you—" he glanced down the receiving line, which still had a long way to go, then sighed ever so softly "—once my duty here is done. Please do me the honor of staying until we have spoken again."

After Shane had shaken the queen's hand, he and Carly moved away, then wandered into the next room, which was resplendent with lights. Shane snagged a glass of champagne for Carly, but declined one for himself. Surprised, she asked, "You're not drinking?"

"I'm driving."

"One drink shouldn't—"

"And one of the side effects of the medication I'm on is an increased tendency toward sleepiness. No," he reassured her when her eyes widened with alarm, "if I felt at all sleepy, I wouldn't have driven here. But alcohol can have the same effect, so I'm not risking it." His voice dropped. "I'm not risking you, Carly."

Just like that, her thoughts skidded down the path they'd taken earlier. She'd never made love with a man whose first and last inclination was a fierce protectiveness of those around him, and she couldn't help but imagine what it would be like. She'd never been a fairy-tale kind of woman. Had never needed rescuing—she could rescue herself, thank you very much! But there was something particularly appealing about an everyday hero. A man who didn't have to think about being heroic, he just was—heroism came as naturally to Shane as breathing.

And Carly knew she was in trouble.

Chapter 6

Marsh slid out from beneath Senator Jones's shadow-black Ford Mustang GT, levered himself up and dusted off his clothes with his gloved hands. He'd stealthily followed the car when one of the valets parking cars at the Zakharian embassy had taken the keys from the senator and driven the Mustang to this location. He'd patiently waited for almost an hour, until no more vehicles had arrived for at least twenty minutes. Then he'd gone to work.

He'd originally intended to wire the bomb to the ignition, but had been forced to rethink that when the car had been valet parked. Fortunately, he was a man who always thought two steps ahead, and he'd had a battery-operated remote detonation device with him. He'd wait until the senator and the reporter were safely inside the Mustang, trail them for a couple of miles to a fairly deserted area, then...

* * *

"Buy American," Shane told Carly as he retrieved his Beretta from the guard at the front door and holstered it, handed Carly her .22, then helped her on with her coat before donning his own. He turned over his valet ticket outside the Zakharian embassy, but kept a watchful eye on their environs as they waited for his car to be brought around. "That's the first thing my political advisors insisted on when I ran for Congress. Buy American."

She pointed toward the pistol already tucked away. "A Beretta isn't American made."

"No, but it's standard issue for the US Marine Corps, and I'm familiar with it. I do own a Smith & Wesson I inherited from my dad—I just prefer the Beretta I'm used to. I figure if the Corps uses it, the public can't complain." He smiled. "Besides, a gun isn't in the public eye the way a car is. So I used the 'Buy American' dictum as an excuse to buy my dream car—a Mustang GT."

"What had you been driving?"

He laughed. "A Toyota Corolla. I'd wanted a Mustang ever since I was a kid. But for one reason or another, I'd always driven practical cars, even before I was married."

He stopped abruptly. He hadn't talked about his deceased wife in years. At first he hadn't mentioned Wendy's name because it made his friends uncomfortable—they didn't know what to say to him. Then it had gotten to be a habit. Not that he didn't think about her. He did. Especially on certain days, such as her birthday, their anniversary and the anniversary of the day she'd been murdered. And at Christmastime. He always thought of Wendy at Christmas.

"Her name was Wendy, wasn't it?" Carly asked. "What was she like?"

Their eyes met, and Shane knew the question wasn't just idle curiosity on Carly's part—she really wanted to know. He automatically turned his gaze back to the street, on the alert for any betraying movement while he thought about what to tell her. "She was special to me. To everyone who knew her, really. We were high school sweethearts—stereotypical, I know. I joined the Corps out of high school while Wendy went to college. And when I realized I wanted to make the Corps my career, she supported my decision, even though she was scared to death whenever I was deployed. We were married the day after I graduated from OCS. That's—"

"Officer Candidates School," Carly finished for him. "Yes, I know."

He glanced at her, then focused on the street again. "It's funny," he said. "Wendy was always worried about me, but I was never injured in combat. All the theaters of war I served in, and not a single scratch. But Wendy…" He trailed off.

"I know what happened, Shane," Carly said softly. "You don't have to tell me."

A pang went through him as it always did when he remembered the details. When he remembered having to identify his wife's mutilated corpse. "She was seven months pregnant," he rasped. "What kind of twisted monsters kidnap a pregnant woman, then use her to send a political message?"

"Subhumans," she stated. "Not sick. Not twisted. Not even men. Just subhuman."

That's the perfect word for them, Shane thought. *Subhuman*. He'd tracked down Wendy's murderers— a terrorist cell operating from Belgium. He'd wanted so badly to take them down himself, to avenge Wendy and their unborn son by wiping their murderers from the face of the earth. But he hadn't been able to do it. Some spark of humanity had remained, and he'd called in the Belgian army instead.

But he hadn't shed a tear when the terrorists had blown themselves up rather than be captured.

Shane was relieved when he saw his black Mustang pull up in front of the embassy. Not that he was in a hurry for his evening with Carly to end, but because he really didn't want to think about Wendy anymore tonight.

He'd been involved with a few women in the fifteen years since Wendy's death. But none who touched his emotions the way Carly did. He'd gone from admiration—and, okay, lust—to anger at how careless she was with her safety in the blink of an eye. Then the pendulum had swung back to admiration and—yeah, yeah, yeah—lust again. She was a complex woman with more facets than a diamond, and he wanted to delve beneath the surface to discover what kind of woman she was at heart.

Tonight when she'd opened the door to her town house, he'd been blown away at how beautiful she was in that shimmering blue dress, and all he'd wanted to do was take it off her. Okay, *rip* it off her, but he'd settle for unzipping it and gently sliding it from her body. A body that was a challenge he wasn't strong enough to resist. And yet, she didn't seem to have any idea how much he wanted her.

He automatically took Carly's arm and guided her down the stairs, a gesture that wasn't strictly necessary since the embassy stairway and the sidewalk in front of it had been meticulously cleaned of every vestige of snow and ice. But he'd had his manners drummed into him by his parents, who'd taught him a gentleman always helped a lady. Always. Old-fashioned? Yeah. Condescending toward women, who could manage for themselves in this day and age? Not at all.

Shane had quickly learned in the Marine Corps that his father's attitude toward women was outdated and sexist. He'd served alongside women who deserved— and got—respect from him. And when his baby sister, Keira, had joined the Corps when she turned eighteen, as all four of her older brothers had done, he'd adjusted the way he thought of her, too.

But respect was one thing. Courtesy was another. Just as he used *sir* and *ma'am* when addressing the older generation, he would continue to treat his date with the courtesy she deserved—including taking her arm in any situation where she might conceivably need his assistance.

Shane accepted the Mustang's keys from the valet and slipped him a generous tip, then superseded him when the man would have opened the passenger door for Carly. "I've got this," he told the valet.

He didn't make a big deal out of it, just made sure Carly was comfortably seated before closing the door and walking around the front toward the driver's side. Then he stopped abruptly when he saw something that shouldn't be there. "Son of a bitch," he whispered under his breath, completely forgetting to place a curb on his tongue. His body was already moving back to the passenger side, tugging Carly out of the seat and away from the Mustang without conscious thought. "Clear the street if you can," he barked at the two valets who approached him. "And if you can't, keep everyone away from the car. I think it's wired to explode."

"Shane, what—" Carly began breathlessly as he hustled her back up the stairs and into the embassy.

"I'll tell you in a minute," he assured her. To the guards on the door he said, "Call the DC police and the FBI. Tell them to send the bomb squad. And don't let anyone leave the embassy until they get here." Such was Shane's air of command that one of the guards immediately turned to the nearest phone to do his bidding. Shane quickly explained to the other guard, "If I'm right, my car has been wired with explosives. I don't know if it's rigged to explode at a certain time or if it's radio controlled, but either way it's a threat to anyone out there. Can you see if the embassy can somehow cordon off the street until the police and FBI get here?"

Marsh hadn't hung around when he saw his targets slip through his fingers. He hadn't been prepared for the senator's sudden suspicion and quick reaction. By the time he grabbed the remote control device on the seat next to him, the senator and the reporter were already near the top of the embassy stairs—too late to set off the bomb with any certainty of killing them. Marsh had cursed under his breath, then hightailed it out of the vicinity.

He didn't waste time bemoaning fate. He didn't believe in it. Fate was an excuse used by lesser men for inadequate preparation or improper execution. As he drove, Marsh mercilessly analyzed his actions tonight, from start to finish, and came to the conclusion that his preparation had been flawless. Which meant his mistake was in execution. *Something* had set off alarm bells in the senator's head this time, same as last time.

A flash of admiration for the other man's instincts in no way mitigated Marsh's determination that next time he would succeed in killing his targets. Hopefully the man on the inside would be able to tell Marsh exactly how he'd screwed up. This was twice now that Marsh had underestimated the senator. He wouldn't make that mistake again.

It was after two in the morning before Carly's FBI and ATF interrogators reluctantly agreed with her assertion that she'd told them everything she knew—which wasn't much—and she'd be happy to continue if she wasn't falling asleep. Which she was. Twice now she'd ignored the agents in the interrogation room with her and had put her head down on the table for a five-minute catnap.

She hadn't gotten much sleep the previous night. And though she'd accepted Shane's invitation to the reception at the Zakharian embassy, the gala affair was to have ended at ten. Which meant Carly would have been asleep by eleven at the latest. *Unless you brought Shane home with you*, a tiny corner of her mind reminded her. But she had no intention of telling the FBI and ATF agents *that*.

"We must ask you to keep what you know to yourself, Ms. Edwards," one of the men said. "This is an ongoing investigation."

Carly shook her head. "Not going to happen. You can't muzzle the press. But," she added, when one of the men looked as if he was going to argue—and she was too tired to argue—"I don't know anything. So you don't have to worry." *Which is true*, she reminded herself. *I don't even know what Shane saw that tipped him off to the bomb.* And there *had* been a bomb. Her interrogators had refused to say yes or no, but the participation of the ATF agents in the interview was a dead giveaway.

The reminder of Shane and how long the questioning had gone on made her worry about him. He'd already had one seizure in her town house—what if it happened again?

She stood, shrugged into her coat and tucked her evening bag under her arm. "I must ask you to return my gun. I have a valid carry permit, and my gun is in no way evidence in this investigation."

"No problem," one of the FBI agents told her. "You can pick it up as you leave."

She nodded. "Okay. Can someone call a cab for me? I went to the embassy with the senator, and—"

The agents looked at each other. "Someone will drive you home, Ms. Edwards. We appreciate your cooperation. We'll be in touch if we have any more questions."

Shane glanced at his watch. He'd been here for nearly four hours, and for the last two he'd done nothing but repeat the same facts he'd already recounted during the first two. Endlessly. The FBI and ATF agents had been deferential—he was a US senator, after all—but their questions had changed slightly with each round, as if they were trying to trip him up somehow. It would almost have been funny—if he wasn't so damned tired. If he wasn't worrying about Carly. If he wasn't feeling so guilty for having put her through this *again*—the same kind of monotonous and probably just as pointless interrogation they'd both gone through after the assassination attempt in Arizona.

"We're done here, gentlemen," he said now, standing abruptly. He picked up his tuxedo jacket, which he'd hung on the back of his chair a few hours ago, and shrugged it on. Then he retrieved his overcoat from the chair beside him. "I've answered your questions to the best of my ability. I have nothing more to offer. I don't know who's trying to kill me, or why. Do I have enemies? Professionally, maybe, but none that I'm aware of. And no enemies in my personal life, as far as I know. As for tonight's incident, if you're thinking it was some kind of publicity stunt—think again. I don't operate that way. I never have."

The four agents in the room glanced at each other, then back at Shane. "Why would you bring that up, Senator?" the lead FBI agent asked in silky tones.

Shane smiled cynically. "I can read between the lines. All I can say is it happened, whether you believe it or not. All I can tell you is what I've said a dozen times already—the car was speckled with dried slush from the streets...*except* for that tiny patch on the panel below the driver's side door, which had been smudged. The light from the streetlamp just happened to hit it at an angle where I could see it when I came around the corner of the car."

"The valet could have touched that spot with his leg when he got in or out of the car."

Shane shook his head. "It wasn't that kind of a smudge. This was *dried* dirt. There was no reason for that area to be smudged when the rest of the car was still clearly speckled, unless someone had grasped the panel. I can't tell you how I knew in that instant my car had been tampered with, I just did. That's the only conscious thought I had. And I knew I had to get Ms. Edwards out of the car and far away from it as soon as possible."

Shane fought off a wave of tiredness, praying he wouldn't experience a seizure in front of these FBI and ATF agents. It wasn't likely—he rarely had more than one a day, and he'd already had one in Carly's town house this evening. Could he hide the symptoms? Hell yeah, he'd been doing it for months. Still…it was a concern. Even though he'd already given Carly the interview this afternoon—which would have aired tonight—he wasn't about to let strangers see him as anything less than perfectly healthy. Especially men who were already suspicious of him for God knew what reason.

The reminder of Carly made him ask, "Has Ms. Edwards been released yet? I'm responsible for her, and I need to make sure she gets home safely."

"We'll check, Senator," one of the agents replied before he headed out of the room. He returned a minute later. "She's just leaving now—signing for the release of her weapon. One of our agents will be driving her home. Did you—"

Shane interrupted him. "I want to talk with her. And I need my Beretta back, too."

Carly turned and saw Shane approaching. And despite being so sleepy she could barely keep her eyes open, warmth suffused her at the expression in his eyes. An expression that conveyed how worried he'd been on her behalf. Worry that was only partially lessened by seeing her. Something about that protective attitude appealed to her far more than she'd ever thought it would.

Long before her parents died when she was seventeen, Carly had always been the one doing the protecting. Looking out for her little sister, Tahra. Fighting battles for every underdog who came into her orbit. Standing up to bullies. Challenging the status quo when that meant someone else's suffering.

After her parents died and Carly assumed sole responsibility for Tahra, she'd only grown more protective of her sister…and everyone she knew. Which was one of the reasons she'd blamed herself for Jack's death—how many times had she told herself she should have been on the lookout for the warning signs?

Carly had never stopped to think that protection was a two-way street. That in a strong, healthy relationship, *both* parties should have each other's back. No one had looked out for Carly in so long she'd forgotten what it felt like.

And what it felt like with Shane was incredibly… comforting.

"You okay?" he asked softly as he came up to her.

"Fine," she answered automatically. Then amended, "Tired. Really, really tired."

"Yeah, me, too." He grinned suddenly. "Want to blow this hotdog stand?"

That idiomatic expression from her childhood made her laugh, and she responded in kind with a phrase her father had often used. "I'll give you a bright, shiny nickel to get me out of here."

"Deal," he said promptly. "Let's get a cab."

"The FBI offered me a ride home."

"That's more than they offered me." He let his gaze slide over her, and teased, "Maybe I should have worn blue."

She laughed again, wanting to hug him for making her see the humor in an otherwise tense and trying situation, and her eyes twinkled at him. "Maybe you should have."

He shook his head with mock regret. "Nah, I can't compete with you in the evening dress portion of the competition." His lips twitched as if he were holding back a smile. "And I doubt I'd be able to win the swimsuit competition, either."

Carly caught her breath, because suddenly the expression in Shane's eyes changed from teasing to something else. Something hot. Something tempting. Heat flashed between them, and her knees did that little wobbly thing she'd already noticed he could engender in her without half trying.

"Take me home, Shane," she whispered, her eyes answering *yes!* to the question his eyes were asking. "Please."

Carly fell asleep in the cab on the way home. Shane cradled her against his shoulder, enjoying the simple pleasure of having her in his arms, even in such a chaste way. It was obvious she'd invited him home because she wanted him the way he wanted her. Because desire flared between them with only a look. A touch. But the only sleeping done tonight would be *sleeping*. And strangely enough, he didn't mind. He'd forgotten how good it felt to hold a woman when the ultimate goal wasn't sex. When the ultimate goal was merely... holding her.

He breathed deeply, luxuriating in the soft, delicate scent of Carly's hair, her skin. And he smiled to himself at the slightly wistful expression on her face in repose. Carly liked to think of herself as invulnerable, and maybe she was. But not when she was sleeping.

When they arrived at Carly's town house, he was torn between waking her and carrying her. He *could* carry her...she was tall for a woman, but she didn't weigh all that much, despite the voluptuousness of her body that she usually tried to disguise. But carrying her on a sidewalk that might be icy held its own risks. And besides, he'd still have to wake her once they got to her front door.

Deciding, he shook her gently. "Carly? You have to wake up now, Carly."

She awoke with a start. "I wasn't sleeping," she told him as her eyelids fluttered but remained closed. She snuggled back against his shoulder. "I was just resting my eyes."

"Right. Well, you have to open your eyes now. We're here."

"We are?" She straightened abruptly and glanced around, then blinked owlishly and said, "Oh. We are."

"Come on," he said. "I'll walk you to your door." He handed his credit card to the cab driver. "Don't leave. I'm coming right back."

"No problem."

Outside the cab, the cold air woke Carly better than he could have done, but Shane took her arm until they were safely on her doorstep, just in case.

She fumbled in her evening bag until she found the key, then unlocked the door and turned to face him. "Shane, I..."

He touched her face, sliding his fingers along the curve of her cheek and coming to rest beneath her chin. "You're dead on your feet," he told her. "Sleepy, early-morning sex might be great, but not for our first time." He kissed her lightly. Then kissed her again, not so lightly, as desire for her surged through his body. "Tell me to go home, Carly," he rasped, drawing back a little, even though it was the last thing he wanted to do.

"Go home, Shane," she agreed, smiling faintly. She tugged his head down until she could brush her lips against his. "You're right—not our first time."

Chapter 7

Carly woke from an erotic dream of Shane, then curled tighter in her warm cocoon of bedclothes, thinking about him. About last night. And about how she wished it had ended. She tucked her hand between her pillow and her cheek and let her imagination run riot.

Eventually, though, she sighed, stretched and yawned. Then dozed off. She soon found herself in another dream of Shane—one that had nothing to do with sex or attempted murder. All he was doing was smiling at her in a quizzical way, his gorgeous brown eyes sending a message she couldn't quite interpret. Not yet. But if she stood there long enough, she knew the answer would come to her. If she could just—

The phone beside her bed shrilled, shocking her awake, and she grabbed it. "Hello?" She couldn't help that her voice was grumpy.

"Good morning, sunshine," her producer said.

She told him exactly what he could do with his *good morning*, and he laughed softly, which chafed her temper raw. "What do you want, J.C.?" she demanded. "I didn't get to bed until after three, and it's…" She squinted at the clock on her nightstand. "It's barely eight. Between last night and the night before, I've gotten less than nine hours of sleep. Don't you have a life?"

"Sure I do. My job is my life."

She told him what he could do with that, too, and he laughed again before turning serious, saying, "A little bird told me there was another attempt on Senator Jones's life last night." That made her sit up with a jerk.

"Who told you?"

"Not you." He let that statement hang there like a silent accusation, then said, "And my little bird told me you were right there in the thick of things."

"I can't tell you anything because I don't *know* anything," Carly was quick to explain. "Yes, I was there, but not as a reporter. I was on a *date*, J.C. You should try it sometime," she added caustically.

He ignored her statement. "My sources tell me someone tried to blow the senator to hell and gone after the reception at the Zakharian embassy. And the bomb could have killed you, too."

"Are you asking for confirmation as my producer? Or as my friend?"

There was a slight hesitation at the other end. "Both."

Carly rubbed her eyes and fought back a sudden yawn. Not that this conversation wasn't important, but she was still sleepy. And she needed to think before she spoke. Needed to choose her words carefully. She trusted J.C., but… "Professionally, I'm standing mute—

I refuse to go on the record. As your friend, the answer is yes. I was in the car. I don't know how he knew, but Shane—"

"Shane? He's Shane to you now?"

"He was my *date*, J.C." Her tone was wry. "Don't you call *your* dates by their first names? Or don't you have any?" She didn't wait for an answer. "Shane saved my life. I don't know anything about the bomb or how it was wired to explode or anything—the FBI and the ATF wouldn't tell me a damned thing." *And I was too sleepy to question Shane afterward*, she thought but didn't volunteer. "But somehow he knew, and he got me out of the car so fast I had no idea I was even in danger until I wasn't. Then the bomb squad showed up and the FBI and the ATF. And I spent most of the next four hours being interrogated by experts. But I couldn't tell them any more than I can tell you—I don't know anything."

"If you say so."

There was just enough of a question in the way he said those four words for Carly to vehemently repeat, "I. Don't. Know. Anything."

There was silence at the other end for a moment. "Okay, but I'm pulling you off anything related to Senator Jones."

"What?"

"You're part of the story now, Carly," J.C. explained patiently. "You can't be objective. Not if you're right in the middle of it."

Carly seethed, although she knew in her gut her producer was right. But she didn't have to like it. "Who are you putting on it?"

"Pearly White." It wasn't his real name, of course, just the disdainful nickname Carly had given Tate Westerly. He was pretty-boy handsome, and his capped teeth gleamed pearly white when he smiled, hence the nickname. He wasn't much of a reporter, but he played well to the cameras, and his likeability index with the viewers was high.

"That bozo?"

"You got the big exclusives," J.C. consoled her. "The first assassination attempt. The epilepsy story. At this point it's just a matter of reporting what someone else uncovers. And no matter what we think of him professionally, Tate *is* good in front of the camera."

"Just keep him away from me," Carly insisted. "He tries to ask me any questions about *my* story, and he'll find out what I really think of him."

"Don't worry, I'll keep him out of your hair." She could tell J.C. was relieved he'd managed to skate right over what he liked to call a "sticky wicket," and what Carly referred to as a disaster waiting to happen.

"If there's nothing else, J.C., I'd like to get a couple more hours of sleep before coming in to work. If I can't work on the attempted assassination story, do you have a new assignment for me?"

"Nothing urgent. We can discuss it when you get in."

"Sounds good. See you then." Carly hung up, then fell back against the pillow and pulled the bedclothes over her head. *Sleep*, she ordered herself. She was pretty good at that. Just like a lot of soldiers, she could sleep anytime, anywhere, given the opportunity.

She was floating in that half-awake half-asleep state when the phone rang once more. She snatched the phone off the cradle, assuming it was J.C. again, and snarled, "What now?"

"And good morning to you, too." Shane's voice, warm and amused, sounded in her ear.

Marsh disconnected his disposable cell phone—cutting off his conversation with his contact on the inside—before he cursed. Disposable or not, he was discretion personified on the phone. He never let his clients—or their hirelings—know what he was thinking. And he especially never let on when he'd made a mistake.

But he was angry with himself for his carelessness. He'd worn gloves, of course—he wasn't stupid enough to leave fingerprints. He wasn't stupid enough to leave DNA, either, if he could possibly prevent it. But in this case the gloves had been his mistake. Who could have foreseen the gloves would smudge the dried dirt splatters on the panel below the driver's side door of the senator's car when Marsh had slid beneath it to set the bomb? Or that the senator would notice that tiny patch where the dirt splatters should have been but weren't?

"Should have thought of that," Marsh muttered to himself. "Planning? Perfect. Execution? Flawed." Respect for his target made him add, "He's smarter and more observant than anyone you've gone up against before. Which means you need to be on top of your game. No more screwups."

"I'm sorry," Carly told Shane. "I thought it was J.C. calling again. My producer."

"Yeah, I met him yesterday, remember?" His voice turned dry. "I have epilepsy, not amnesia."

Carly winced at first, until she realized something. "Hey, if you can joke about it, then—"

"It's getting a little easier to talk about...with you. I haven't received any feedback from my constituency on the interview that aired last night, but my mom called while we were at the reception and left a message on my answering machine—I heard it when I got in this morning. *She* thinks it went okay, but we'll have to see what the polls say."

She was suddenly reminded that since Shane hadn't seen the broadcast, he still didn't know... "I have to tell you something," she began, but he interrupted her.

"Can it wait? The Senate will convene at nine and I just arrived at the office—I slept late this morning. I have several things I need to do before going down to the Senate floor, but I had to call and see how you're doing this morning after last night."

"Sleepy, but otherwise I'm fine," she assured him. "But I have to tell you—"

"Will you have dinner with me tonight? Lunch is impossible, I'm afraid, but—hang on a second, please," he said, and Carly could hear voices in the background. When he came back on the line he said, "I have to go. Dinner?" His voice dropped a notch. "Please, Carly."

"Okay, dinner."

"I'll pick you up. What time?"

Surprised, she asked, "You have your Mustang back?"

"Not yet, but my executive assistant arranged a rental car. So what time should I pick you up?"

She thought quickly, and said, "Seven." It was always possible he'd call and cancel...if he found out what she hadn't told him about last night's broadcast. If he didn't cancel, then...

"Seven it is. See you then."

* * *

Carly was jumpy and nervous all day. Every time her office phone or her cell phone rang, she was sure it would be Shane, calling to say she'd betrayed him by not telling him about the computer-generated reenactment and the interview with the woman he'd saved that had been included in last night's broadcast. But every time it wasn't him. She was so worried about Shane's reaction that when the overnights came in—the ratings on her interview with Shane—they barely registered, even though her colleagues praised her for the journalistic coup that had also been a ratings success. She was so distracted that when J.C. laid out three potential stories he wanted her to pursue, she just said *fine* without picking one to focus on first.

She still hadn't heard a word from Shane by the time she left work. So she went home and dressed for their upcoming date as if she were facing a firing squad. She tossed aside a "little black dress" she loved in favor of a killer red, practically backless one whose hem floated several inches above her knees. *Men prefer red*, she reminded herself feverishly. She didn't go overboard with makeup, but she remembered the expression in Shane's eyes when he'd seen her last night, and did pretty much the same with her eyes and lips. She couldn't do her own hair the way Maggie had, so she brushed it until it crackled and coiled it into a simple chignon at the nape of her neck. Classic and elegant.

Dangly ruby and diamond earrings she'd inherited from her mother—and which she cherished more for that reason than their obvious beauty—completed her ensemble. She left her throat bare. Someday she'd have to worry about the signs of age every woman eventually fretted over, but that day—thank God!—had not yet arrived.

She lightly touched the pulse points on her wrists and behind her ears with her favorite gardenia-scented perfume, hesitated, then dabbed it between her breasts. Then she looked at herself in the full-length mirror.

Carly knew she was quietly beautiful—if your preference was for dark-haired women and not blondes. But for the first time since Jack, she wanted to be especially beautiful for a man. For Shane.

The doorbell rang and she jumped. *Don't let him be upset*, she prayed silently. Not for herself, but for him. Because it had suddenly become unbelievably important that she not hurt him. She grabbed the little clutch purse she'd already prepared, and hurried down the stairs.

When the door swung open Shane started to speak, but the breath left his lungs at the sight of Carly in red, and he had to remind himself to breathe. Last night, in her sparkly blue evening dress that matched her eyes, she'd been regal and radiant. Tonight, she was stunning.

When their eyes met he said huskily, "There are no words, Carly."

He hadn't realized she'd been anxiously awaiting his approbation until the anxiety was banished, replaced with a smile that made him want to forget dinner, walk her backward into her town house, and make love to her on the first surface he found. Which he couldn't do, of course. But he wanted to.

"Come on in while I get my coat," Carly said with a little catch in her voice.

Shane didn't trust himself inside. "I'll wait out here."

She shook her head, took his arm, and drew him into

the house, closing the door behind him. "That's ridiculous. Forgetting the fact that it's cold outside, you'd make a terrific target standing under the porch light. A ten-year-old boy could take you down, much less an experienced marksman."

She turned toward the closet as she was speaking, and that's when Shane saw the back of her dress. Or rather, what *wasn't* there. And before he knew it, he'd spoken her name in a voice that couldn't hide his desperate need.

She froze for a second, then faced him. And the invitation in her eyes was unmistakable. "I'm not really hungry," she whispered. "Except..." She caught her breath, then let it out, the faintest tremor running through her body. "For you, Shane," she finished on a rush. "Except for you."

He closed his eyes, then opened them again. And suddenly Carly was in his arms, her lips locked on to his. A rushing sound filled his ears, and he realized it was his blood coursing through his veins as his heart pounded furiously. He let Carly go only long enough to fight out of his overcoat and jacket, dropping them unheeded on the floor. Then his arms closed around her again.

Shane retained just enough sanity to know he couldn't take Carly right there on the floor in the foyer...or on the staircase...or bent over the arm of the sofa in the living room. But he honest to God didn't know if he could make it to the bedroom.

He slid his hands beneath her skirt and up. Up over silky thighs, until he grasped her hips and lifted, pulling her flush against the hardness of his erection. "Hold on tight," he whispered, and she wrapped her legs around his hips and rocked against him, moaning a little, her hands frantically clutching his shoulders for purchase.

Afterward he could never explain how they ended up in her bedroom, except that somehow he'd carried her up the stairs just like that—her arms around his neck, her lips glued to his, her thighs clutching tightly. He tumbled her onto the bed and followed her down.

Claws of need ripped through him. She'd lost her shoes somewhere along the way, but the .22 was still strapped securely to her right thigh. He hadn't felt it before—hell, he'd barely known his own name earlier—but now he unbuckled the strap and dropped the holstered gun over the side of the bed. He would have dispensed with her nylons and underwear by ripping them away, but Carly raised her hips and wriggled the offending garments off far enough for Shane to peel them down the rest of the way. The nylons and satin panties joined the gun on the floor.

His fingers stroked between her thighs and found her damp and oh-so-ready for him, and he praised her in a guttural voice. Her arousal fueled his own—as if he needed anything to make him harder. He slid one finger inside her, and she arched and moaned his name, her hands clutching his arms. He gently inserted a second finger beside the first, stroking in and out until she bucked against his hand and whimpered with need. Then she was whispering something he had to strain to hear. "Please, Shane. Please."

Oh, hell yeah, he was going to please her. And please himself at the same time. He dug his hand into his pocket for one of the condoms he'd placed there, just in case, and came out with three. He dropped two of them on the comforter, then put the third packet between his teeth and ripped away the packaging. He unzipped quickly, freeing himself, and rolled on the condom faster than he'd ever managed before. Then he guided his erection to her damp entrance.

"Tell me yes," he panted, his lips a fraction away from her ear.

She'd barely answered in the affirmative before he plunged deep, and her hips arched upward to meet him. It could have been all over in seconds—he wanted her that much. But he'd never left a woman unsatisfied, and he was damned if Carly would be the first. So he gritted his teeth and held back, even as he slid in and out. In and out. Faster, and yet faster. The tiny part of his brain that was still functioning kept saying each thrust *had* to be the last, but he held on. He managed to work his left hand in between their bodies, until he found the tiny nub he sought…and that was just enough to send Carly flying over the precipice, as she came. And came. And came.

When he felt her throbbing around him he thrust himself deep one last time and let go with a gasp of relief in a cataclysmic orgasm that seemed to be matched by hers.

Chapter 8

Shane made as if to withdraw from Carly's body, but she clutched at his arms and tightened her legs around his hips, refusing to let him leave.

"Let me go, Carly," he pleaded. "I hurt you."

"No. Oh no. You didn't hurt me." She caught her breath on a shuddering sob, then asked, "Why do you think that?"

"You're crying."

"I am?" She let go of his arm with her right hand, and touched her cheek, bemused to find it damp. "I am." Then her brain cells kicked in and she said quickly, "But you didn't hurt me, I swear."

"Then why...?" He rolled over, taking his weight off her. And though part of her was sorry, another part of her acknowledged it felt better being on top. And they were still connected. She didn't think she could bear it if he withdrew just yet. It had been years since she'd felt this way after sex—as if the two of them shared a bond far beyond the physical—and she wanted to hang onto it as long as she could.

That's when she realized they were both mostly clothed. And Shane was still wearing his shoulder holster. A sudden urge to laugh swept through her, but she managed to turn it into a strangled gurgle instead.

"What's so funny?"

Okay, so she wasn't all that good at hiding her laughter. "You. Me. Us. Don't shoot me for laughing in bed," she teased with mock seriousness as she ran her hands over his chest and slid the fingers of one hand beneath the shoulder holster for emphasis.

Then Shane was laughing, too, and she could feel it everywhere. He shook his head regretfully. "Obviously I have a one-track mind where you're concerned."

Carly didn't know why, but that statement only made her laugh harder, because she felt the same way. She hid her face against Shane's chest, but she couldn't hide her reaction from him any more than he could hide his from her.

When they were all laughed out, she reluctantly let him go. He disappeared into the bathroom and returned a minute later, minus the condom, the shoulder holster and the rest of his clothes. And Carly caught her breath at the sight. He was lean, but muscular, without a spare ounce anywhere. And he was already semi-aroused again.

She had just enough self-control to try to keep things light. "You know that swimsuit competition you mentioned last night? You'd win hands down."

He grinned and sat on the bed next to her, then

reached down to cup her cheek with one warm hand, his smile fading. "If I'm assuming too much, just tell me," he said quietly. "But if I have a choice, that was merely the appetizer. I'm hungry for the main course. And dessert, too."

She breathed sharply, because her appetite for him had only been whetted, not sated. She'd never been shy about expressing what she wanted, either, and something about the way he said it appealed to her. Not cocky. Not assuming. Just a statement of what he wanted…if she wanted it, too.

And she did.

"One of us is overdressed for dinner," she replied, letting her eyes do the asking.

He smiled slowly, the smile that made her tummy quiver. He drew her up into a sitting position, his hands stroking over her bare back. "How does this thing come off?"

"This *thing*, as you call it, cost me four hundred and ninety-five dollars on sale," she chided.

His eyes never left hers, but his hands slid lower. "It's gorgeous. How does it come off?"

"Keep going," she breathed. "There's a zipper at the waist."

The dress had a built-in bra because there was no way to wear one otherwise. And since Shane had already dispensed with her pantyhose and satin undies earlier, once her dress and half slip were gone, she was as naked as he was.

"Hang on a sec," he told her when she grasped a corner of the comforter and sheet to pull them down. He grabbed something from the middle of the still-made bed, and when he dropped them on the night stand, Carly saw they were condoms.

"How many did you bring?"

"Six," he admitted. "There are three more in my pants pocket."

"Six?" she repeated in a stunned question.

He shrugged lightly. "Condoms can tear. Especially if you're impatient." He cradled her face in his strong hands, tilting it up for his kiss. "I've never wanted anyone the way I want you," he whispered when he raised his mouth from hers. "I figured I'd have one mishap. Maybe two. I had to make sure I didn't run short."

Helpless laughter overcame her. Again. "Oh, I *do* like a man who plans ahead," she whispered as her arm curved around his neck and pulled him closer.

Shane surfaced from a pleasurable dream in the early morning hours to find it wasn't a dream after all—Carly was sprawled across his chest. She slept with the abandon of a child—completely oblivious to her surroundings, and to the slight movements he made to arrange her more comfortably in his arms.

Light from the bathroom spilled into the bedroom, allowing him to see her face clearly. *Must have forgotten to turn the light off the last time*, he thought, letting himself be distracted momentarily from his contemplation of Carly. Then his focus returned to her.

Two more used condoms had joined the first in the bathroom trash basket—and neither had been wasted. He'd made love to her the second time for more than half an hour. Wanting—*needing*—to make it up to her for the wham-bam-thank-you-ma'am of their first time. He'd used his mouth on her, and she'd gone crazy. A suspicion resided in the back of his mind that maybe no one had ever done that for her before. *Their loss*, he told himself now. Because Carly wasn't just multiorgasmic, she was *generously* multiorgasmic. He'd brought her to completion with his mouth, then slid into her tight sheath while she was still spasming and she'd come again for him. Higher. Harder. And she'd taken him with her, gasping his name in a way that still echoed in his mind.

The third time they'd made love was just icing on the cake. *Dessert*, he thought with a flash of humor, remembering his statement to her earlier. He'd pulled Carly on top of him, leaving his hands free to toy with her breasts. The breasts he'd tried to ignore from day one—but had failed miserably at doing. He couldn't really blame himself because her breasts were perfect. Absolutely perfect. They filled his hands as if they were made for him—just enough and not a fraction over. With silky nipples that tightened at the slightest touch.

And the way she'd moved on him? *Should be a crime*, he told himself with another stab of humor. He felt like a horse who'd been ridden hard and put away lathered. Drenched, in fact. But he wasn't complaining.

Just thinking about it was making him hard again, and he tried to shift so he wasn't touching her. Or rather, so she wasn't touching him. It shouldn't be possible. Yeah, it had been months since the last time he'd made love to a woman, but he was forty-one, not fourteen. He shouldn't be popping up at the slightest provocation, but there it was. He tried to talk some sense into his body—*three times should be plenty*. His body wasn't listening.

Carly stirred, and with her lips pressed against his chest she murmured something he couldn't hear.

His arms tightened around her. "What did you say?" he whispered almost soundlessly, not wanting to wake her up if she wasn't up already.

She stretched a little. Sighed with contentment. Then rubbed her cheek against his bare chest like a satisfied kitten and said, "Again?"

He chuckled softly. "Have pity on me, Carly."

She snuggled closer to his body, which responded with a surge of desire that left him hard and aching. "I wasn't asking for *me*," she explained. "I was voicing the question your body seems to be asking." Her hand slid down to stroke his already-aroused flesh. "Doesn't feel as if you need pity. Feels as if you need tender, loving care."

"You're exhausted."

"Mmm." Her lips curved into a Mona Lisa smile.

She toyed lazily for long minutes, until the breath caught in Shane's lungs. "God, Carly, stop. I can't—"

"Yes, you can." She raised her head to look at him, a challenge in her sparkling blue eyes. "Come on, Marine, oorah. You can do this."

Whether it was the challenge, the US Marines battle cry or Carly's clever hand—which was soon joined by her unbelievably talented lips—somehow he found he could after all. No condom needed.

Shane made it to the Senate floor when it convened at nine by going there directly instead of to his office first, as he usually did. He'd texted Dee-Dee from home—where he'd gone to shower and change clothes—to let her know he was running late, and had asked her to have his senior legislative assistant and legislative correspondent meet him on the Senate floor with the paperwork he needed. He knew he could count on Dee-Dee and she didn't disappoint him—his aides were already there waiting for him when he arrived.

As was often the case, nothing much was happening on the Senate floor that morning, except a vote on a bill that was meaningless because the president would veto it and the Senate leadership didn't have the votes to override that veto. Shane hated that kind of nonsense—grandstanding for the constituency at home—but he still voted because he wanted to go on the record as opposing the bill—he always voted his conscience.

The rest of the day passed in a whirl of committee and subcommittee hearings, a strategy lunch with the two other senators who were cosponsoring his domestic terrorism bill, meeting with a delegation—some of whom were constituents from his home state and needed to be handled with kid gloves—regarding the upcoming vote on the pipeline bill and a policy meeting with his staff that took up most of the afternoon.

But he found time to text Carly twice. The first was just three words—thank you again. He'd thanked her this morning when he'd left, of course, but he wanted her to know he was thinking of her, which he was. A lot. Everything he thought of saying seemed impossible to convey in a text, though, and he concluded his mother was right—texting might be great for some things, but it was a piss-poor way of communicating complex emotions.

The second text was equally terse—we need to talk about the interview. Because right in the middle of the staff meeting he remembered he'd never discussed it with Carly last night. He'd intended to—until she'd opened the door and every rational thought was driven from his brain. He hadn't been angry—well, okay, maybe a little angry, although *upset* was a more appropriate word. He'd been upset they'd used the domestic terrorism incident at the bookstore in the broadcast. That they'd interviewed the woman whose life he'd saved. That wasn't *news*—it had been at the time, but it wasn't now—and he felt Carly's network had crossed an ethical line it shouldn't have.

And he'd been upset Carly hadn't mentioned anything about it when he nixed her interview question on the topic. She had to have known what was planned, but she hadn't said a word, and that had bothered him.

When he'd watched a replay yesterday morning of the broadcast his press secretary had taped for him, it had bothered the hell out of him at first because he saw it as some kind of betrayal. But then he'd realized he was looking at it through the lens of their date that night…and into the next morning. When she'd interviewed him on Sunday, he'd been nothing more than a story for her. The subject of an interview. Sunday night had changed all that.

Then he'd deduced that's what Carly had wanted to tell him on the phone early yesterday morning—too late to change it, but at least in time to warn him what to expect from the news media. Because he was more than just a story for her now. Because he mattered to her. Because his *opinion* of her mattered to her. He hadn't given her the chance to tell him, so he couldn't blame her for that. At least she'd *tried*.

But he still wanted to discuss it with her. He had no intention of letting last night and this morning be the end of his relationship with Carly. Which meant he needed to get a few things straight before they went any further.

Marsh whistled tunelessly to himself as he walked casually away from the reporter's town house in Georgetown and down the block. He'd already taken care of the senator's house with no one the wiser. Now he'd done the same here. The reporter had a better security system than the senator—which didn't surprise him with her being a woman. But neither had been too much of a challenge for him to overcome.

He turned right at the corner and walked three more blocks, "checking six" twice, before turning left. He always watched his back for a tail—it was as automatic for him as breathing. He'd never been followed. Not once. But he always looked.

Halfway down the block he clicked the remote to unlock his truck, and waited. When nothing untoward happened, he circled his truck as he always did when he'd left it unattended in a public place, because a professional hit man had a lot of secrets. Secrets that could be dangerous to those who hired him.

Marsh wasn't a blackmailer. When he accepted payment for a job, he did it, collected his money and his employers never heard from him again. But sometimes his employers figured him for a liability once he'd completed the job they'd hired him to do. He'd set enough booby traps himself that he had no intention of being someone else's victim.

Once he was satisfied none of his nearly hidden markers had been disturbed, he hopped in, started the engine and pulled away from the curb.

He never even saw the man who'd been shadowing him.

* * *

Carly returned home to find her street roped off and yellow tape stretched across her front door. She parked as close as she could, got out and headed for the first official-looking person she could find—a DC police officer standing guard in the street, watching her closely as she approached, then heading to intercept her.

"What's going on?"

"Sorry, ma'am, I can't tell you. Do you live on this street?"

"I live there," she said, pointing to her town house and the group of FBI and ATF agents clustered on her lawn, a couple of them blowing on their hands and stamping their feet to keep warm. "I'm Carly Edwards. What's going on with my house?"

"Hang on a sec," he told her, blowing his whistle to get the agents' attention, then signaling for them to come over.

"Ms. Edwards," he said, indicating Carly when two agents responded with alacrity. "She's the home owner." He moved back to his original post in the middle of the street, just out of earshot.

"Ma'am, I'm going to have to ask you to come with me," said the FBI agent.

"Why? What have I done?" were the first words out of her mouth. Then she said to the ATF agent, "Wait, I know you. Weren't you interrogating me after the attempt on Senator Jones's life?"

"Yes, ma'am," he said without even the hint of a smile.

"What's going on? Why is my house being searched?" And being Carly, she had to add, "Do you have a search warrant?"

The two agents exchanged glances, then the man from the FBI removed something from an inner pocket and handed it to her. "Search warrant," he said. "Ma'am."

She stood and read the thing in its entirety, as an icy wind blew down the street, making her shiver. *Or maybe it's not the wind*, she acknowledged. Because there in the middle of all the legalese were words to the effect that the FBI had good reason to believe a bomb had been planted in her town house. Target? Her and anyone visiting her.

Shane. Oh my God—Shane. That's all she could think of in that instant. *Another attempt on his life.*

She raised frantic eyes to the two agents. "Senator Jones," she blurted out. "If there's a bomb in my home, has anyone searched Senator Jones's home?"

The FBI agent spoke for both men. "Ma'am, we can't give you any information on an ongoing investigation."

"That's not why I'm asking," she said urgently. "He's the real target. Someone has to warn him." She fumbled in her purse for her smartphone. "Oh my God," she breathed as she realized her phone had somehow been turned off. She frantically turned it on and scrolled to find Shane's cell phone number in her contacts, her fingers trembling. "Oh my God."

The ATF agent put a hand over both of hers, preventing her from completing the call. "He's safe, ma'am," he assured her. He glanced at the other agent, then back at her. "This is *not* for publication—I know you're a reporter, and this can't go beyond here," he insisted, drawing a circle in the air indicating Carly, the FBI agent and himself. He overrode the other agent's angry protest to say, "They already found and disarmed a bomb in his home."

For the first time in her life Carly's knees buckled, but she caught herself and stiffened her knees before she could fall. She had more difficulty dealing with the sudden lightheadedness that struck without warning—not even when word had come about Jack had she reacted this way…as if she might faint. And that realization terrified her nearly as much as the idea that something bad could have happened to Shane.

But she didn't have a lot of time to dwell on that, because her phone suddenly dinged for an incoming text. She glanced down and saw she had several from Shane, time-stamped throughout the past hour. She clicked on the last one and read, Get out of your house NOW!

Carly had barely processed Shane's warning when the attention of the two agents was drawn to something behind her. She swung around, her heart thumping in her chest, and saw television trucks approaching…including one from her own cable network.

"Keep them back," the FBI agent barked to the DC policeman standing outside the rope cordoning off the street, and the cop quickly advanced on the approaching TV reporters and their camera operators.

"You'd better come with us, ma'am," the ATF agent said quietly, taking Carly's arm and attempting to lead her away. "You don't want to get involved in that circus."

She'd just opened her mouth to argue that freedom of the press was *not* a circus, it was a necessary adjunct of democracy, when a car squealed around the corner and jerked to a stop at the first parking spot it came to. A man jumped out. The TV cameras all swiveled in his direction and followed him as he raced toward Carly, his open overcoat flying behind him.

Her heart nearly leaped out of her chest when she recognized Shane. Then she dropped her purse and ran to meet him, TV cameras be damned.

Chapter 9

"Another attempt on the life of Senator Shane Jones, independent from Colorado, was foiled today in a remarkable turn of events," the news anchor announced. "Correspondent Tate Westerly is on the scene. Can you tell us what we know so far, Tate?"

Carly snatched the remote from Shane's hand and muted the sound before Tate could speak. Then she settled back against Shane's shoulder. They watched the silent news coverage of Tate looking self-important in front of Shane's relatively modest house just across the Potomac River from Georgetown, where Carly lived.

She gave a delicate snort. "I can't stand him. And he *never* gets anything first. He just looks good in front of the camera."

"*You* look good in front of the camera," Shane replied mildly.

"Yes, but that's not my *only* qualification for the job," she insisted, sitting up straight to confront him. "I'm—"

"Yeah, I know." Shane smiled. "Tiger Shark. No one can forget that, especially me." He put a restraining hand on her arm, exerting gentle pressure. "Put that head back where it belongs," he told her in no uncertain terms. And when she'd done so, he kissed her forehead. "I think I went a little crazy this evening when I thought…well…you know what I thought."

"Me, too," she confessed. "All I could think of was, if someone planted a bomb in *my* house, what about yours?"

"You know what this means, don't you, that your house was targeted?"

She nodded. "Someone knows you stayed there last night."

He shook his head. "That bomb wasn't meant for me, it was meant for you. Which means you're a target, too. Five will get you ten those two bombs were constructed and planted by the same man who sabotaged my car. I'm also betting he's the same guy who tried to kill me at the Mayo Clinic. The assassin whose face you saw. He knows you saw him, Carly. He knows you can identify him. That's why he wants to take you out. Me? Whatever he has against me, that's one thing. With you it's personal."

She didn't say anything for the longest time, and Shane wondered what she was thinking. He knew what *he* was thinking—this thing with Carly had rocketed to the top of his personal hierarchy of needs in nothing flat. The time from the moment he'd met her in his hospital room to today hadn't even encompassed a week. But when he'd heard someone had been spotted leaving her town house in DC—the same someone who'd been spotted leaving *his* house in Virginia—all he could think of was warning her. Then getting to her side. All he could think of was keeping her safe the way he *hadn't* kept Wendy safe.

His wife had been targeted because she was married to a US Marine assigned to NATO. The terrorists had reasoned striking a blow at the United States, as well as NATO, would have more political impact on delivering their message than if they'd targeted an unrelated civilian. And they'd been right—the news coverage had been lurid and unrelenting.

Now Carly was in danger because of him, too. And that was *not* going to happen. Not if he had anything to say about it.

The FBI and ATF had refused to allow Carly inside her town house so she could pack a suitcase. They'd told him the same thing—they needed time to sweep both houses to make sure there wasn't another bomb or a booby trap somewhere. *Sorry, Senator*, the lead FBI agent on the scene had told him. *It's just not safe. If we don't find anything, you and Ms. Edwards should be able to get back into your homes tomorrow.*

So he and Carly had stopped at the nearest discount store for the bare minimum of essentials they would need overnight, and here they were in a hotel room in DC—with FBI agents outside the door.

He didn't know how long that federal protection would last—they hadn't volunteered the information and he hadn't thought to ask earlier. He could take care of himself, but he was frantic to keep Carly safe long-term. He didn't know who he needed to talk to, but he'd find out first thing tomorrow morning and argue his case—he wanted the FBI guarding Carly until the lunatic trying to kill them was caught.

Which might be later rather than sooner, he acknowledged, because the FBI had run the license plate on the truck the man had used…and it had turned out to belong to a Honda minivan in Maryland and not a Chevy truck in DC. The plates had been stolen the day before, while the minivan was parked outside a grocery store. And there was no camera covering the parking lot… only one on the store entrance and several inside. So Shane wasn't holding out hope the man would be spotted on surveillance footage.

If the FBI couldn't—or wouldn't—keep the protection on Carly indefinitely, he'd have to find another way to ensure her safety.

When Carly finally spoke, though, it wasn't what Shane had expected. "How did they know the bombs had been planted?" she asked as if it had just occurred to her.

Shane knew, but he wasn't going to say. Not because she was a reporter and he didn't trust her, but because he'd called in a huge favor from someone who was technically AWOL—if that terminology was used outside the military. There was no way he was chancing that getting out and negatively affecting the man's career. So he temporized. "Someone must have been watching our houses. After the incident with my car the other night…"

"You need an affidavit for a search warrant…except in very circumscribed circumstances," Carly insisted. "So how did they know about the bombs?"

"Yeah, well… I'm not going to complain. Are you?"

"It's the principle of the thing," she argued. "I totally get that in this case we got lucky, but Big Brother isn't supposed to be spying on people who haven't done anything, and—"

He kissed her to distract her. Okay, not just to distract her, although that was part of it. He kissed her because it still terrified him how close he'd come to losing her. If that bomb in her town house had exploded while she'd been inside…he couldn't even bear thinking about it.

Shane deepened the kiss when Carly kissed him back, and he slid his hands down, over her hips, to pull her body flush with his. When he finally let her go, his heart was pounding and he was hard as a rock. Her breathing was as ragged as his was, and that pleased him to no end. He didn't want to be the only one vulnerable here.

But then Carly drew away from him and said, "We have to talk about something."

He desperately wanted to make love to her and she wanted to talk? *Stand down*, he ordered his body. *The lady has something to say before you see action.* "Okay."

She jumped to her feet suddenly and walked away, pacing nervously. And Shane knew whatever it was she planned to tell him was a hell of a lot more serious than he'd first thought.

"We have to keep a certain…distance," she said finally.

"Distance?" The word didn't compute. Not where he and Carly were concerned. "How distant can we be if we share the same bed?"

"I don't mean sexually. I mean…emotionally."

He didn't know where she was going with this, but

he already knew it was a load of crap. She'd run to him this evening. She'd been as terrified for him as he'd been terrified for her. That didn't equate to emotional *distance*. But all he said was "Uh-huh." As if he was following her logic.

"We... *I*...can't... That is, I was engaged years ago. Did you know that?"

He'd known...but only because of Dee-Dee's in-depth report. The one he'd asked her to compile the day he met Carly. That was another thing he wasn't about to reveal, but he wouldn't lie to her. "I'd heard."

"If you heard, then you probably know Jack...died," she added in a rush. "And it was my fault."

What the hell? That was all he could think of in that instant. Because he knew the story. It had all played out on the six o'clock news, had been plastered across the bottom half of the front page of *The Washington Post*. Jack Tremaine, rising star in DC politics, and his fiancée, Carly Edwards, a war correspondent for a prominent cable news network, had been in a horrific car accident involving a drunk driver, an icy road and a faulty airbag.

But Carly hadn't been driving. And Jack Tremaine hadn't died in the crash, anyway, so... "How was it your fault?"

"The doctors warned us—Jack's parents and me—that the traumatic brain injury he received in the crash could cause...mood swings. Depression. They *warned* us, Shane." Her voice broke. "They told us what to watch for. They explained how critical it was for everyone around Jack to be on the lookout, especially that first year after the crash."

Tears stood in Carly's eyes, and the sight of them

made Shane's heart ache the way hers was obviously aching. She blinked rapidly to hold back her tears, as if she could hold her emotions at bay that way, too. "I should have seen the signs," she whispered. "But I was so busy with the story I was working on…and so caught up in the preparations for our wedding, that I…"

Then it clicked for Shane. He remembered from the news clipping in the file Dee-Dee had compiled, that Jack, suffering from untreated depression the doctors theorized had been the result of the traumatic brain injury he'd received, had committed suicide. He'd jumped from the Eleventh Street Bridge into the Anacostia River three days before his wedding.

And Shane had suffered a TBI, too.

He shook his head vehemently. "There's no parallel between Jack and me," he began. "They're two completely different situa—" Then he stopped cold. Yeah, he hadn't been depressed—*unduly* depressed—after the explosion that had ended his career in the Marine Corps five years ago. And suicide was the *last* thing he could ever see himself doing. But…he had epilepsy. And one of the known side effects of many of the drugs used to control seizures was…depression.

Including the medication he was taking.

The words he'd intended to say died a quick death, and he alternately clenched and relaxed his left fist, attempting to come to terms with what Carly was trying to tell him without actually coming right out and saying it.

Bitter rage swept through him. Not against Carly, whose heart had been broken once and who never wanted to suffer that again. He could relate—he'd loved and lost before, too. Fifteen years was a long time, but he could still remember what it felt like.

No, his rage wasn't externally directed, it was directed against himself. Against the traitor within his own body. Against the damned seizures he couldn't even control without medication.

"I…see," he said finally. He stood and walked slowly to the window. The curtain was drawn, but he pulled it back slightly to stare out at the DC skyline, bitterness still churning inside him. But instead of the lights of the city, all he could see was his own reflection, and it gave him pause. Because the man in the window was a stranger. A stranger who asked in a voice Shane didn't recognize, "Would you rather we had separate hotel rooms?"

He *had* to make her that offer. If she said yes, that would be that. But if she said no, he still had a chance. A chance to change her mind. A chance to make her see they had something special, despite everything going against them. Something worth the risk. Not just sex, although they were incredible together that way, too.

She didn't answer right away, and he turned to face her. "I hurt you," she said at last. And some latent emotion in her voice gave him hope. "I didn't mean to."

He dug his hands in his pockets to keep from reaching for her and smiled faintly, forcing a lightness he was far from feeling. "I'm a big boy. I've been hurt before, and I've always survived."

"Yes, but *I* hurt you," she reiterated, placing the emphasis on *I*. As if it was important to her that *she* not hurt him, and Shane drew a small amount of comfort from that knowledge. He meant something to Carly, even if she didn't want to admit it.

"No more than I hurt you."

"You didn't!" Her eyes flashed blue ice. "You never hurt me."

He didn't agree, but he wasn't going to argue with her. "So what's your answer? Would you rather we had separate hotel rooms?"

She shook her head slowly, then crossed the room to stand in front of him. This close he could see the fine tremor in the hand she placed against his chest. "But it has to be…just sex," she reminded him.

And pigs can fly, he thought but didn't say. Carly wasn't that kind of woman, no matter what she said. She was dreaming, but he wasn't going to argue with her on that, either. "Okay." He forced himself to grin at her. A wicked, lighthearted grin that promised things he was going to have to work hard to deliver, because he didn't want "just sex" with Carly, even if that was all she was offering…for now. "So when does the 'just sex' part start? I bought a box of condoms."

Carly couldn't sleep. Shane was already out like a light, one arm thrown possessively across her bare waist as he spooned behind her, as naked as she was beneath the covers. She usually slept in the nude at home, and apparently so did he. He radiated heat, and she loved the way his big body made her feel, all warm and cherished. So it wasn't that keeping her awake, even though it had been a long time since she'd had a man in her bed. It wasn't the strange bed, either. She'd slept in enough hotel rooms in her career that that never bothered her. She'd slept on army cots, too, and a few times even in a bedroll on the cold, hard ground. She'd never had trouble falling asleep before—the exact opposite, in fact. Once she was asleep she had a hard time waking up.

No, she decided, there was one reason and one reason only why she remained awake—the way Shane had so readily agreed to her insistence on emotional distance. The way he'd willingly accepted her "just sex" decree.

It didn't make sense that it bothered her, but it did. *She* was the one who'd set the boundaries, after all. Shane was merely going along with them. But…

But what? she asked herself. The answer, when it came to her, was terrifying. *You're falling for him*, she chastised her heart. *You're not supposed to fall for him.*

Can't help it, her heart replied. *He's just so lov—*

She tried to cut the thought off, but it was impossible. Lovable. Shane was just so lovable. Her heart knew it, and now her head did, too. Which was why she didn't want him to willingly settle for "just sex" with her.

Not that sex with Shane wasn't mind-blowing. It was. Just *thinking* about some of the things he'd done last night and tonight made her shiver and tingle all over. But she wanted exclusivity. She wanted him all to herself. She didn't want him making any other woman tingle and ache and moan and…

She shifted uncomfortably, squeezing her thighs together to suppress the sudden throbbing in her loins that thoughts of Shane ignited.

She froze when his arm tightened around her waist. "What's wrong?" he rumbled in a way that told her he was only half-awake. "Can't sleep?" His warm hand slid down until it was curled at the juncture of her thighs. "Maybe I can help."

Her sudden laugh was mixed with something that sounded suspiciously like a sob to her ears. She was going to decline his offer, but before she could open her mouth one of his fingers stroked down and in…and she melted. That was her last coherent thought.

Chapter 10

Carly was not—never had been, and never would be—a morning person. She could never be an anchor on one of those morning TV programs—even if she even remotely wanted to be one, which she didn't—because she couldn't get up to be at work by four in the morning on a regular basis. There were exceptions to her rule, of course, if the story she was working on absolutely demanded it—such as when the combat unit she was embedded with in Afghanistan moved out before dawn.

But waking in the early-morning hours to strong hands stroking her bare skin, a night's scruff on an unshaven chin nuzzling her cheek and firm lips nibbling on her earlobe? Not to mention a certain male body part letting her know US marines—retired or not—were always ready for action?

She wouldn't object to *that*...especially since *that* was how Shane woke her in the wee hours of the morning. "Oorah," he whispered in her ear when her quickened breathing gave away that she was awake…and appreciating everything he was doing, thank you *very* much!

Her gurgle of laughter ended on a sharply indrawn breath when his fingers brushed an area of her anatomy she hadn't realized was so sensitive—the inside of her elbow. *Or maybe it's just him*, she acknowledged against her will. Maybe every part of her body was especially sensitized when Shane touched her…the way he touched her. Which meant attempting to keep an emotional distance while sleeping with him was a fool's errand.

She turned in his arms to tell him she'd changed her mind…and he kissed her. His kiss sent streamers of desire rippling through her body, making her toes curl. And just like last night, all rational thought fled.

Shane reluctantly and surreptitiously slid from beneath the covers, hoping not to wake Carly. But the minute he was gone her eyelids fluttered open. "Where are you going?" she whispered.

The room was dark save for the light Shane had deliberately left on in the bathroom last night, because he'd wanted to see Carly when he made love to her. Because he'd wanted her to see him. To know who was there in bed with her. To understand that "just sex" wasn't possible for him, no matter what he agreed to.

Carly's sleepy eyes focused on him, and he wanted nothing more than to fall back into bed with her. But he had commitments he needed to keep. "Home first, if the FBI and the ATF will let me inside," he explained in a low voice. "I showered last night, but I need a change of clothes this morning, if possible. Then I have a breakfast meeting scheduled for seven-thirty before hitting the Senate floor at nine o'clock."

She stretched sinuously beneath the covers, and somehow Shane knew it wasn't for his benefit. Unfortunately. Everything about Carly was unconsciously arousing—even when she'd been impersonating his fiancée in the hospital to get a story, she'd exuded what the French called je ne sais quoi, the indefinable certain something that set some women apart. Carly had it in spades, although she seemed to be largely unaware of it. Sexy? Hell yes. Quietly beautiful in a classy way? Assuredly. But neither of those things held a candle to her charm. She might be a tiger shark when she got her teeth into a story, but getting that story in the first place was due in large part to the charm that came as naturally to her as breathing. She'd be charming the socks off someone in pursuit of a story when she was old and gray—looks had nothing to do with it.

Shane's thoughts in no way impeded his dressing, so by the time he'd reached this point in his silent assessment he was knotting his tie as he stepped into his loafers. He leaned over and pinned Carly to the bed for a quick kiss. A quick kiss that soon threatened his good intentions to keep to his itinerary no matter what. A bomb scare wouldn't derail his schedule, but Carly might.

Despite already having taken the edge off his hunger for her earlier this morning, desire came surging back when Carly returned his kiss. He was three heartbeats away from chucking his commitments and sliding back into bed beside her when she turned her head and broke their lips' connection.

"You have things to do, Marine," she breathed. "And

so do I. Sleeping," she added. She sighed suddenly, a sound that said he was a temptation she was determined to resist, and her hands gently pushed at his shoulders to remove him from her proximity.

Or to remove her from mine, Shane thought with a stab of humor. He stole one last kiss before heading out of the hotel room.

As he drove toward the Francis Scott Key Bridge that would take him back to Virginia—tailed by a vigilant FBI agent—Shane's thoughts returned to the woman he'd just barely managed to leave. He hadn't wanted to. Temptation and Carly went hand in hand, and he craved her like a chocoholic craved chocolate. Problem was, he didn't want to be cured.

And he loved the way she called him Marine. It seemed more intimate than calling him Senator, which she'd started out doing. It even seemed more intimate than calling him by his name. He'd been a US Marine for half his life when he'd been forced to accept a medical discharge at age thirty-six, and he still thought of himself as one, even though he'd been retired for five years now. Major Jones—he'd been on the promotion list at the time of the incident, so by law they'd retired him as a lieutenant colonel even though he'd never served as such—had laughingly joked to his baby sister he bled marine blue…right before the explosion that had proved he bled bright red just like every other human being.

Traffic going into DC was starting to build up, even this early in the morning, but Shane was driving against traffic, so he made good time. As he turned off North Fort Myer Drive, out of habit he rubbed the fingers of his left hand against the long white scar on the side of his head. It didn't hurt anymore. And it was barely visible—if he wore his hair longer, it wouldn't be visible at all. In fact, if not for the medical discharge, there would have been times he completely forgot about it. But he could not forget he'd never serve as a major again. Or a lieutenant colonel. Colonel. General. Commandant of the Marine Corps. He'd never make his onetime ultimate goal—which he'd only shared with his brother Niall—of serving as one of the Joint Chiefs of Staff.

Not that being a US senator was anything to sneeze at. It was service to his country, too, just in a different way. And if he couldn't be a marine, this was the next best thing.

But he still loved it when Carly called him Marine.

"The chair recognizes Senator Jones from Colorado," the president pro-tem of the Senate intoned. "Senator Jones, you have the floor."

Shane rose to his feet. He had notes, but he didn't need them. "I agree with my esteemed colleague from Texas," he began, nodding in the direction of that senior senator, who'd just given a long-winded speech in favor of the proposed pipeline under discussion. "The vote on this pipeline bill has been postponed long enough. But I must beg to differ with him in one crucial way—I cannot, in good conscience, vote for a bill that would rape—yes, *rape*," he repeated sternly when a gasp went up from the press and the public following this debate from the gallery, "rape our environment and the public coffers the way this pipeline will do if this bill is passed."

A chill struck him with no warning whatsoever—

the way it always did—and Shane could have sworn aloud. Now? A damned seizure was happening *now*?

He glanced at his notes, pretending he'd paused for effect, and counted the seconds until the chill and the goose bumps disappeared. Then he continued smoothly from where he'd left off, as if he'd never stopped. "As usual, the battle cry is jobs—this pipeline will bring well-paying jobs that are desperately needed in every state the pipeline will pass through, including my own state of Colorado."

His lips formed a thin line. "The pipeline is needed, I don't dispute that. But *this* bill," he said, hefting the voluminous document for a moment before dropping it with a disdainful thud on his desk, "isn't the way to go." He tapped a finger on the offending bill. "This reads as if it was drafted a hundred years ago, when no one worried about the environment. When no one cared about the world their children and grandchildren would inherit.

"We know better now. This bill as written, with all the riders and amendments that have been shoehorned in, is a short-term solution to a complex problem, but a solution with disastrous long-term results."

He breathed deeply. "And there's more. This bill is rife with potential for corruption and greed at the expense of the American taxpayer. There's big money backing this pipeline. Fortunes are riding on it. I can't speak for every senator here, but I can tell you this—I was approached months ago by several different lobbyists seeking my approval on this bill. I was offered 'campaign contributions'—a euphemism for bribes, in my opinion—if I would give the bill my tacit support.

And even bigger 'campaign contributions' if I would openly support it."

Enough on that issue, Shane reminded himself. He wasn't going to belabor the point about who *had* taken the money because it didn't matter. All that truly mattered was garnering enough votes to defeat the bill. To make his fellow senators vote their consciences and not their wallets.

"And so I urge each and every one of you here today to examine your conscience—as I have done—and vote against this bill when it comes to a vote. Not just for the environment and your children's children. But for the average American taxpayer, as well, struggling to make ends meet and pay his or her fair share toward the common good. Don't add to the taxpayers' burden by allowing the beneficiaries of this bill to feed unchecked at the public trough. Thank you."

He sat down abruptly. Sporadic applause from the gallery—strictly forbidden, as the pounding gavel wielded by the president pro-tem indicated—followed Shane's impassioned speech. He glanced up at the gallery to acknowledge the applause without openly acknowledging it with a raised hand, and was surprised to see Carly seated up there in the first row, a short distance from one of the C-SPAN cameras.

She was too far away for him to see her expression, but she nodded. And in that instant he knew she agreed with him about the pitfalls of the pipeline bill. It *sounded* good…until you delved into the details. Until you followed the money trail. Until you ferreted out how this bill would circumvent both federal and state environmental protections that had been put into place over the years to guard against the very thing this pipeline would bring about—deregulation on a massive scale.

Carly's reaction warmed him. Not that he hadn't meant every word he'd said. Not that he wouldn't have argued vehemently against this bill even if Carly hadn't agreed with him. But it felt good to know he'd earned her approval. Again.

Carly couldn't believe it when Shane stood up to oppose the pipeline bill. She'd been following the bill for months as it made its way slowly but inexorably through committee hearings and onto the Senate docket for this legislative session. Like Shane, she'd read every word of it, including the riders and amendments. And like Shane, she was appalled.

She'd done a preliminary piece on the bill back when it was still in committee. It had been bad enough when it had first been introduced, and had only gotten worse with everything that had been tacked on to it. But nobody—and by that, Carly meant the TV-viewing public—had seemed to care. The ratings on that segment had been abysmal. So J.C. had shelved the idea of a follow-up story, although Carly still had hopes of convincing him otherwise, which was why she was here today.

Now if only J.C. didn't get it in his head that because Shane had openly opposed a bill sponsored by other senators, and Carly was involved with Shane, that made her incapable of being objective where the bill itself was concerned. Maybe some reporters couldn't be objective under those circumstances...but Carly wasn't one of them. "This is *my* story, J.C.," she muttered under her breath. "I'll be damned if you're giving this one to Pearly White."

* * *

Carly returned home, accompanied by the FBI agent who'd shadowed her footsteps all day, but who wouldn't be replaced when he went off duty. The yellow crime-scene tape that had festooned her front door was gone, and the police cordon around her town house was gone. But even though she could stay here if she wanted to—which she didn't—the FBI and ATF had warned her against it earlier, when they'd told her they were releasing her town house as a crime scene. The man who'd set the bomb yesterday had managed to disable her alarm system as if it were child's play, so she wasn't safe. Carly didn't need the FBI and ATF to tell her that.

Which meant she had two choices. She could stay in a hotel for the duration—however long *that* was. Or she could stay in the cabin on Lake Barcroft she and Tahra had inherited from their parents years ago. They'd inherited the family home, too, which Carly had maintained until Tahra went off to college, after which the sisters had made the decision to sell it.

But the cabin was a different story. While they rented it out through an agency during the summer months, it was usually vacant in the winter…as it was now. It was roughly ten miles southwest of her Georgetown town house, but would add more than an hour one way to her daily commute during rush hour.

Carly had just reluctantly decided the commute wasn't worth it—"It's not as if you can't afford a hotel," she murmured under her breath as she packed two suitcases—when her smartphone dinged for an incoming text.

Shane.

Need a place to stay? the text asked.

She texted back, Hotel.

Better idea, was the response. If your offer still stands.

"What in the world?" She didn't get it at first, then realized Shane was referring to the "just sex" offer she'd made him last night, and she didn't know if she should laugh or cry. "Oh, Shane."

Carly no longer believed she could maintain an emotional distance if she continued seeing him—that had been nothing more than a last ditch effort on her part to justify doing what her body wanted, to sleep with him again, when her heart warned her she was stepping into quicksand.

She could get hurt. Badly. The question was, was she willing to risk it?

Her phone dinged for another text. Carly? was all it said, but she knew he was waiting for her answer.

Yes, she typed. Her fingers weren't quite steady, but she hit Send anyway.

Pick you up in 30.

K.

"If you don't take care of the problem soon, it will be too late. It might already be too late."

Marsh knew his employer was referring to the speech the senator had given today. And he knew the man was right—it might already be too late. The truth stuck in Marsh's craw, but he couldn't hide from it. "I know," he admitted.

"You came highly recommended," the voice on the other end of the phone said, in a tone that indicated skepticism of the recommendation, and that flicked Marsh on the raw.

"I've always delivered," he said harshly. "Always."

"See that you do."

The dead air at the other end told Marsh his employer had disconnected. He didn't bother to curse the man, though he wanted to, because Marsh had only himself to blame. "No more excuses," he muttered. "No more failures." His reputation was on the line. Which meant his livelihood was on the line.

Which meant the senator *had* to die. Before it was too late.

Shane put Carly's two suitcases down and fished a key out of his pocket. He inserted it in the lock, then punched in a digital code. He waited five seconds, then punched in a second code before turning the key. A faint bell-like sound told him he'd been successful, so he twisted the doorknob and opened the door.

"Hang tight," he told Carly as he slipped inside and closed the door behind him. He didn't turn on the lights, just moved swiftly to the lighted panel on the wall near the door. He keyed in the code his brother had given him, then waited.

After a few seconds a green light flashed. "Code confirmed," said a computerized voice. "Thumbprint, please."

Shane pressed his thumb against the touch screen.

After a few seconds a second green light flashed on beside the first. "Thumbprint confirmed. Name, please."

"Shane Thermopolis Jones." Thermopolis wasn't his middle name. It actually belonged to his youngest brother, Liam. Shane's real middle name was Breckenridge, because his mother had named him for the place he'd been conceived—which she'd done for all her children, to their secret and not-so-secret embarrassment.

But Niall had used Liam's middle name deliberately, in case someone had forced Shane this far at gunpoint. All Shane had to do was use his real middle name, and the silent alarm would go off, notifying the alarm company, the police and Niall's agency.

After a few seconds a third green light flashed on, making three in a row.

"Name confirmed," the computerized voice said. "Welcome, Senator. Please make yourself at home." The hallway and living room lights came on automatically, and the lights on the panel turned off.

Shane opened the door. "Come on in," he told Carly, picking up her suitcases and bringing them inside, then bolting the door behind her. Carly was carrying Shane's one suitcase, which she put down when she reached the living room. She turned in a circle, taking everything in with wide-eyed astonishment before asking, "What *is* this place?"

Chapter 11

Shane couldn't blame Carly for her reaction. Niall's condo was like something out of a futuristic sci-fi movie, with sleek chrome and glass tables, white leather modular couches and recliner, and techno-geek gadgets everywhere. Shane had been here a few times before when his brother was in town, but it still amazed him. And it seemed as if every time he visited, something new had been added.

The high-tech security system was just the beginning. Shane picked up a remote from the coffee table and pressed a button. White enamel-coated vertical steel blinds parted smoothly, electronically, in the center of the south wall, revealing a picture window that took up most of that wall and presented an incredible view of the DC skyline, albeit a slightly muted one.

Carly was drawn to the window at first, then turned,

a puzzled expression on her face. "The glass," she began, but Shane anticipated her question.

"Double-paned. And each pane is an inch thick. Tempered glass."

She touched one of the blinds, obviously testing its weight. "This is steel," she stated, as if she couldn't quite believe it.

"Yeah. The glass will stop most bullets, but when the blinds are closed this place is like a fortress." He smiled faintly. "The walls are reinforced concrete and rebar. Both doors are steel, too."

"Who lives here?" She glanced around again before meeting Shane's eyes. "Not you."

He shook his head. "Not my idea of home. Too sterile, for one thing. And though it's more comfortable than it looks, I'd hate being constantly reminded that violent death is only a heartbeat away." He pressed another button on the remote, and the blinds slid closed as quietly as they'd opened.

"So if this place isn't yours, who *does* it belong to?"

"My brother Niall."

"The black-ops warrior?"

Shane stiffened and his smile faded. "What do you know about Niall?"

"I have my sources," she said with a smile that warned him not to ask for specifics…because she wasn't about to give them. "But they couldn't tell me much. I know he's a year younger than you. I know he served four years in the Marine Corps, just like your other brothers and your sister. When he left the Corps he joined a federal organization that operates in the shadows. Even their federal budget is buried." This was obviously a sore point with Carly, but she didn't elaborate on it. "Other than that, I know nothing. He's a blank slate."

Tension ebbed out of his body. "Niall is...he's the best brother a man could have—and my best friend. I can't think of anyone I'd rather have at my back than him—and I've served with some damned fine fellow marines. You wouldn't want Niall as your enemy, but as a friend there's none better." He started to add something to this, but changed his mind at the last minute. Not because he didn't trust Carly, but because it wasn't his secret to share.

"So your brother lives here...when he's in town."

"Yeah."

"If he's letting you stay here, that means he's not in town now."

Carly hadn't posed a question...and Shane wasn't volunteering anything. Niall's whereabouts were a closely guarded secret—even Shane never knew from one day to the next where his brother would be. He could reach him in any one of three ways...but not all at the same time—cell phone, email and Facebook. And of the three, Facebook was the most reliable, although response times could vary and coded messages were a must.

Shane had often wondered—but had never asked Niall—if Niall's email and social media accounts were monitored by someone within his agency, someone who made it a point to contact Niall some other way when there was an urgent communication from his family, like this last time, when Shane had desperately needed to reach Niall. Some people might think that smacked too much of cloak and dagger work, but Shane had been on the receiving end of military intel gathered through the most unlikely sources. He didn't care *how* his messages to Niall got through…just that they did.

"Too bad," Carly continued, having no idea how far Shane's thoughts had wandered. "I would like to meet your brother. He sounds fascinating. I've never met anyone in his line of work…at least I don't think I have."

He laughed softly. "You know what they say, don't you?" he teased. "I could tell you about him…but then I'd have to kill you."

"Ha ha ha." Carly's dry tone and the expression on her face said she wasn't amused. "Seriously, though, does he really need to live in a fortress?"

Shane's humor fled. "Probably not. But at the moment I'm grateful he does. There's no way anyone could break in to plant a bomb here, so at least we can get a decent night's sleep without worrying about that."

"What about the FBI? Why can't they keep us safe?"

"They could…if they could spare agents to babysit us indefinitely, which they can't." He thought about how to put it. "I know why the guy who tried to kill me in Phoenix is trying to kill you—you can identify him, or he thinks you can. But I still have no idea why he wants me dead in the first place. Do you?" Carly shook her head. "If the FBI or the ATF or the Phoenix police have any clue, they're not sharing it with me. Which means it's open season, and I might as well be walking around with a bull's-eye target on my back."

A stricken expression entered Carly's eyes, but she didn't say anything, and Shane continued implacably. "I can't just hole up here for the duration—I have a job to do. For all I know, this could be some kind of campaign to intimidate me into hiding out, and the hell with my job. But if I do that, he wins even without killing me."

Carly dropped her purse on the coffee table and held up one hand, an arrested look on her face. "Stop right there," she told him. She pursed her lips and her eyes creased thoughtfully. "Why would someone want to kill you?"

Shane started to speak, but she waved him to silence. "I'm an idiot," she said finally. "I should have asked that question from day one. It's Homicide 101—cui bono? Who benefits?"

"It can't be money—I don't have any. At least, not enough to kill for."

Carly kicked her shoes off and curled up on the leather sofa with her feet beneath her before flashing a cynical smile Shane's way. "You'd be surprised how little money is necessary to turn someone into a killer." Then her smile dimmed. "But in this case, I think you're right. But if it's not money someone is after, what else could it be?"

Shane perched on the arm of the couch facing Carly. "I wasn't sleeping with any man's wife or girlfriend," he volunteered.

"Are you sure?"

The pointed question took him aback for a moment, but all he said was, "I'm sure."

"How can you know?"

Carly was surprised when she blurted out the question, and all of a sudden she realized she wasn't asking as a reporter, she was asking as a woman. A woman who wanted to know the answer, but at the same time didn't.

One corner of Shane's mouth twitched into a half

smile. "Because before you it had been months since I slept with anyone."

She wanted to believe him. She really did. But a tiny corner of her mind insisted it wasn't possible. Shane was an incredibly sensual man with no reason to abstain from sex. So why would he?

When she didn't respond, just gave him a questioning look, he stated quietly, "I have no need to lie about this, Carly. And I wouldn't anyway."

"Why?"

He gave a little huff of laughter. "Why wouldn't I lie?"

"No." All at once his answer mattered to her more than she ever thought possible. "Why would you...abstain?" She almost asked him if it was related to his epilepsy, but then she knew the answer was no. She already had ample proof neither the seizures nor the medication he was taking affected him sexually.

His smile deepened. "Now that sounds like a sexist question if I ever heard one. You wouldn't ask a woman, would you?"

He was right. She knew he was right, damn it, and she hated that she'd asked the question in the first place. But since she had... "Please tell me. It's important."

He didn't answer for the longest time. Then, "Because I have to care about a woman in order to sleep with her, okay? Is that a crime?"

The question tacked on at the end was delivered with deliberate lightness, but there were overtones that told Carly it bothered Shane—a lot—that he had to justify himself to her this way. "I'm sorry," she whispered. "That was unforgivable. And none of my business."

Shane's expression became shuttered. "It *is* your business…if you want it to be. But that's your call."

He didn't say the words *emotional distance*, but she knew he was laying that out there. If she wanted it to be her business, she'd have to admit there wasn't a snowball's chance she could distance herself from Shane emotionally. In which case it would be important for her to know she wasn't a fling to him. That she wasn't merely an itch he wanted to scratch. That he…cared about her.

But if she didn't want it to be her business, if what was between them was "just sex," as she'd insisted last night, then she had no right to force him to reveal something personal and private about the man he was. If she wasn't willing to admit to him that *she* cared, she had no right to insist he admit he did, either.

Carly didn't say anything because she *couldn't*. She couldn't answer Shane's unspoken question. Because she was just coming to terms with what she felt herself, and she wasn't ready to expose those vulnerabilities. Not yet.

But he obviously took her silence as a rejection of the verbal hand he'd outstretched to her, and he returned to their original discussion. "Since I wasn't sleeping with anyone's wife or lover," he said matter-of-factly, "it can't be someone in a jealous rage. Besides, the man targeting me is too professional. Too calculating. Three attempts. Three different ways. Yes, twice it was a bomb, but one was in my car—remote detonation, by the way—and the other was a timed device in my home. And before you ask how I know, the ATF confirmed both points this afternoon."

"That's more than they told me."

Shane's smile held a trace of cynicism. "A US senator has a little more clout than an investigative reporter. Even with the power of your network behind you."

"Okay, so we rule out jealousy. Do you have any enemies that you know of?"

He shook his head. "Not to my knowledge. It could be someone who disagrees with my politics, I suppose," he said doubtfully. "Or someone with a mental problem," he added.

Carly ran a finger over her bottom teeth as she considered this possibility. "Maybe. But again, the attacks on you are too well thought out. Too meticulous. I could buy that the first attempt was a crazy with a rifle—anyone who could get their hands on a gun could take shots at you. But the bombs? Uh-uh." She shook her head vehemently. "Building and planting a bomb is a specialized skill, just as disarming them is. I knew this guy when I was covering the war in Afghanistan—a sergeant—who used to disarm roadside bombs. It was fascinating, and I wanted to do a piece on him," she said as an aside, "but he flat out refused.

"Anyway," she continued, "he told me it's not all that difficult to learn how to build a bomb, and you'd be surprised how relatively easy it is to acquire the component parts. But building a bomb *safely*, so you don't blow yourself up in the process, isn't as easy as you'd think. So whoever built and planted those bombs knows what he's doing. Which means he's done this before. Which means he's a professional."

"Which means," Shane said slowly, "he's a hit man. A hired gun."

She nodded. "Probably. Which brings us right back

to why. Why would someone hire a hit man to kill you? What does killing you accomplish?"

He hesitated. "The only thing I can think of is… No. It can't be that."

Carly pounced. "Can't be what?"

"It was five years ago. And besides, last I heard, that organization was teetering on the brink of collapse."

"What organization?"

He bent a hard stare on her. "I can't tell you as a reporter. Only as—"

"Someone you're sleeping with?" she tossed off with forced insouciance.

He stood abruptly. "Don't." His voice was low but there was an angry edge that had come out of nowhere. "Don't be flippant about what's between us, Carly. Okay, I get you don't want to be emotionally involved. I get that. And I'm doing my best to do as you ask. But don't treat it as casual sex. Because I don't do casual sex. I haven't for a long, long time."

With that he stalked out.

Carly followed Shane and found him in the kitchen pulling a bottle of water from the fridge. He half emptied it in one long gulp, then turned when she said his name.

"I don't do casual sex, either," she admitted. Knowing what else she was admitting to.

"I know you don't."

She tilted her head to one side as she considered this. "Then why did you agree?"

He took another long swig of water before answering. "Because you'd backed yourself into a corner last night. And no," he assured her, "I wasn't humoring you. At least, not in a condescending way. I wanted to give you space. Well," he amended, smiling a little, "not physical space. Because this thing we've got going? I don't see that burning out anytime soon. I wanted in your bed in the worst way. And you wanted me there, too."

Carly flushed at the wicked light in his eyes.

"We're not kids," he said, finishing off the bottle and dumping it in the recycle bin. "Although around you I feel like one sometimes." He tugged her gently into his embrace and kissed her forehead. "That's why I agreed. Because I'll take whatever part of you I can get. Even if it's 'just sex.'"

"You're making me feel... I don't know. Silly, I guess. And guilty." His arms tightened around her infinitesimally, but she felt it. "I wasn't using you, Shane. Honest. But I've never experienced some of the things you make me feel when we... That is, when we're in bed together I can't think of anything else except the next time." Her voice dropped a notch. "I didn't want to give that up."

"Same here."

They stayed in each other's arms for a minute, then Carly reluctantly drew back. "Let's finish our other discussion before we forget where we were, okay?"

"Okay." He nodded. "Let's see about dinner while we talk."

Over lasagna and cauliflower florets, courtesy of Niall's freezer, and a bottle of Italian Chianti from a large wine rack in the kitchen pantry, Carly said, "Earlier you brought up an organization that might have something against you." She smiled reassuringly. "Deep background, you have my word."

He considered this for a moment. "The New World

Militia, an anarchist paramilitary organization," he said finally. "They believed that any government—federal, state, or local—was inherently bad and should be overthrown. They were fanatically dedicated to bringing that about in this country. A while back my sister and the man who's now her husband were instrumental in uncovering a link between them, a political action committee called NOANC founded by a man named Michael Vishenko, and the Russian Mafia."

"Vishenko. I know that name."

"I'm sure you do. Michael Vishenko is Aleksandrov Vishenko's nephew. The uncle was initially one of the defendants in the human trafficking conspiracy case you covered."

Carly's forehead wrinkled. "Yes, but I've heard the name Michael Vishenko, too. Isn't he in prison for murder and bribery? And wasn't his Political Action Committee—"

"NOANC."

"Right, NOANC." She took a sip of wine. "Wasn't that exposed as a front funneling money to corrupt politicians?"

"Give the lady a gold star."

"Nothing special about me knowing that," she pointed out. "It was a huge political scandal. I'd just moved from war correspondent to covering Capitol Hill, so of course I remember. But how does the New World Militia come into it?"

"That domestic terrorist organization actually predates NOANC and Michael Vishenko. Long story short, the New World Militia had been dismantled at one point, and the federal agencies responsible for bringing it down thought it had been destroyed. But Michael Vishenko revived it, as a way to fund his PAC so NOANC could fly under the radar of the Federal Election Committee."

"I see."

"Yeah, but the problem was, no one realized that when the New World Militia was brought back to life, its members were true believers in the cause it espoused. Several splinter groups formed, including one in Denver. The bomb that exploded outside that bookstore five years ago…"

She caught her breath. "The New World Militia? *They* set off the bomb that almost killed you?"

Chapter 12

Shane nodded. "They were trying to make a political statement, but it backfired on them. And no, I wasn't able to help in the investigation. I don't even remember actually saving that woman. The last thing I remember is shopping with my sister the day after Christmas, heading for the bookstore and seeing the woman walking in a little ahead of us. Everything else is a blank—Keira had to tell me what I did beyond that point. But after all the media hype about me, several people came forward with what they knew about the New World Militia, saying I'd inspired them to have the courage to speak up. The bomber and many in his splinter group were identified, arrested, tried and convicted."

"So that organization—or at least some of its members—holds you responsible."

"Yeah, but it was five years ago. And since then the

agency—you know the one I'm talking about, right?" Carly nodded. "The agency has quietly put most of the New World Militia members out of commission permanently."

"Most, but not all."

"No," he agreed. "Not all." Finished with dinner, he rose from the table, carrying his plate and utensils to the sink. Carly hurriedly ate the last bite of her lasagna— surprisingly good, given that it had come out of the freezer—and brought her own plate to the sink. Shane took it from her, saying, "I've got this. Why don't you top off our wineglasses and take them into the living room? I'll just be a minute."

Carly did as he asked, pouring the last of the bottle of Castello di Monsanto Chianti Classico Riserva into her own wineglass, because Shane's had hardly been touched. He obviously wasn't drinking much because of the medication he was taking—even though he wasn't driving anymore tonight—and that abstention impressed her. *Just like his abstention from sex.*

Carly admired self-control in a man, because in her experience it wasn't all that common. *Especially* when it came to sex. She didn't believe all men were animals, but she'd seen enough of what they could do to women when war loosened the social bounds of acceptable behavior to not take her safety for granted. Which was why she carried her .22 with her most of the time now, either in her purse or—when her purse was too small, such as the night of the reception at the Zakharian embassy—strapped to her thigh.

She rinsed the empty wine bottle at the kitchen sink—Shane silently made room for her when she approached—then placed it in the recycle bin, thinking abstractedly, *Niall has good taste in wine.* She'd perused his wine rack before picking the Chianti earlier and had been impressed. Not by how expensive the wine was—she didn't think any bottle there cost more than twenty dollars—but by the array of lesser-known but highly regarded vintages from all over the world. And she wondered now if Shane was a connoisseur as his brother was, admitting to herself, *There's so much you don't know about Shane.*

But she knew the important things. She knew he was a gentleman…and a protector. She knew he had a strict moral code—*probably higher than your own, if truth be told*, she acknowledged. She knew he cared deeply for his family—not just by the things he said, but by the *way* he said them.

And let's not forget the way he treats a woman in bed, she reminded herself. *That* told her a hell of a lot about him, the way he put her needs above his own. The way he wasn't satisfied until *she* was satisfied.

Carly couldn't help the tiny smile that played over her lips as she remembered everything Shane had done to her. Things that—if she had her way—he'd be doing again, soon. Very soon.

They settled side by side on one of the couches in the living room, sipping from their wineglasses, and Carly asked, "So you really think it's them? The New World Militia?"

He shrugged. "No idea. But they're the best answer I can come up with. Especially since I'm cosponsoring that domestic terrorism legislation again this session. Some sections of that bill would directly impact the New World Militia."

She thought about this for a minute. "I think you need to tell the FBI and the ATF."

"I think you're right. But not just them." She cocked her head to one side and gave him a questioning look, and he said, "Did I happen to mention my brother-in-law, Cody Walker, is the head of the Denver branch of the agency?"

"No, you hadn't mentioned it," she said drily. "But I knew."

A faint smile touched his lips. "Ahh, I see. You researched me."

"I'm a reporter," she exclaimed in a huff. "It was necessary to know everything I could about you for my story."

He placed his wineglass on the coffee table in front of him, then took hers and placed it beside his. "I'm not criticizing," he said mildly. "Just acknowledging how thorough you are."

"That was before I knew you," she clarified. "Before I...before we..."

"Became involved."

Her breath whooshed out. "Yes. I would never do that to you now. Not now. Please believe me."

He cupped her cheek and brushed his lips against hers. "I believe you." His conscience nudged at him, and he confessed, "I did the same to you. And I can't even use the excuse that I was researching a story."

Her eyes widened. "You checked me out? When?"

"The day I met you." She seemed blown away by his admission, so he added softly, "I was drawn to you, Carly. I had to know everything I could about you. Especially..."

"Especially what?"

"If you were married. Involved. Batting for the other team. Or otherwise unavailable."

"You checked me out." She couldn't seem to get over it. "So that's how you knew about Jack," she whispered, more to herself than to him.

"Yeah. Hell of a thing to learn the woman you're smitten with almost married someone else." He didn't say it lightly, jokingly. He was serious, and he didn't care if she knew it.

Carly's eyes closed for a moment, and a variety of expressions crossed her face. When she looked at him again, she was as serious as he was. "That was a different woman. *I* was a different woman eight years ago. I've changed since then. In some good ways…but also in some bad."

"Name one."

"I'm…harder now, I think. More cynical."

He tugged gently until she was cradled against his shoulder. "In what way?"

"My profession, for one. I used to be…oh…a little naive, I guess, when it came to journalism. I used to believe all reporters were as idealistic as I was. But I'm not that way anymore."

He smiled to himself. Carly was still idealistic—she just didn't realize it. "What happened to change you?"

"All the news coverage about Jack, after he… The way the press hounded me, hounded Jack's parents. The way our private pain played out on the six o'clock news for everyone to gawk at."

Shane processed her words, finally understanding why—after she'd tricked her way into his hospital room the week before—Carly had left without a story. "That's why you said my epilepsy was no one's business but mine that first day."

She nodded. "Some things aren't news. Not legitimate news. Some things should remain private."

"I agree with you there. But Carly," he said, kissing her temple, "that doesn't make you hard and cynical. Just the opposite."

"No, but it does make me cynical about my profession. Because I know there are some of us out there who will do *anything* for a story. No matter what. No matter who it hurts. Ambush journalists, I think you called them," she added with a sad little smile.

"And sleazy paparazzi, let's not forget them."

She laughed as he'd intended. "Right. Can't forget them."

Shane's hands were moving, stroking over her body's curves, and his lips were doing the same over the curves of her face as he murmured in the deep voice that never failed to move her, "I'm so sorry, Carly. Sorry they hurt you. You didn't deserve that."

Her breath caught in her throat at what Shane was doing, and she barely managed to reply, "No one does."

"Let me make it up to you."

"You're not responsi—oh, Shane…"

"Is that 'oh, Shane, yes'? Or 'oh, Shane, no…'"

She couldn't even answer. Could only arch against his wicked hand and whimper, praying he'd accept that as *please, yes!*

The world condensed down into here and now. Into this moment and the next, and the next. Into Shane and Carly and the way he touched her so reverently, as if he cherished everything about her. Into the emotions that speared through her heart and into her brain. Into the whirling maelstrom where the only anchor holding her safe was Shane.

Eons later, after an orgasm that had left her in tears again, after Shane had lifted her into his strong arms and carried her into the bedroom, after he'd undressed them both without haste, after he'd smoothed on a condom to protect her, he paused at the portal to her womanhood and whispered, "Look at me, Carly."

Still too dazed to do anything except follow his order, she gazed up into his eyes and nearly drowned in the darkness there. He pressed inward a tiny fraction, saying, "This."

She arched, trying to take him deeper, but he pulled back slightly, saying, "Isn't."

She couldn't think. Couldn't focus on anything but his body moving on hers. In hers. Inch by inch. "Just," he growled, as if he was fighting to hold back.

"Please, Shane," she whispered.

He filled her. And when he was seated to the hilt, he held her eyes captive and uttered one word. "Sex." He pulled out almost completely, then surged back in. "This isn't just sex," he repeated implacably. "Not for either of us."

There were no more words after that. Just sighs and moans and…at the very end…wordless cries of satisfaction. From both of them.

Carly woke in the darkness. Alone. She reached out a hand for Shane, but the place where he'd lain beside her when she'd fallen asleep was empty, and the sheet was cold to the touch. So she knew he'd been gone a while. Long enough for his body heat to dissipate.

She sat up and turned on the bedside lamp, then glanced around the room, hoping to find her suitcases. No such luck. The clothes she'd worn earlier were lying in tidy piles across the arms of the chair in the corner, and they brought a smile to her face. Shane had taken his time undressing her earlier, she remembered. And she had been content to let him.

But for some reason she didn't feel like donning her work clothes again. Especially since she had every intention of luring Shane back into bed with her. So she tugged the top sheet free from the comforter, wrapped it around herself sari-style and went in search of him.

She found him in the living room, standing naked except for his boxer shorts in front of the picture window. He'd cracked the blinds open slightly, and was staring out into the night lights of DC as he spoke into his cell phone.

Carly took a moment to admire the shadowy picture he made in the darkened room—muscle, bone and sinew backlit by the skyline behind him. *Okay, I can't really see his muscles*, she admitted, but she'd felt them enough to know they were there. And she *could* see broad shoulders tapering down to a narrow waist and hips—obvious because his boxers rode low on his hips—a classic outline of male beauty.

She sighed soundlessly, remembering the way she'd clutched those hips earlier as he'd brought them both to completion…long and slow. Never rushed until the very end, when he—

Shane's voice crashed into her consciousness. "No, Cody," he said firmly. "I haven't a scintilla of proof. It's a theory, that's all. But I thought you'd want to know."

A long silence was followed by "I've already shared

the theory with the FBI and the ATF, and they're going to check into it. I figured the agency deserved a crack at it, too, given your long history with the New World Militia."

He chuckled softly, obviously in response to what his brother-in-law was saying. "Yeah, and you're very welcome. Always happy to be a target for a good cause." He listened for a minute, then said, "Give Keira my love and tell her I'm sorry I called so late and woke you both up, okay? And give her a kiss from me. Not that you need an excuse to kiss your wife," he joked. He laughed after another minute of silence. "Give Alyssa a kiss, as well. Tell her Uncle Shane plans to be back in Denver at the end of March, and can't wait to see her on the two-wheeler she got for Christmas—if the snow has melted enough."

Shane nodded in response to something said to him, then ended the call with "Thanks, Cody. I appreciate this. Let me know what you find out."

He disconnected and turned. When he caught sight of Carly he froze for an instant, then relaxed. "I didn't hear you come in," he said. "How long have you been there?"

She padded barefoot toward him. "Long enough to know you've already notified the FBI and the ATF." She touched his chest and found his skin cool beneath her fingertips. "You're cold," she chided. "You should have put more clothes on." She was unwrapping the sheet as she spoke, then enclosing both of them in its enveloping folds.

"Mmm, this is nice," he told her, sliding his hands around her waist. "I didn't want to wake you," he explained. "I just grabbed my boxers and my cell phone and left." He kissed her lightly. "I got distracted earlier, but I didn't want to wait until tomorrow to get the ball rolling on the investigation."

"Let's go back to bed where it's warm." She shivered slightly, because everywhere his skin touched hers was cold. "You can tell me the rest there."

"Okay." His hands moved and he lifted her up, even though his cell phone was still clutched in his left hand. "Wrap your legs—yes, like that," he told her as her thighs automatically clasped around his hips. He began walking them back toward the bedroom. "Hold on tight."

"You always say that," she murmured, teasing him a little.

Laughter rumbled out of him. "I don't always. Sometimes I can't even form words," he teased back. He tumbled them both onto the bed, then pulled the comforter over their already-cocooned bodies.

"Mmm, this is nice," he repeated, letting his hands wander at will, but Carly caught them before they could go too far.

"Don't start anything until you tell me everything," she insisted.

"Everything's a pretty tall order."

"You know what I mean." She wrapped one hand around a certain portion of his anatomy and squeezed lightly. "We have ways of making you talk," she said in a mock-threatening voice with a fake Russian accent, forcing another laugh out of him.

"Marines don't surrender to threats." When her fingers tightened he sucked in his breath and said, "Okay, okay, you win." But then he began tickling her fiendishly until her grasp loosened and she choked on her own laughter, begging him to stop. "Ha-ha," he gloated like a cartoon villain. "You are at my mercy, fair maiden." But he stopped the tickling. After they'd both had a moment to catch their breaths, Shane's face tightened with sudden seriousness. "I wish you were," he said in an undertone.

"Wish I were what?"

"At my mercy." He rolled her over until she was beneath him, and all at once he was hot and heavy between her thighs. "Because, God help me, I'm at yours."

A complex wave of emotions washed through her, and her chest was so tight it ached. In that instant she knew there was no turning back from this point on. She fought to free her hands from the sheet, then cradled Shane's face as she blinked back tears. As serious as he was, she whispered, "God help us both." Then she kissed him.

Marsh wasn't given to panic. He planned his life as methodically as his hits, and vice versa, always leaving a margin for error. And he rarely had trouble sleeping. Dreamlessly.

But he'd woken in a cold sweat at 3:17 a.m., his heart pounding, the ragged remnants of a nightmare of epic proportions clinging stubbornly to his consciousness. And try though he might, he hadn't been able to go back to sleep again.

He turned over in bed, punching the pillow and bunching it beneath his head, as if the inoffensive object was his most recent target. He knew why he'd had trouble falling asleep last night, which was also the reason for the nightmare—his target had disappeared. Marsh had no idea where he was. Even the man on the inside didn't know—just that the senator had notified his staff he couldn't be reached at his home, only via cell phone...and that was an area where Marsh was *not* an expert. He had no idea how to hack into someone's cell phone.

The kind of disappearing act the senator had pulled usually meant a woman was involved, the man on the inside had suggested. Marsh hadn't volunteered anything, but he knew the senator wasn't at the reporter's house, either, because no one was there.

And time was running out.

He'll be at work tomorrow, though, Marsh consoled himself. *Not that I can kill him on the Senate floor...but I can trail him from there, find out where he's hiding.*

Then take care of the senator once and for all.

Chapter 13

Despite not being a morning person, Carly was dressed and getting into the car beside Shane at seven-thirty. "I have time to drop you at your office before I go to work," he'd told her in the wee hours of the morning.

"You don't have to," she'd stated. "The network's studio is out of the way for you." Niall's condo wasn't all that far from the Capitol Building, and if Shane didn't have to take her to work, it would be a straight shot for him. "I can take a cab," she'd added. *And sleep in*, she'd thought but hadn't voiced.

"Humor me," he'd said stubbornly. "I can't guard you 24/7, but I can at least make sure you get to and from work safely. What time should I pick you up after work?"

Now Carly watched Shane through sleepy eyes as he drove his Mustang GT through the DC traffic, shifting gears effortlessly. Occasionally she sipped from the travel mug of coffee he'd handed her just before she'd walked out the door. She hadn't had time for breakfast—she never had time for that in the morning as a general rule before heading to work—but she couldn't survive without coffee.

At first she'd been surprised Shane knew how addicted she was to coffee, then she realized she shouldn't be. He was incredibly observant…and they *had* spent one night together in her town house—and a morning after. She hadn't been able to offer him much in the way of breakfast that morning, but she *had* brewed fresh coffee for him—her Café Du Monde coffee and chicory blend that she bought from a little Chinese grocery not far from her house. It cost her an arm and a leg because she couldn't buy it most places—only in New Orleans's French Quarter, online or in Chinese grocery stores almost everywhere, though at a premium price. But she'd fallen in love with the coffee the first time she'd visited New Orleans, and it was her only indulgence.

Shane turned toward her when they stopped at a stoplight and smiled the heart-stopping smile that had garnered him a few extra votes in the last election. "Awake yet?"

"I've *been* awake since you woke me at six…mostly," she assured him. "But you'll never make a morning person out of me."

His smile turned wicked. "A challenge. I love a challenge."

The light changed and he turned his attention back to the road, for which Carly was grateful. He wouldn't see her flushed cheeks as the memory of *how* he'd awakened her this morning floated through her mind. Not to mention the memory of how he'd kissed her when he'd brought her home from the interrogation following the reception at the Zakharian embassy, and said, *You're dead on your feet. Sleepy, early-morning sex might be great, but not for our first time.*

There's no "might" about it, she barely stopped herself from saying out loud. Sleepy, early-morning sex with Shane *was* great. And if she *had* to wake up early, that at least made up for it.

Carly was kept busy reviewing video footage with her producer on a story that was about to break wide open: a police shooting of an unarmed black man in Philadelphia, which had been caught on dash-cam video that the Philly police had refused to release to the public until several networks—including Carly's—sued under the Freedom of Information Act.

The dash-cam video had just been released that morning, and the story would air that night. The victim—who'd turned out to be a uniformed police officer on his day off, doing nothing more than picking up a pizza for his family—had miraculously survived despite being shot seven times, and Carly had snagged an interview with him in the hospital two months ago, along with his wife and children. Her initial interviews had aired at the time, but now the video of the actual shooting made the story explosive.

"Should I go up there?" she asked J.C. "Do we need something else to make the story pop?"

He considered it for a moment, then shook his head. "We've got enough footage of you on the street from when the shooting occurred. We can splice that in with your in-depth interviews with him and his family along with the dash-cam video footage—it's black and white and kind of grainy, but I think our guys can enhance the image a little without damaging the integrity."

"What about the renewed protests? Shouldn't I cover that?" The initial protests had died down as the shooting had quickly faded from media coverage. But now they were flaring up again.

"The network's sending Rafe Coburn out of New York to cover it."

She didn't like it, but she'd learned to pick her battles. This wasn't one she could win, not when the network brass had already made the call.

After lunch Carly filmed the lead-in and the wrap-up, as well as two teasers that would run during the nightly news and the early-evening programming. At three she and J.C. watched the entire segment twice with a slew of staff members, taking feedback and making tiny tweaks here and there. By five they were done.

"Go home, Carly," J.C. told her as everyone filed out of the room, leaving only J.C. and her.

"What about—"

"Go home. Nothing more you can do here." His voice softened. "You did a good job on those interviews, by the way."

"Thanks." She stashed her notebook in her purse, then looked up again. "I just hope something comes of this."

A cynical expression crossed J.C.'s face. "Keep dreaming."

She didn't know why she did it, but something made her argue. "There *has* to be a better way, J.C. There just has to be."

J.C. smiled, not unkindly. "Go home, Carly."

Carly headed for her office once she left the conference room. She needed her coat and the travel mug Shane had given her this morning, but she was operating on autopilot, because she couldn't stop thinking about J.C.'s cynical statement—*Keep dreaming.* As if things could never change.

All at once she desperately wanted Shane. Wanted his reassuring arms around her. Wanted him to convince her J.C. was wrong, that things *could* change for the better…if you fought hard enough to change them. Shane, who tilted at windmills. Who fought for what he believed in, no matter how impossible the odds.

That's when she realized she hadn't called or texted Shane all day. She'd been so busy she'd—well, not forgotten him, because she'd thought of him several times throughout the day. But she hadn't taken the time to let him *know* she was thinking of him. And he hadn't called or texted her, either. She grabbed her smartphone from her purse and double-checked to be sure it was on. It was, but there were no messages, no missed calls and no texts.

Fear clutched at her heart. What if something had happened to Shane, *and she hadn't contacted him?* She'd done this to Jack, too, let herself get so caught up in other things—a story, their wedding plans—that she'd neglected the man she loved.

The man she loved?

"Oh no. No," she whispered, not wanting to believe it. "You didn't, Carly. You *didn't*."

Only…she had. She'd fallen in love with Shane. Two days ago she'd insisted they maintain an emotional distance. And now…now her heart was telling her what her head didn't want to acknowledge—she loved Shane so much she was suddenly frantic with worry merely because she hadn't heard from him all day.

She hurriedly checked the time, remembering she'd told Shane to pick her up at five, and it was now almost half past the hour. She fumbled with her phone, intending to text him, but before she could, the device buzzed and vibrated. When she looked at the touch screen, she saw it was from him.

Waiting downstairs, if you're ready. If not, just let me know. Don't rush. Take your time.

Shane was waiting for her downstairs. Had *been* waiting patiently for almost thirty minutes. That's all she could think about. She shrugged on her coat, grabbed the empty travel mug and crammed it into her purse, then flew out the door, heading for the elevator.

She rushed out, hitting the circular glass door with such force it was still going round when she was already on the sidewalk outside. Cars lined both sides of the street in front of the building, but none of them was Shane's, although she looked twice just to be sure. She didn't despair, though. He'd told her he was here, waiting, and he would be. She just had to be patient and—

Out of the corner of her eye she saw a car coming down the street. She heaved a sigh of relief when she recognized Shane's Mustang, and she was at the curb waiting by the time he pulled up. He made as if to hop out, probably to hold the door for her like the gentleman he was, but she jumped in before he could.

"Hi," she said breathlessly, buckling herself in. "Sorry I made you wait."

"No problem." His smile went right through her, and

she sighed softly. "Busy day, I take it?" he asked as he pulled into traffic.

"Kind of." But she didn't really want to talk about her day. Maybe later. For now, all she wanted to know was what kind of day he'd had. "You?"

"So-so. Nothing happening on the floor of the Senate, but Cody called me."

"Your brother-in-law? Has the agency found out something already?"

"Not exactly. But he talked with his boss here in DC, and they sent a couple of local agents to interview me this morning."

"And?"

"And nothing. They'll let me know when and if they learn anything. In the meantime, they gave me some advice."

"Which is?"

"Watch my back." He chuckled softly. "As if I wasn't already."

She shook her head at him. "I don't know how you can laugh at something as serious as this."

He didn't answer right away. Just glanced at her, then back at the road. "I was a US Marine for a lot of years, Carly," he finally explained. "You don't get—I guess *complacent* is the word—you don't get *complacent* about death, but you can't stress over it, either. You have to laugh whenever you can, 'cause otherwise you'd be a basket case. Gallows humor, maybe. But you have to see the humor in everything to stay sane and sharp. You should know—you were an embedded reporter in Afghanistan."

"Yes, but..." She started to say it was different when someone you loved was in danger. Humor was the last thing on your mind then. But she stopped herself before she could say it, because she wasn't ready to let him know he'd slipped under her defenses. She wasn't her sister, Tahra—old-fashioned enough to think a man should speak first—but she wasn't sure exactly what Shane was feeling. It was one thing for him to insist he didn't do casual sex, that he had to care about a woman in order to make love to her. But that was a long way from love. And until she *knew*…she wasn't going to put her heart out there. Not to mention she wasn't going to put that burden on Shane, as if she was pressuring him to return her feelings by telling him how she felt.

She sighed again. At least she was with Shane. At least she could guard his back. She turned to look at him, and that's when she realized something was wrong. Shane's whole body language had changed.

"We're being followed," he told her quietly. "No! Don't turn around. I don't want him to know he's been tagged. Not yet."

Carly stopped herself from looking backward, but it was an effort. She tried to peer into the side mirror, to see if she could spot what Shane was seeing, but the angle was all wrong. "How do you know?" She was proud her voice didn't waver.

"Trust me, I know. He's two cars back at the moment, but now that I think of it, he's been there since I left my office. He's good. Really good. He doesn't ride my tail, and he varies how many cars are between us. But he's there."

"Could it be the FBI?" she asked. "Or the agency?"

"Maybe." Shane smiled grimly. "But I doubt it. It's not a government car *or* a federal license plate number. But I'm going to find out for sure—one way or the other." He fished his smartphone out of his pocket and hit one number for speed dial. Steering with his left hand and holding his phone with his right, which he also needed to shift gears, told Carly just how dangerous Shane thought their situation was. He spoke into the phone without identifying himself. "I need a huge favor. I need a Virginia plate number run on an older model white Chevy truck. XKF dash..." He reeled off three numbers, then said, "The last number could be either a three or an eight. It's already dark, the plate was dirty and I only saw it for a second." He laughed softly in response to something said on the phone, and agreed, "Yeah, yeah, yeah, I'm losing my touch. My eyes aren't what they used to be, my hearing is going and I've got one foot in the grave. Forget that crap and run that number, okay? If it's who I think it is, the plate could be stolen, but on the off chance it's not..." He nodded, even though his listener couldn't see him. "Right."

The person on the other end of the phone must have asked a question, because Shane said, "Yeah, I'm pretty sure my tail isn't from the FBI or the agency. Or any other kind of law enforcement. I'm a minute away from ditching whoever's back there, but it'd be nice to know for the future if the feds are following me. The FBI *told* me they couldn't spare the manpower, which is why— right again. Call me when you know something."

Shane disconnected, then dropped his phone into one of the empty cup holders between their seats, and replaced his hand on the gear shift. "Hang on tight," he warned Carly. "I'm going to lose this tail."

Afterward, Carly could only remember the next ten minutes as a hazy blur. The Mustang accelerated with a throaty roar as Shane worked the clutch and the gear shift with practiced ease, darting in and out of lanes of traffic with a seeming disregard for safe distances between cars. Twice he swerved around corners without stopping, right after the lights turned red but before cross traffic could start. And each time his eyes slid to the rearview mirror.

Knowing that whoever was following them had to know by now he'd been spotted, Carly swiveled her head around as much as she could without removing her seat belt—and there wasn't a chance in hell she would do that the way Shane was driving. After a minute of watching anxiously over her shoulder she said, "There's no white truck back there anymore."

But Shane didn't slow down. "Maybe not, but I want insurance." So he continued driving like a lunatic for another four minutes, until he spotted a police car coming the other way. He braked abruptly, downshifted and the Mustang slowed to the speed limit.

She let out the breath she hadn't realized she'd been holding when the police car rolled right on past them without turning on its red-and-blue lights and signaling for them to pull over. Then she laughed.

"What's so funny?"

"Me," she explained, still laughing, but softer now. "I just realized the only time I panicked in the last ten minutes was when I thought you were going to get a ticket."

Shane grinned at her, and there was more than a touch of the unrepentant wild teenage boy he must have been at one time in his expression. "Would you believe I've never—not even once—gotten a ticket?"

She smiled and shook her head at him. "No, I don't believe it."

He raised his right hand from the gear shift and held

it up as if he were taking an oath. "True as I sit here." Then he amended, "Came close a couple of times. But both times I was stopped I was in uniform, and the cops let me off with just a warning."

The laughter that pealed out of her this time wasn't just for Shane's narrow escape from the law all those years ago, but also for their escapes today—from the police *and* the man tailing them.

Shane sedately turned left onto the road that would take them to Niall's condo. Curious, Carly asked, "How did you learn to drive like that?"

"I learned a few defensive driving tricks in the Corps. But to be honest, I already knew how to drive a muscle car to an inch. My dad…" He smiled to himself. "My dad had a candy-apple red sixty-nine Camaro he'd rebuilt practically from scratch. He rarely drove it—a man with a living to earn and a wife and five children to support doesn't have a lot of free time for nonessentials—but he *owned* it. And the guys he worked with envied him that car. That was more important to him than actually driving it."

He chuckled. "That car in the garage drove Niall and me crazy. We couldn't understand leaving it to sit there in all its gleaming glory. So one day when our parents were out of town visiting relatives, taking Alec, Liam and Keira with them, Niall and I 'borrowed' the Camaro. We were just going to take it out for a quick spin, then put it back as if had never been touched."

"Uh-oh."

"Yeah. Uh-oh. Best laid plans and all of that. Do you remember the Porsche scene from *Risky Business*? The movie that made Tom Cruise a star?"

"Oh, no," Carly said, dismayed. "I mean, yes, I remember, but please don't tell me you drove your dad's Camaro into a lake."

"Not quite that bad. But we *did* end up in a ditch. Nobody injured, but one fender took a beating. We managed to drive the car home after Niall and I wrestled it back onto the road, but there was no hiding the damage."

"How old were you?"

"Seventeen. And my brother was sixteen."

"What happened?"

They'd arrived at Niall's condo by this time. Shane pulled into the underground garage and parked the Mustang before turning to her and answering. "We 'fessed up, of course, when our dad got home. After he made it very clear we were paying for the damage—and it wasn't cheap, by any means!—and after he tanned our hides, he took Niall and me out once the Camaro was repaired and taught us how to drive it."

At first Carly smiled at the happy ending. Then she focused on the other thing Shane had said, and her brows drew together into a frown. "I don't believe in corporal punishment."

"Neither do I, as a general rule. But in this case restitution wasn't enough. We stole a car, Carly," he explained patiently. "The fact that it belonged to our dad only partially mitigated our crime. He couldn't let us off scot-free. And he couldn't just reward us by teaching us how to drive a car like a Camaro. Actions have to have consequences. Otherwise the whole fabric of our society will shred."

"Yes, but—"

"Niall and I weren't bad kids, but we'd stepped onto a slippery slope. My dad had to make sure we didn't take that next step downward. It didn't 'damage our psyches,' and it didn't 'scar us for life.' A few minutes of pain taught us a lesson we've never forgotten."

She considered this for a long time, then said, "I see your point, but I still don't think it's right."

"We'll have to agree to disagree on this one," he told her. He was out of the car and holding the door for her before she gathered up her purse.

It wasn't until they were walking into Niall's condo that Carly realized with a sense of shock *why* Shane's stance on this issue mattered so much to her—she was already envisioning him as the father of her children. The same way she had with Jack.

And she didn't even know if Shane loved her.

Chapter 14

Under the cover of darkness, Marsh parked his truck down the street from a busy Virginia grocery store, took a screwdriver from the glove compartment, grabbed something from beneath his seat and got out. He set his little markers that would tell him if someone touched his truck while he was gone—the insurance was worth the time investment—then headed for the store's side parking lot. He'd scoped out this place several months earlier, and at that time he'd learned it had no surveillance cameras except inside the store and in the far parking lots. He double-checked, and found it still held true—the store was counting on lights and foot traffic to keep the close parking lots safe.

He waited in the shadows until he saw a truck park in his target area and the driver get out and hurry inside. Then he moved. It took him less than a minute and a half to unscrew the back license plate and replace it with one of the ones he'd brought with him. Then he moved to the front. He was almost done when he heard footsteps clicking on the pavement, heading his way, and his hand slid inside his jacket. But the footsteps continued on past him, and Marsh left the Ruger where it was.

He quickly finished with the last screw on the replacement license plate. He waited until the unknown driver turned on the engine and the lights and pulled out of the parking lot before tucking the two plates he'd just stolen inside his jacket.

Five minutes later he was driving away.

He always swapped out plates if he could. It was less likely a driver would notice his license plate number had changed—many people didn't even know what their own plate numbers were—but most people would notice a missing plate and report it right away. It was a little thing, but something Marsh had learned years ago. One of the little tricks of the trade that kept him from prison.

He was almost home before his disposable cell phone rang, and Marsh knew his employer was calling for a status update. He didn't answer. He wasn't about to reveal his target had given him the slip. He wasn't about to reveal he'd been outplayed.

He didn't know how the senator had known Marsh was back there, but somehow he had, and once again his admiration for him rose. Never mind the frustration he felt at letting the senator slip through his fingers again. Never mind the postponement of the final payment for a job he should have accomplished a week ago. There was a thrill in knowing his target was a worthy one. It was a game of cat and mouse, and for once Marsh wasn't sure which role was his. Which added a touch of spice to a profession that had grown somewhat stale over the years of nothing but success after success.

He would need to call upon all his skills for this one. Would need the cunning of a fox, the keen eye of a hawk and the nose of a bloodhound to win this game. But one thing was certain—Marsh had no intention of losing.

Carly slipped from the bed as quietly as she could so as not to wake Shane. She grabbed her robe from the chair beside the bed, belted it firmly around her waist, found her slippers, then crept from the bedroom, closing the door softly behind her.

She padded to the table by the front door where she'd left her purse and pulled out a pen and her notebook. She always thought better with them. Her mini recorder was great for recording conversations with her interview subjects, but her notebook was where she made sense of everything. And she needed to make sense of something now because she couldn't sleep until she tried.

She headed for the kitchen, debating whether she wanted to make a pot of coffee or not, and decided against it. Not that the caffeine would keep her awake— she could drink coffee any time of the day or night and it didn't bother her—she just didn't want to waste the time right now. An idea was buzzing in her brain and she needed to get her thoughts down on paper ASAP.

She sat at the kitchen table, opened her notebook to a fresh page and started jotting down random words and phrases. Every so often she circled one, then drew a line connecting it to another. And another.

She propped her elbow on the table and leaned her

head on one hand—thumb beneath her chin, two fingers supporting her cheek, her ring finger across her lips— as she stared down at what she'd written. She shook her head a couple of times and drew Xs over a few words and phrases, then wrote something else in their place.

The hair on the back of her neck began to rise as a picture started taking shape. She scribbled one word and circled it three times, then drew lines from it to the rest of her notations. "It fits," she whispered. "Oh my God, it all fits."

"Can't sleep?"

Carly jumped and gasped when Shane spoke from the doorway, fear-induced adrenaline coursing through her body. "Oh my God," she breathed, "you scared the hell out of me."

"Sorry, I didn't mean to." He pulled out a chair and took a seat across from her, then tapped a finger on her notations. "What are you working on?"

She glanced from his face to her notebook, and back again. "I think I know why you've been targeted. And it doesn't have anything to do with the New World Militia."

In Carly's experience men had a tendency to dismiss a woman's ideas, especially if they contradicted his. That was one of the main reasons she'd switched from her previous network to her current one, even though some people might have viewed the move as something of a demotion career-wise. As much as she clashed with J.C. at times, he never dismissed her ideas. He challenged them, made her defend them, but he never dismissed them out of hand.

So she knew an instant of surprise when Shane didn't automatically dismiss her statement. But then she chastised herself for lumping Shane in with the rest of mankind. *That's not who he is and you know it in your heart.* She couldn't have loved Shane if he was like that.

"So if it's not the New World Militia," he said, his words slow and measured as he obviously tried to read her notes upside down, "then who?"

"Follow the money," she said softly, holding his gaze.

It took him a minute, then his eyes widened in disbelief. "The pipeline?"

She nodded. "Not retaliation. Just greed."

He looked blown away. "That's...not possible." When she just continued to stare at him steadily, he said, "I'm not even the leading voice of the opposition to the pipeline bill."

"But you *are* the pivotal vote," she reminded him. "As it stands now, the vote is split right down party lines, and you're an independent. But it's not just that. You're passionate and eloquent in your opposition, and you'll sway others to your side." She thought for a moment. "Remember what you told me about the people who came forward to testify in that domestic terrorism case, the ones who said your actions that day inspired them to have the courage to speak up?" She put her hand on his. "You have that effect on people, Shane. You make them examine their consciences. You make them do things they might not otherwise do."

He was silent for a moment, then shook his head. "That might be true, but it doesn't track. There were two assassination attempts before I went public with my opposition. So no one knew how I intended to vote."

"No one?" She gave him a skeptical look. "I find that hard to believe."

"Only my—" He stopped short.

"Only your...staff?"

"Oh God." He closed his eyes, and Carly's heart went out to him. When his eyes opened again, there was something cold and hard in their depths that hurt her, because she knew the potential betrayal of his trust devastated him.

She squeezed his hand in encouragement, and said, "Who knew? All your staff? Or just certain ones?" She turned to a clean page in her notebook, swiveled it around and gently pushed it in his direction. She held out the pen. "Write down their names."

He took the pen from her, but didn't start writing. "Not Dee-Dee," he said, and the note of thankfulness in his voice wasn't lost on her. "She probably guessed, but she didn't *know*—not until I returned from Arizona."

"Okay, that's good. She's probably in the clear. Who else?"

"Not Mike Adamson, my press secretary. There's a lot I don't tell him until I'm ready to go public. *Not* because I don't trust him, but because he gets asked a lot of questions by the press, and I don't like to put him in the position where he has to dissimilate. If he doesn't know, he doesn't know, and he can answer with a clear conscience."

"That's two who probably didn't know and couldn't betray you. Now tell me who for sure *did* know...because you discussed it with them."

Shane stared over Carly's shoulder, remembering the strategy session in his office two weeks before he'd flown out and checked himself into the Mayo Clinic. Then he glanced down at Carly's notebook, clicked the pen in his hand and wrote six titles, followed by six names.

Chief of staff—Marie-Therese Guidry.
Deputy chief of staff—Bobby Vernon.
Chief counsel—LaWanda Jackson.
Legislative director—Hank Warren.
Senior legislative assistant—Miguel de Santos.
Legislative correspondent—Terry Chan.

"That's it," he said. "That's everyone who knew for certain." Then he grimaced. "Of course, any of these six could have mentioned it to someone else, either on my staff or off it. There's no way to know for sure."

"Let's assume for now these six are an all-inclusive list," Carly said with practical matter-of-factness, "because we have to start somewhere. Now of these six, who would you rule out?"

"The two women," he replied immediately.

"Because they're women?"

"No," he said patiently. "Because Marie-Therese is an ardent environmentalist who opposes ANWR drilling," he explained, referring to drilling for oil in the Arctic National Wildlife Refuge. "So of course she's against the proposed pipeline that will have such a devastating environmental impact. And LaWanda is the one who ferreted out the money men behind the pipeline bill. Half of what I know about the bill's supporters and its egregious clauses comes from them."

"Okay, I'll buy that," Carly said. "That leaves four. Are there any you would cross off the list?"

He thought long and hard, then shook his head with real regret. "No. I…no."

She ran her pointer finger over her bottom teeth, then tapped them with a fingernail—a little habit she had when she was thinking hard, he realized suddenly. Then she said, "If you can't rule any of them out, are there any you'd particularly rule in? And before you answer that," she rushed to add, "ask yourself if any of them expressed dissatisfaction with the way you intended to vote, and tried to get you to change your mind. Put that on one side. On the other, have any of them shown signs of unexplained affluence? Money they shouldn't have?"

"Miguel," Shane said slowly, thinking back to the strategy session. "He kept emphasizing the jobs the pipeline would create, never mind the drawbacks. But that's not unusual for him—that's sort of the role he has taken on, playing devil's advocate." He thought some more. "Hank came into quite a bit of money recently, but it wasn't unexplained. His father died, and Hank's an only child."

Shane paused, and Carly said, "Keep going. What about the other two?"

"There's Bobby. But with him it's not unexplained wealth—just the opposite. He's paying child support to two ex-wives, and he always seems to be strapped for cash. But I've known him since high school—we played football together—and I can't believe…"

He seemed lost in thought, and after a minute of silence Carly asked, "And the last guy? Terry?"

"Terry's the newest member of my staff, so if I had to pick one it *might* be, I guess I'd pick him for that reason—although it doesn't seem fair to suspect him for that reason alone. But the other three have been with me since the beginning, when I ran for the House. Terry just came on board nine months ago when he graduated from college. I don't really know much about his private life. He's kind of a loner."

Shane scoured his mind for anything else, but came up blank. "That's all I can think of."

"That's okay," Carly reassured him. "Four names. Four suspects. It could be any one of them, or it could be none of them. Turn their names and the new theory over to the FBI first thing in the morning, and let them take it from there."

"And the agency," he reminded her.

"And the agency," she agreed. "Although if the New World Militia isn't involved…" She didn't finish the sentence, but she didn't have to. If that was eliminated as a possibility, the agency would probably defer to the FBI and bow out of the investigation.

Carly yawned suddenly, glanced at the clock on the microwave and made a face. Shane's gaze followed hers, and he saw it was past two. He stood and held out his hand. "Let's go back to bed," he invited. "There's nothing more we can do tonight."

She yawned again. "You're right." Her eyes met his, and there was contrition in those bright blue orbs. "I'm sorry," she said, her voice very quiet yet full of understanding as she rose and took his hand. "I know this isn't something you wanted to hear."

He wrapped his arms around her and she did the same to him. There was such consolation in her embrace, such silent caring, and all at once Shane wondered how the hell he'd ever survived without Carly in his life. She'd become the most important person in his world so quickly, he'd been blindsided.

Would he change it if he could? Hell no! He'd been alone for so long he'd almost forgotten what it was like *not* to be alone. Not to have to deal with life's hard knocks on his own. He'd almost forgotten the tender comfort of a woman's presence.

His life was now divided into two distinct parts, as if a line of demarcation separated them. BC—before Carly. And now. He wouldn't trade *now* for anything you could offer him, not even freedom from the seizures and the diagnosis that had brought his world crashing down on him a week ago.

Then he wondered what the hell he was going to do when she called it quits. Because even though what was between them wasn't just sex, even though they were far beyond casual bedmates, the bottom line was Carly had never retracted her emotional distance requirement. Which meant at some point she would be gone. Leaving him bereft…and devastated.

Carly raised her head from his shoulder, disrupting his desolate thoughts, and said, "At least now we have a deadline. And in a funny way, that's a good thing. If you're not dead before the vote on the pipeline bill, killing you no longer matters. You'll no longer be a target. When is the vote?"

"Tuesday…assuming the debate ends by then, which the president pro-tem assures me it will be." Then he added, "But even if I'm in the clear, that doesn't mean you'll be." His face hardened to match his voice. "You saw him, Carly. He thinks you can identify him. Which means we have to catch him. Otherwise…"

He couldn't fathom letting anything happen to her. He hadn't protected Wendy fifteen years ago—he would protect Carly no matter what. Even if it meant putting his life on the line to draw the assassin out. Even if he died for it.

Chapter 15

Shane was just taking his seat on the Senate floor when his smartphone dinged for an incoming text. He usually switched the notification sound off and the vibrate on when heading down to the floor, but he'd forgotten this time.

He glanced at the text, then cursed silently. U R right. Plates stolen.

It was too much to hope for that whoever was following him last night would have slipped up enough to use his own license plates, especially since Shane already knew the hit man had used stolen plates before when he'd left the bombs at his house and Carly's. But it would have made tracking him down a lot easier. And a lot less deadly.

He already knew the answer—who but the would-be assassin would use stolen plates?—but beneath his desk he surreptitiously tapped out, FBI? Agency?

No. Just the one word, but it decided him.

He glanced left and right, but no one was paying him the least attention. As was often the case, senators filed in late and took their places as if they had all the time in the world. Shane never did that, but he was the exception rather than the rule.

Need another favor, he typed.

He smiled to himself at the response. Tell me something I don't know. Before he could reply, another text arrived. My place. Tonight. 7.

He replied, You're not working?

24/7. Window.

Shane chuckled softly, shaking his head. So Niall had a window of opportunity with his job, did he? As if Shane were stupid enough to believe *that*.

The good news was that he didn't need to rely on the FBI or the agency to set up the sting. Not that he didn't trust them, but he didn't need someone telling him he couldn't put himself out there as live bait. Because he had every intention of doing just that to catch the hit man before he could kill Carly.

Carly looked up from her desk when J.C. stuck his head inside her door. "You're early...for you," he said, moving to fill the doorway. "Don't tell me, let me guess. The senator is a robin, and night owl you is rolling over and exposing your tender underbelly in surrender."

She told him what he could do with himself, and he merely laughed before taking a seat in front of her desk. "But you *are* sleeping with him, right?"

She ignored the question. "What do you want, J.C.?"

she asked pointedly. "And you'd better have a good reason for being here. Because, you know, I could file a sexual harassment claim. And don't think I won't."

He grinned unrepentantly. "Overnights are in. I thought you might be interested."

That made her sit up. "What do they say?"

"We smeared the competition. Your interview with the wife and kids was the kicker. Especially spliced in between those scenes from the dash-cam video. The viewers were riveted."

Carly allowed herself a tiny smile. That had been her idea, and J.C. had enthusiastically endorsed it. "So what's our follow-up?" she asked.

"Philadelphia mayor and chief of police are holding a press conference this afternoon. Damage control. Too little, too late, but…" He shrugged. "I've got a crew standing by in Philly to cover, but I'd rather it was you." He glanced at his watch. "You'd have to leave within the hour, though, to make it…if you want to go."

She frowned. "*If* I want to go? What kind of question is that? Of course I want to go."

"You don't have to check in with the senator first?"

"What century are you living in, J.C.?" she asked fiercely. "This is my *job*. I don't need to ask anyone's *permission* to do my job."

J.C. held up both his hands, palms out. "Hang on, Carly. That's not what I meant."

"Then what *did* you mean?"

"Look, the FBI was here early Monday morning. And again Wednesday."

"What?"

"I'll be honest. I pretty much refused to answer their questions on Monday because I could tell from the get-go they were leaning toward the bomb in the senator's car being some kind of publicity stunt. How do you think I found out so quickly that morning and called you?"

"I…" She was nonplussed. "You have sources, J.C., just as I do. I never really thought about it."

"I knew it wasn't a publicity stunt, and the FBI should have known it, too—the assassination attempt in Arizona should have clued them in if nothing else," he said drily. "Unless they thought *that* was a stunt, too." His expression left no doubt what his opinion on that theory was. "And I'd met Senator Jones the day before, so I knew the FBI was barking up the wrong tree. Besides, I know *you*. You'd never lend yourself to something underhanded like that."

"Thanks."

"But after the bombs were left in your homes…the FBI seemed to take the threat more seriously. And they wanted to know whatever I could tell them about what you witnessed in Arizona. Journalistic confidentiality be damned." He snorted. "I told them they should view the video you made of the sniper—which they already had. And I said they should talk to you directly. Then I told them to bugger off."

Carly bit her lip to keep from laughing because the offensive slang phrase was so unusual coming from J.C. "Thank you," she said politely when she had herself under control.

"You're welcome. But I didn't tell you this to earn your appreciation. I'm concerned for your safety, Carly. I've tried to keep an eye on you here—and besides, this building is pretty secure—but my sources indicate you've spent your nights with Senator Jones. And *that*, let me tell you, has taken a load off my mind."

Carly stared at J.C. in growing disbelief. "Are you kidding me?" she demanded. "I can take care of myself and have been doing so for eighteen years. I've covered two wars and—"

"Three 'police actions,'" J.C. said, cutting her off. "Yeah, I know." His smile held a hint of admiration. Then the smile vanished. "But you've never been an assassin's target. You've never had someone gunning for you. It's not the same thing at all. Trust me, I know."

Perplexed, she asked, "How do you know?"

His lips tightened. "Seven years ago. Colombia. Medellín Cartel. And that's all I'm going to tell you."

Carly considered this. "How come you're still alive?"

He grinned suddenly. "Long story, which you don't have time for if you're going to make that press conference."

"I can be ready to leave in five minutes," she said. She pointed to her emergency suitcase standing in the corner of her office, the one she kept packed and ready so she could leave at a moment's notice.

J.C. shook his head. "Not until we settle this security thing—you can't be on the lookout for a killer when you're covering a story."

Frustrated, she said, "What do you suggest?" Her eyes narrowed with determination. "I'm going, J.C., no matter what you say. This is *my* story."

"Let's compromise. The network has a chopper standing by to take you to Philly—you'll be safe enough on that. I can have someone from a private security firm meet your flight and guard you while you're there, then put you safely back on board the chopper afterward. How's that?"

It was an acceptable compromise—Carly wasn't stupid enough to risk her life unnecessarily, not when she could do her job and still remain fairly safe. "Works for me."

She called Shane from the helicopter as soon as she was strapped in, while the pilot did his preflight checks. But after four rings her call went to voice mail, and she figured he was probably in the Senate chamber where he couldn't answer. So she left a message, telling him where she was going, that she didn't know exactly when she'd be back but it might be late and for him not to wait for her. She'd take a cab from the heliport to Niall's condo.

She considered sending Shane a text, too, but decided against it—the voice message told him everything he needed to know.

As the helicopter began its slow ascent, she pulled her notebook from her purse and began jotting down the questions she'd ask at the press conference as well as the points she wanted to make on camera based on the answers she was anticipating receiving.

She spared one thought for Shane, remembering how he'd taken her back to bed early this morning and just held her. They hadn't made love, they'd just…cuddled. And she'd fallen a little deeper under his spell.

Shane spent most of the day on a low simmer. Never boiling over, but he knew it wouldn't take much to set him off. His staff—with the exception of Dee-Dee—gave him a wide berth, as if they sensed he was bottling something explosive inside and wanted nothing to do with it or him.

His wrath wasn't aimed at the four men whose names were written in Carly's notebook, although he'd started the day with a cold determination to discover which one had betrayed his trust. But his conversations that morning with the FBI and the agency had taken the edge off his anger where his staffers were concerned, and right now they were the least of his worries.

No, his ire was reserved for one quietly beautiful, blue-eyed brunette who'd made a mockery of his attempts to protect her. Who'd gone off cool as you please to cover a story, leaving Shane a message that she'd get herself back to the security of the condo on her own. Every time he thought of her message, he ground his back teeth until his jaw ached.

Part of Shane knew he was overreacting—until a week ago he'd barely been aware of Carly's existence, and only from seeing her on TV. But now that he knew her…now that he'd held her in the stillness of the night…now that his life had forever been changed by the way her eyes smiled before her lips did…he couldn't bear the idea of anything happening to her. Especially not because of him. If *he* hadn't been at the Mayo Clinic last Saturday, she wouldn't have been there. If someone hadn't tried to kill *him*, she wouldn't have tried to catch the would-be killer on her smartphone. And if he hadn't been so damned sure he could keep her safe when she wasn't at work, he would have hired bodyguards to watch her every minute of every day until the man trying to kill them was caught.

He'd called Carly's producer at the network…for all the good that did him. J.C. Burrows had been close-mouthed until Shane admitted Carly herself had told him where she was heading. Burrows had then condescended to inform him the network had hired some rent-a-cop to protect her while she was in Philadelphia—as if that was good enough against a hired killer who might very well have her in his sights.

Shane texted Carly three times throughout the day just to make sure she was alive, and her replies had told him she was. But he didn't trust himself to call her. Didn't trust he'd be able to keep the anger out of his voice, which he needed to do because Carly didn't belong to him, much as he wanted her to. She hadn't given him the right to care about her. Worry about her. In fact, she'd given him no rights at all where she was concerned—except sexually. He could take her to his bed...but he couldn't take her to his heart.

And that thought was killing him.

It was close to six-thirty when the cab Carly was riding in pulled up in front of the condo building. Night had already fallen, and though she wasn't normally nervous at night, she slid her .22 out of her purse and into her overcoat pocket, then flicked the safety off. She hadn't taken the gun to Philadelphia—she'd left it in a locker at the heliport. But she felt a little safer now that it was back in her possession.

She paid the cab driver, grabbed the small suitcase from the seat beside her, glanced around to make sure no one was hiding in the shadows and slid out of the cab. Her purse was slung over her left shoulder, and her right hand was buried in her coat pocket, her fingers wrapped around the comforting touch of steel. But her heartbeat accelerated uncomfortably just the same. She didn't dawdle once she was out of the cab, just entered the condo building as quickly as she could.

She identified herself to the guard on duty because she didn't have a key to Niall's condo or the passcode to the elevator. The guard said, "I'll have to call to confirm, ma'am." He picked up the phone. "It'll just take a minute."

Carly hoped Shane was already upstairs because she really didn't want to wait in the lobby for his arrival. The well-lit interior turned the tall glass windows into mirrors, and she couldn't see outside. That made her nervous. Made her heart jump. And made her breath come a little faster.

"You can go up, ma'am," the guard told her. He held out a piece of paper. "Here's the code for the elevator. Key in the code before you press the floor number."

Shane and J.C. are right, Carly acknowledged, putting the safety back on her .22 as she rode up in the elevator. She hated admitting they were right and she was wrong—but it *was* different when you were a killer's target. She could take care of herself under normal circumstances—but these weren't normal circumstances. She'd been on edge all day, even with the temporary bodyguard provided by the network. Even though nothing untoward had happened. She'd tried not to let that feeling interfere with her job performance, but she wasn't sure she'd been 100 percent successful. She was still jittery.

Shane was waiting for her when she got off the elevator, and she'd never been more thankful to see anyone in her life. She dropped the suitcase, threw herself into Shane's arms and surprised herself by bursting into tears.

* * *

Shane held Carly tight as she sobbed and sniffled and cried herself out—which took about a minute and a half. Then she pulled away in obvious embarrassment and fumbled in her purse, but he anticipated what she was looking for and handed her the clean hanky from his pocket.

"Thanks," she mumbled, wiping her eyes and face and wiping away what little makeup she wore at the same time. "Sorry for crying," she said, stiff with what looked like shame over her weakness. "But you're right—we have to catch him because I can't go on like this." She blew her nose with emphasis, then seemed to realize what she'd done and glanced contritely from the decidedly soiled cloth in her hand to Shane's face. "Sorry about your hanky, too. I'll buy you a new one."

That was the moment Shane fell in love with her.

He'd been falling in love with her since they'd met in his hospital room, of course. And he'd known all day he wouldn't be this angry with her seeming carelessness over her own safety if he didn't care so much. But this moment—with Carly so ashamed because she'd cried, her pride in tatters yet having the grace to admit she was wrong and offering him an apology over something as meaningless as a dirty hanky—Shane knew there could never be another woman like her in the whole world. Not for him.

They were sitting in the living room, their arms wrapped around each other and Carly's head on Shane's shoulder when he confessed, "I was so angry with you today for going out where you'd be a sitting duck, when you *know* what this guy is capable of. It was like when you ran after the sniper to try to film him. Reckless."

"It's my job. You can't ask me not to do my job."

"I'm not." Shane was silent for a moment. "But I *can* ask you to be careful, to not take unnecessary risks."

"Is that what you were doing when you joined the marines? When you saved that woman five years ago? Not taking risks?"

"*Unnecessary* risks, I said. Every risk I've taken has been necessary. At least… I think that's true."

"Yes, but who decides what's necessary and unnecessary?"

"I do," he said promptly, then laughed ruefully and Carly laughed with him. "Okay, so that sounds pompous and self-important, along the lines of 'If I ran the world…'"

"That's pretty common, so don't beat yourself up over it," she said. "We all think our own judgment is better than anyone else's."

He drew a deep breath and let it out slowly. "I can't *make* you do anything, Carly. And I hope I wouldn't even if I could. All I can do is ask, so I'm asking. Please be more careful. It matters to me, more than you know."

"I will." She raised her head so she could look him in the eyes. "You too, Shane. I'm counting the days until you're no longer a target. We're at T minus four days… but until then please don't take *any* risks, whether you think they're necessary or not."

Compunction prevented him from agreeing to her request the way she'd agreed to his—how could he promise not to take risks when he intended to make himself a target?

A knock at the door saved him from having to answer. A quick glance at his watch told him it was seven on the dot, and—*oh crap!*—he hadn't told Carly.

She sat up straight. "Are you expecting anyone?" she asked in an undertone, as if she didn't want whoever was outside to hear her and know someone was in the condo.

"Yeah, I am." The knock sounded again. "I meant to tell you…but you'll know soon enough." He kissed her quickly, then went to answer the door.

Chapter 16

Carly stood nervously, buttoning her blazer and tugging down her black pencil skirt—which had somehow ridden up her thighs—as she wondered who this could be and why Shane hadn't mentioned someone was coming over.

Male voices from the entryway—deep male voices that sounded impossibly alike—exchanged badinage and...laughter?

Before she was ready Shane was back with another man, a shade taller than he was but with the same broad shoulders, same narrow waist and hips. Only instead of the power suit Shane wore to perfection, this man was wearing faded jeans and an olive-green Henley, his shearling jacket hanging open. His light brown hair was shaggy, not the near-military cut Shane sported. But his dark brown eyes were familiar to her and she instantly knew who this was.

"You must be Niall Jones," she said, moving forward and offering her right hand. "I'm Carly Edwards."

The man's hand enfolded hers with a firm handshake she also recognized. He glanced at Shane, who shook his head. "I meant to tell her, but ran out of time. She must have figured it out on her own."

"Pleased to meet you, Ms. Edwards," said the stranger who wasn't a stranger. "But now I have to ask. How'd you know who I was?"

"It's Carly, and you have Shane's eyes."

"Ahh." He nodded, admiration evident. "You notice things, Carly, and you're quick. I like that."

She let a tiny smile escape. "I knew a guy in Afghanistan who said you were either quick or you were dead."

A look of surprise flitted across his face for a second, then he said, "That's right, you were an embedded reporter in Afghanistan, weren't you?" He smiled, and Carly realized Niall and Shane shared another family trait—charm. He could charm the birds from the trees with that smile…or a woman's clothes from her body. "I was there myself a million years ago," Niall continued. "Shane, too." He glanced at his brother, then returned his appreciative gaze—and killer smile—to Carly.

Shane moved to Carly's side, sliding an arm around her waist, and she could have sworn he was staking a claim. "Yeah, that's something we have in common," he told Niall. The glint in his eyes and the way his chin lifted were dead giveaways she wasn't mistaken— Shane was giving his brother a definite "hands off" warning.

If Carly had been a different kind of woman, she would have purred at the two very male animals facing off over her. As it was, she wanted to kick Shane.

Kick Niall, too, for that matter. She wasn't a prize to be won, and she had no intention of letting either of them think she was.

She moved away a little, enough so Shane's arm fell from her waist, but her quelling expression informed Niall she was immune to his charm, too. "I have to thank you for letting us stay here," she told Shane's brother. She lifted a hand to encompass their surroundings. "You have an impressive home—for a fortress."

The charming alpha male smile morphed into one a mischievous boy might use. "You're welcome. I knew from the news coverage about the first attempt on Shane's life, but he downplayed the danger. Then when I badgered him after the second attempt, he finally broke down and asked for my help, so I knew it had to be pretty serious—you might have noticed he has a *slight* tendency to think he can handle everything on his own."

Carly's eyes slid toward Shane, then back to Niall. "A slight tendency, yes," she agreed drily.

"I had to finish a job in…well, anyway, I had to finish a job, but I flew back to DC as soon as I could. Sorry, bro," he said softly, regretfully, looking at Shane. "It was a long flight and I barely made it back in time."

Shane shook his head. "You'll get no complaints from me."

Niall returned his attention to Carly. "I had a hunch—which I didn't tell him about—and as soon as I got off the plane I headed to his house. I was just in time to see someone walking out, and I—"

"It was you?" Carly caught her breath. "You're the one who reported the bomb?"

"Yeah. I didn't know it was a bomb, of course, and

I didn't have time to check it out. But I knew whoever it was had no business being in Shane's house, so I called Shane to warn him and stayed on the guy's tail. Followed him right to your town house, which I didn't know was yours." He grimaced. "Pissed me off no end when my phone call to nine-one-one didn't get faster results. The guy was in and out of your town house in five minutes. I followed him back to his truck, and was faced with a dilemma. Continue to follow him? Or go back to meet the first responders at your place and sign the affidavit for a search warrant." He shrugged. "You know what I decided."

Overwhelming gratitude surged through her. Not so much for what Niall had done to save *her*, although that was part of it, but that he'd been instrumental in saving his brother. She took two steps forward, placed her hands on Niall's arms and kissed his cheek. "I can never thank you enough for saving Shane," she murmured as she released him and stepped back. "And for saving me."

The wicked gleam returned to Niall's eyes, and he tapped his other cheek. "You can try," he said, waggling his eyebrows suggestively.

Shane cleared his throat ominously, and Carly couldn't help but smile. She knew Niall was just teasing—using her to get his brother's goat. That close bond of brothers only a year apart not unusually also contained a little one-upmanship. A little competition. Okay, maybe a *lot* of competition, but friendly, not adversarial.

"Let's sit," Shane said abruptly. Niall took the recliner, while Shane drew Carly to his side on the couch opposite, and this time she didn't protest. His brother might be amused at triggering latent jealousy in Shane, but she didn't want any part of it—she'd never believed that inciting jealousy in a man belonged in a serious relationship.

Serious relationship. That's what she and Shane had. Forget that they'd only known each other eight days. *Eight days?* she asked herself suddenly, and counted back, confirming that yes, she'd walked into Shane's hospital room eight days ago. But the amount of time she'd known him didn't matter. She *knew* him. She knew the man he was. The man he tried so hard to be. And he knew the woman she tried to be, too.

Much of the time they'd spent together had been fraught with danger, and practically from the beginning Shane had done his best to protect her—even when he barely knew her—but that wasn't what drew her to him. Not entirely. It wasn't just his stellar character, his strong moral compass, although that was part of it, of course. It wasn't that he was a hot stud who could turn her on faster than a light switch, either—not that she was complaining. And it certainly wasn't the star quality attached to his being a US senator—although the drive and determination that had pushed him into the role appealed to her. *It's a combination of all those things*, she acknowledged. And one thing more. Shane, for all his physical and moral strength, for all his courage, wasn't invulnerable. Not just to the malady he'd been diagnosed with, but emotionally, as well.

A thought crept into her mind on catlike feet and refused to leave, no matter how she tried to nudge it away. *He loves you, Carly. He won't say it—because you told him you didn't want his love. But he loves you.*

Suddenly the conversation Shane and Niall had been carrying on while she was lost in her thoughts impinged on her consciousness.

"Are you crazy?" Niall was asking. "Or do you think I am? I'm not going to let you do that."

Shane's response was low and implacable. "It's the only way. If Carly's right, once the pipeline vote is cast I'm off the hook—there's no need to kill me. But she'll never be safe…until this guy is locked away."

"Do what?" she asked, glancing from Shane to Niall.

"Idiot here thinks I'm going to let him act as live bait to draw out the hit man," Niall said fiercely.

Her gaze swiveled sharply back to Shane as she placed a hand over his heart. "You can't." Breathless. Panicked. "No risks, remember? Necessary or not."

Shane's hand gently closed over hers, intertwining their fingers. "I never promised," he said, his voice very deep. "It's the only way, Carly."

All she could think was that she couldn't lose Shane, too. Losing Jack had devastated her. Losing Shane—the man she'd tried so hard not to love—would destroy her. She couldn't let it happen. "No. You're not doing this."

He kissed her hand, then lowered it to her own lap. "Yes," he said softly, "I am."

He stood and shifted his attention to his brother. "You can help me or not," he said, his voice as hard as steel. "But you can't stop me. If you won't do it, I'll find someone else who will."

"Damn it, Shane!" Niall stood in confrontation.

"It's not open for discussion. Yes or no?"

Niall's voice was tight with frustration. "Yes, damn it. Of course yes. You know I can't say no."

Carly watched as a faint smile touched Shane's lips, and he held out his left fist to his brother. The two men fist bumped, then did some kind of complicated hand gestures she figured were left over from their childhood. Then Shane said, "Knew you wouldn't let me down."

"Damn it, Shane," Niall repeated, still upset. "I'll never forgive you if you let yourself be killed."

Shane's smile spread. "Now *that*," he said with deliberate provocation, "will be entirely in your hands, bro."

Niall had headed out an hour later, after he and Shane had worked out a few specifics. He'd declined when his brother had reminded him the condo had two bedrooms, saying, "I've got other plans." The very male gleam in his eyes had sent a clear message those plans involved a woman. "Besides," he'd added, glancing at Carly, "three's a crowd."

After he'd left, Shane had gone into Niall's study and quietly closed the door—to do *what*, Carly had no idea. She'd gone into the kitchen to see about a late dinner, needing something to distract her from the fact that Shane was going to do what he was going to do, even though she'd begged him not to. *Well, not begged*, she acknowledged after a moment's reflection, as she pulled another frozen meal from the freezer—pot roast this time. She'd flat out told Shane, *You're not doing this.* To which he'd replied in a voice that brooked no gainsaying, *Yes, I am.*

Would it have made a difference if she'd begged? she wondered. If she'd made it a choice between her and his decision to deliberately let himself be a target...to save her?

She read the instructions on the back of the pot-roast package, cracked the lid, popped the box in the microwave and keyed in the time. Then she leaned her hands on the counter and bowed her head, tears of shame forcing her eyes closed.

* * *

Shane sat at Niall's desk and dialed the number for his press secretary, Mike Adamson. "Is that request for Sunday still open?" he asked when Mike answered the phone and identified himself. Shane had been invited by Old Town University yesterday to fill in for one of the speakers on a panel who'd had to back out at the last minute for personal reasons. The topic—Climate Change: Fact or Fiction?—was one of his hot button issues. But Shane had originally declined at his staff's insistence—they didn't want him appearing in public if he didn't have to. But now…

"I think so," Mike replied. "I don't think they've lined up anyone else yet. But are you sure you want to do this?" Unspoken were the discussion at the staff meeting yesterday and its conclusion.

"Sure." Shane's mind was already plotting ways and means.

"Let me make a call and get right back to you." Three minutes later Shane's cell phone rang. "They're thrilled you can make it after all," Mike said. "Want me to let Denise know?" Denise was Shane's part-time speech writer. Shane wrote a lot of his speeches himself, but he usually gave them to Denise for final polishing. And she occasionally composed speeches for him when there just weren't enough hours in the day for him to do everything.

"Would you?" Shane asked now. "We've got that policy paper she can use as a starting point, and the press release you wrote two months ago. If she can put something together for my review by tomorrow night, that would be great. I know tomorrow's Saturday, but—"

"Don't worry," Mike interrupted. "She's not doing anything special."

"How do you know that?"

"Well, uh…" Mike fumbled for words. "Because she and I were just going to hang out together. Maybe take in a movie. But this is more important."

Well, well, well, Shane thought, amused. His press secretary and his speech writer. They were perfect for each other, he realized now, but it had never occurred to him before. "If you're sure Denise won't mind…"

Carly gripped the counter, holding back the tears with effort. *You can't*, she told herself. *You can't ask Shane to be less than the man he is. Less than the man you love.*

She'd come close this evening. Horribly close. Just because she was afraid of losing the man she loved—again—she'd wanted to diminish him. Wrap him up safe and secure and tuck him away where he couldn't get hurt so her heart wouldn't break.

But just as he'd known he couldn't ask her not to take *any* risks, especially where her job was concerned, she couldn't expect that of him, either. In his mind this was a necessary risk, because by his very nature he was a protector…*and because he loved her*.

Carly wiped the tears from her eyes with the heels of her hands—she'd cried more in the past week than she'd cried in the eight years since…Jack. Since she'd encased her heart in ice after Jack's death.

Loving Shane had melted that ice. Had drawn her emotions back to the surface from the dark place where she'd buried them, and now the least little thing seemed to set her off.

Not that this was a little thing. It wasn't. But she had to love Shane as he was. Which meant being *vulnerable* again. Which meant letting him do what he needed to do because of who he was. Which meant...risking everything.

On that note she set her mouth in determined lines. Then she went looking for Shane.

Shane hung up the phone on his fifth and last call. After locking down the speech invitation with Mike, he'd called the four men on the suspect list. He'd let them know exactly where he'd be Sunday afternoon. Exactly when. One of them—he didn't know which one—would get the ball rolling. Would contact the would-be killer...and set Shane up to be assassinated.

Which one? he wondered. It hurt not knowing because he'd trusted these men. Laughed with them. Strategized with them. Except for Terry, they'd all been with him since the beginning. Not that long as political careers went, but still...

He didn't know what—if anything—the FBI had uncovered so far on the four suspects. *Suspects?* he asked himself, but was forced to admit that's what they were. And that reminded him that when this was all over, things wouldn't be the same. There was no way the other three wouldn't learn they'd been suspected, right along with the man who *was* guilty. Which meant it would be a long time before trust would be restored... both ways. If it could ever be restored.

A tap on the door interrupted his thoughts, then the door opened and Carly stood there. "We need to talk," she said. And from the deadly serious expression on her face, he feared the worst, mentally girding his loins against what he thought she might try to convince him to do.

"Come on in."

She walked in, not bothering to close the door behind her. She glanced around the room, then took a seat in front of the desk, facing him. "Why do I feel as if I've entered a time warp into the future?" she asked, her lips curving upward with a touch of humor.

Shane's lips twitched in response. "Maybe because Niall was always hooked on sci-fi and fantasy?" He relaxed slightly. "Niall and I used to tease Liam that he was born in the wrong time—that he was a swash-buckling twelfth-century knight-errant who somehow ended up in the twentieth century. But Niall was just the opposite. He was born to roam the stars as a kind of intergalactic Wyatt Earp, bringing law and order to lawless galaxies…but the technology doesn't exist yet."

"How about you? Who was your childhood hero?"

He hesitated. "Didn't have one."

She cocked her head to one side and considered him. "Now you see, you shouldn't have hesitated before you answered. That gave you away." Her eyes held under-standing. "You had a hero. Who?"

There was just a hint of coaxing in her voice, and Shane wasn't proof against it. "George Bailey."

"*It's a Wonderful Life*?" she asked. "That George Bailey?"

"Yeah." He didn't volunteer anything more, but somehow Carly knew.

"Because he made a difference," she said softly, her eyes glistening with tears she blinked back. "Because he was an everyday hero."

She made a little hiccupping sound. "Oh, Shane."

Her gaze met his, and there was something in those tear-damp blue eyes that made him feel invincible. As if he could accomplish anything. As if he were her hero. "I—" She stopped, swallowed hard, then said, "I owe you another apology."

"Why?"

She shook her head. "I can't tell you."

He stared at her, perplexed. "Why can't you?"

"I'm too ashamed," she admitted finally, her voice very low.

Something dinged from the direction of the kitchen, and Carly jumped up. "Dinner's ready." She practically ran from the room.

Shane went after her, and caught her before she'd gone ten steps. He grasped her arm and swung her around to face him. "Carly."

Then he was kissing her because he couldn't *not* kiss her. Because the hard hot knot of need that gripped him suddenly had to find release somehow, release that could only be found in Carly's arms. And she was kissing him back, her body plastered against his as if she wanted to crawl inside his skin to get closer.

He tried to lift her up so she could straddle him, but she made the little strangled gurgle of laughter deep in her throat that he loved, and said, "I can't. My skirt's too tight."

He reached behind her and made quick work of the zipper, sliding the skirt over her hips until she could wriggle free. She was already unbuttoning her black blazer, which she shrugged off and dropped to the floor. Leaving her standing there wearing a semi-sheer pale blue blouse—through which he could see the outline of her bra and a hint of cleavage—a black-and-red scarf, pantyhose and the tiniest scrap of satin and lace. All of which he wanted to tear off.

"One of us is overdressed," she said with fake solemnity, and Shane realized this time it was him. He stripped in nothing flat, watching as Carly did the same. She had no false modesty—and he loved that about her. She knew what she looked like without clothes and was proud of how she'd kept herself in shape. Not that Shane would have cared one way or the other—a few pounds here or there wouldn't have made a damned bit of difference to the desire that raged through him. He just wanted *in*.

"Bedroom," he managed to say when Carly placed her hands on his shoulders and hopped as he lifted her naked body to his. "Condom."

Those were the last words he spoke…until he moaned her name at the end.

Chapter 17

The pot roast was cold and dry by the time they made it back into the kitchen, but Carly added a little water and put the box back into the microwave for a couple of minutes. "It won't be gourmet, but it should be edible," she told Shane. "Wine will help."

She went to the pantry and came back with another bottle of wine, a merlot this time—Tire Pé Diem. She removed the cork and opened the microwave, splashed a little of the wine over the meat, then restarted the microwave. She turned and caught Shane watching her, an amused smile on his face. "What?"

"Cook much?"

She shook her head. "But I do know how to pair wine with food. And I know how to add a little zest to stuff from the freezer. My mom taught me the basics of cooking years ago, but I never was all that interested.

Jack was—" She cut off what she had been about to say, and turned away to grab wineglasses from the cabinet.

Shane came up behind her and put his hands on her arms. "You don't have to do that, you know."

Her hand was trembling a little as she poured the merlot into the wineglasses. "Do what?"

"You don't have to pretend Jack never existed. Not with me."

She put the bottle down because she was in danger of dropping it. Then she turned around and looked directly up at him. "You said it was a hell of a thing to learn I'd almost married someone else. I didn't want to…" She trailed off, unsure exactly what she wanted to say.

"Yeah, but *you* said that was a different woman."

"Yes." She tried to make sense of her chaotic thoughts. "But when Niall was here…"

"Ahh." Shane smiled and slid his hands down to her waist. "Now the light dawns. You thought because I was jealous of the way Niall looked at you that I'm jealous of Jack."

"Aren't you?" She hadn't meant to ask him that question. Okay, yes, she *had* meant to, but not so bluntly. Now that she had, though…

His smile twisted a little. "I'm only jealous because you loved him enough to marry him. Not for any other reason."

That sounded suspiciously like a declaration of love, and Carly's heart leaped. She loved Shane. Despite her brain's insistence that she protect her heart, she just hadn't been able to do it, and she loved him more every hour. If he loved her, too…

The microwave dinged again, and the moment was lost. Shane turned away to take the pot roast out and put it on the counter, then served up generous helpings for both of them and set them on the table. Carly brought over the wineglasses, then fetched the silverware and napkins. She found it surprising and a little intriguing that Niall had cloth napkins, not paper ones. And again she wondered if that was Shane's preference, too. So she asked him.

"Yeah, we get it from our mom. She always had cloth napkins, so paper ones seem chintzy and not very substantial." He forked a bite of meat and chewed thoughtfully. "You're right. It's not gourmet, but it's not bad. And the wine does help."

"Tell me about your mom." She couldn't help the little pang of pain that always hit her when she remembered her own mother, who'd died when she was seventeen, along with Carly's father. In a way it was good for them they'd gone together, because they'd loved each other so much. But that had meant Carly and Tahra had been orphaned in one fell swoop—and Tahra had only been ten at the time.

She brought her attention back to Shane. "Five kids," he was saying. "Four strapping boys and then finally the little girl she'd always wanted. She'd never admit it," he said, sipping at his wine, an appreciative expression on his face. "But we all knew." He chuckled softly to himself. "Keira wasn't the daughter she'd expected, though. Far from it."

"How so?" Carly's plate was almost untouched, so she quickly took a bite.

"Oh, I think my mom was looking forward to ribbons and bows, that sort of thing—the kind of girl *she'd* been raised to be. But Keira wasn't interested in anything 'girlie.' She was a scrapper. I think my dad had a lot to do with that."

"In what way?"

Shane said reflectively, "My dad was an old-school marine. You know the type. Tears were for sissies. Don't get me wrong—we all loved him, and when he passed away, it just about killed us. My mom, too. But he wasn't perfect. And one of his...well, imperfections, had to do with how he saw gender roles."

"I see."

"I wonder if you do." His face took on a thoughtful mien. "Growing up, my brothers and I didn't give Keira much respect. We loved her, but she was a *girl*, even though she tried to be one of the boys." He ate the last bite from his plate. "Keira always had to fight for respect. She was ten when I left home, but she was feisty even then, and only became more so as she got older. She used to try to scrap with Alec and Liam, but they knew better—Dad would have killed them." He smiled slightly. "I quickly learned in the Corps that my attitude toward women—which I'd gotten from my dad—needed a little—" he cleared his throat "—adjustment."

"Ah." Carly couldn't help but smile. "I wondered about that."

Shane laughed and sipped at his wine. "It still shows, huh?"

"Just a tad," she said, tongue in cheek.

"Guess it's a good thing you never met me back then." Carly shook her head at him, but didn't say anything. She looked down at her nearly full plate and at Shane's empty one, then pushed her plate toward him. "You're not hungry?" he asked.

"Not really. I had a late lunch in Philly after the press

conference." She watched as Shane made quick work of her leftovers and smiled to herself because it seemed to be another little sign of how he felt about her. Her dad used to do that with her mom, finishing what her mom wasn't hungry for. Most Americans wouldn't even consider eating off someone else's plate—but husbands and wives did it all the time.

Stop right there, she ordered herself sternly. *Shane isn't your husband.*

But she wanted him to be. And that realization almost made her gasp.

Marsh disconnected the call on his disposable phone and reviewed the notes he'd taken. Sunday, 3:00 p.m. Old Town University. Adams Hall.

Plenty of time, he thought. The senator had gone to ground, but he would surface for the panel and discussion on climate change. Marsh could scope out the venue tomorrow, plot his sight lines, stash his weapon and be ready come Sunday afternoon.

Once the senator had been dealt with, he still needed to take care of the damned reporter. But that could wait for a more propitious time. Unless, of course, the reporter tagged along with the senator, as she seemed to be doing a lot lately. Then he could kill two birds with one stone.

Once again Carly woke to an empty bed beside her. And once again the sheets were cold where Shane had lain, which meant his place had been empty for a while. This time, though, when she glanced at the clock on the nightstand, she saw it was past eight. Which meant she'd gotten her requisite eight hours of sleep and then some.

She went in search of Shane, thinking she'd find him in the kitchen, but he wasn't there. A pot of coffee had been made, and she gratefully poured herself a cup before continuing her search, cup in hand. She knew he wasn't in the living room—she'd already passed through it on the way to the kitchen. But he wasn't in the office, either. Puzzled, she went farther down the long hallway and tried the two closed doors she'd never entered. The first was the spare bedroom—empty. The second door swung open to reveal the man she sought— in a workout room that rivaled a gym.

Shane was jogging at a rapid pace on a treadmill set on a steep incline, wearing earphones, running shorts, socks and running shoes…and nothing else. His body gleamed with sweat, his abs rippling with exertion.

When he saw her, he smiled and took off his earphones but didn't turn off the treadmill. He glanced at his watch and said over the noise of the machine, "Three more minutes."

She nodded, then turned to peruse the rest of Niall's workout equipment. Weight bench—that made sense. But this one looked professional grade, not the kind of thing usually found outside a gym. Not far from it was a machine she recognized as an elliptical trainer, and next to that was a recumbent stationary bicycle. There was also a leg press machine like the one in her physical therapist's workout room, where she'd gone after she'd had arthroscopic surgery on her left knee following a skiing accident.

She took a large sip from her coffee cup, then saw the chin-up bar that stretched across the far corner of the room, and all she could think was *Wow! No wonder Niall's in great shape.*

The sound of the treadmill suddenly ceased, drawing her attention back to Shane. She watched as he wiped his face and chest with a towel, then draped it across his shoulders, and thought, *Shane must work out religiously, too.* Because there was just no way he could look that good at forty-one unless he did.

Carly belonged to a fitness club and usually went three times a week when she was in town. When she traveled, she tried to use whatever workout equipment was available in her hotel. She had to maintain her weight for her job—TV tended to add a few pounds to the way she appeared on the screen—and she worked out for the same reason. It wasn't fair, but women were held to a higher standard than men when it came to TV news. A well-fitting suit on a man could hide a lot of faults, but not so with women.

Shane came up to her and stole a kiss while she was musing. "Morning," he said. "Sip?"

She held the coffee cup up to his lips, but he took it from her hands and turned it so he could put his lips where hers had been before he drank. "Sweet," he said with a wicked gleam in his eyes before he gave the cup back to her.

"I don't know how you can say that," she argued. "I don't put sugar or sweetener in my coffee."

"I know."

He raised and lowered his eyebrows suggestively, and then she got it. "Oh." A flush of warmth spread through her body, as if she'd been the one on the treadmill.

The smile was suddenly wiped from Shane's face, and he went completely still. And Carly *saw* the goose bumps forming on his arms. "Son of a bitch!" he whispered in a furious undertone. She put her coffee cup down on the nearest surface and placed a hand on the tense muscles of his left arm. His skin was warm to the touch, but she knew to him the room was suddenly freezing.

"It's okay." She didn't know what else to say to him. She wanted to reassure him somehow, but all she could say was, "It's okay, Shane. You're okay."

The seconds ticked by like hours. *Thirty seconds*, she reminded herself feverishly. He'd told her the episodes lasted roughly thirty seconds, then the symptoms disappeared like magic.

She mentally counted—*one thousand eighteen, one thousand nineteen, one thousand twenty*—and had just passed twenty-seven when the goose bumps beneath her fingers vanished.

She let out the breath she'd been holding, sucked in air and let that out, as well. She opened her mouth to say something—*anything*—when, with a muttered oath, Shane pulled away from her and stalked out the door.

She went after him. He was *not* doing this. He was not going to lick his wounds in private, like some kind of alpha wolf, and if he thought he was, he'd better think again. "Shane!"

She caught up with him as he was stripping his clothes off in the master bathroom. The shower was already running, warming up the water, but Carly grabbed his arm when he went to step into the shower stall. "You're not doing this," she told him fiercely.

"Not taking a shower?" He peeled her hand off his arm. "Sorry to be the one to break the news to you, but I usually shower after a hard workout. Most men do."

"That's not what I mean and you know it." She

grabbed his arm again and shook it. "You're not running away and dealing with this on your own."

His face was closed, his eyes hard. "One, I'm not running away. Two, I'm dealing with it the only way I know how."

Damn you, she wanted to say. *Damn you for being such a stubborn, pigheaded man.* Instead she said, "Talk to me, Shane. Please. Tell me what you're feeling."

"I'm not feeling anything except exhausted from twenty-five chin-ups, a hundred push-ups, a hundred sit-ups and an hour on the treadmill. And sweaty. I'm feeling sweaty, too. Does that satisfy you?"

It would have hurt less if he'd slapped her. She let go of his arm and stepped back away from him. "Fine," she said, forcing the words past stiff lips. "You win. But then you always do, don't you? Everything has to be your way or the highway." Emotions rose up, choking her, and she couldn't say anything more. Then she turned and walked out, refusing to let herself look back at him.

Shane thrust his head under the punishing shower spray, letting the hot water pummel him. He soaped himself all over, scrubbing his hide as if he could scrub away the memory of Carly's face, pale and still, from his mind. As if he could wash away the memory of her stricken eyes as she said *You win*.

He'd hurt her, and that was like a dagger to his heart. The fact that he hadn't meant to hurt her cut no ice with him. A man didn't hurt a woman—that had been engrained in him as far back as he could remember. Not physically—*never* physically—but not emotionally, either.

Emotional distance. That's what she'd insisted on four nights ago, although he'd known from the start it was a crock—Carly could no more maintain an emotional distance than he could fly unaided. But had she known somehow this was coming? Had she sensed that if she *didn't* keep an emotional distance, he'd inevitably hurt her as he'd just done?

He abruptly turned off the shower and sluiced the water from his skin, then dried quickly and headed for the bedroom. Carly wasn't there. But then, he hadn't really expected her to be. He dressed in the first clothes he could find and walked out of the bedroom with only one thing on his mind—apologizing to Carly.

It wasn't until he'd gone through every room in the condo twice that he realized he couldn't apologize to her…because she was nowhere to be found.

Carly had walked out without her purse, gloves or scarf. She'd thrown on jeans and a sweater, had tugged boots on and had grabbed her jacket, but she was already out the front door of the condo building and two blocks away before she realized what she'd left behind. She stopped so quickly the man behind her walking his dog ran into her, and Carly was forced to apologize.

When she was alone again she stood there in the middle of the sidewalk, her hands in her pockets against the cold, her breath making a little cloud in the near-freezing air as she realized she'd left behind more than just her purse, gloves and scarf. She'd left Shane behind, as well. She'd given up without a fight, and that was so unlike her she couldn't believe it.

She turned around and headed back the way she'd come, but before she reached the second light Shane came flying out the condo building's front door, frantically looking left and right as if he were searching for someone. As if he were searching for her.

He suddenly spotted her in the sparse Saturday morning crowd and broke into a run. Carly barely waited for the light to change before she was running, too. They met in the middle, and Shane caught her in an embrace that threatened to crush her ribs, all the while peppering her face with kisses.

"I'm sorry," he said over and over. "God, Carly, I'm so sorry."

"Me, too," she said, achingly glad she'd turned back. "I shouldn't have run away."

"I didn't mean it. Please believe me. I just didn't know what to say."

"I know."

They kissed and hugged and murmured apologies to each other until two teenage boys passed them and shouted rudely, "Get a room, for Chrissake!"

Carly spluttered with laughter, and then Shane was laughing, too. "We have a room, Marine," she whispered. "What say we take their advice?"

Chapter 18

Once Carly and Shane were inside the condo, however, the smell of coffee drew them to the kitchen. "Oh, my cup," she said. "I left it…"

Before she could go fetch it herself, he said, "I'll get it."

By the time he'd returned she'd poured a cup for him—straight black, the way he liked it—and was rummaging in the pantry and fridge for breakfast. Shane tossed the dregs of her drink in the sink before refilling her cup, then turning off the coffeemaker.

"There's not much in the way of breakfast," she informed him with the air of someone delivering bad news.

"I thought I saw oatmeal in the pantry."

"Oh. You're right." She took down the tall, cylindrical container. "I was looking for those little packets of instant," she explained. "You know, the ones you just add water to and put in the microwave."

"This is almost as quick," he said, taking the container from her. "You can nuke it, but I'd rather cook mine the old-fashioned way." He found a pot, filled it halfway with water, and set it on the stove to boil.

"Let me guess—this is how your mom makes it."

He leaned a hip against the counter and grinned at her. "Give the lady a cigar."

"Tell me more about her," she invited. "You started to last night, but then we got sidetracked to your dad, and…"

He picked up his coffee and drank deeply, a reminiscent light creeping into his eyes. "She's one tough lady. She's had to be. Four rambunctious boys and a little girl determined to be as fearless as her older brothers." He checked the pot on the stove, then looked back at Carly. "Then losing my dad before he ever reached retirement age. He was the light of her life and it nearly broke her. But she refused to surrender to grief." Love and admiration were evident in his voice. "My dad was the marine, but I think my brothers and sister and I get our grit and determination from her."

He chuckled suddenly. "Every one of her children has scared the you-know-what out of her by nearly getting killed, but that never stopped her from loving us with everything she has."

"I know about you and Liam—what happened with the others?"

"Keira stepped in front of a bullet meant for someone else to save him. Alec was nearly killed when two terrorists attempted to kidnap his date and him in a coffeehouse in the tiny Middle Eastern country where he was serving as the regional security officer at the embassy."

Surprised, Carly paused in the midst of raising her

coffee cup to her lips and named the country. "That was Alec? I read about it, but the State Department never released the name of the DSS agent involved."

"Yeah, that was him." The water was boiling, so he turned the fire down and added oatmeal, stirring occasionally. "And Niall…" He chuckled softly. "I can't disclose any of the details," he said with his back to her. "Suffice it to say that if you ever see him without his shirt, you'll know just how close he came to dying." He turned around and added drily, "Not that I want him to take his shirt off in front of you, you understand."

She started to respond with a snappy comeback, until it sank in he was only half-kidding. She put her coffee cup down. "No matter how ripped Niall is—and by the looks of his home gym I'd be willing to bet women drool when he strips—" she told Shane as she crossed the room to him. She took the spoon from his hand and turned off the fire under the oatmeal, then placed her hands lightly against his chest. In all seriousness she said, "No matter what he looks like naked, he can't possibly hold a candle to you."

He breathed sharply, and she added with a note of incredulity in her voice, "I can't believe you didn't know that."

"It's irrational, I know," he admitted in a low voice. "I love him—don't ever think I don't—but I've been in competition with him nearly my whole life. That's good in some ways, but… And he delights in yanking my chain whenever he can. Last night…"

"Men are going to look at me, Shane. I can't help that. And they're going to like what they see," she said bluntly, "unless I wear a burka. But I thought I made it perfectly clear last night where my interests lie."

That forced the beginnings of a smile from him. "Yeah. You did."

"So what is the problem?"

The faint smile was still on Shane's face, but she sensed the effort he was making to keep it there. "Niall doesn't have epilepsy."

His answer was so unexpected she couldn't think of what to say. Then she remembered the first day she'd met Shane, and her assessment of him as a wounded warrior trying to come to terms with the diagnosis that had to have devastated him. She'd thought he'd dealt with it. Put it behind him. She'd thought wrong.

"No, he doesn't," she said with deliberate emphasis. "He doesn't have epilepsy." Her right hand reached for his left one, and she raised it to her cheek. "But he's not you, either."

Her gaze held his, and in those dark brown depths she saw what she knew he didn't want her to see…and her throat ached. "Take me to bed, Shane," she whispered. "Let me prove it to you."

Alpha male that he was, Shane tried to take control once they were in the bedroom, but Carly was having none of that. This was her seduction, and she was going to erase that sliver of insecurity from his eyes if it was the last thing she did.

"No," she told him firmly, catching his hands in hers when he tried to undress her. "I want to do it." And when he started taking his clothes off himself, she stopped him there, too, shaking her head. She let her eyes promise he wouldn't be disappointed, then removed his shoulder holster and his clothes one deliberate piece at a time. Caressing. Stroking. Every move dictated by her heart.

When he was completely naked, she breathed deeply and let it out very, very slowly. "There's no contest," she told him, her voice soft, seductive. Gliding her hands over his pecs, his abs. And lower. "No one can compete."

His body responded with a surge of desire, and she didn't need to hear the low growl coming from his throat to know how much he wanted her. But she was just getting started. She was going to teach him that he was the only man she wanted, as well as something new and amazing about postponement of pleasure, by the time she was done.

Carly gently pushed Shane onto the bed and dragged the bedclothes over him, saying, "I can't concentrate," then stepped away. She'd never set out to seduce a man before. But she knew enough about men—about this *particular* man—to know what would drive him crazy.

She removed the clip from her hair, which she let fall over her shoulders, before running her fingers through the sable tresses to muss it up the way his hands always did. Then she arched her arms over her head and stretched, watching for his reaction to her provocative move. He loved her breasts, she knew…but she could also see in his eyes that he loved the way her hands slid down to caress them, fondle them through her sweater the way he wanted to do.

Men are visual, she reminded herself as she crossed her arms, grasped the bottom of her sweater and lifted. Slowly. Revealing the bare skin of her midriff, then the satin-and-lace bra that cupped and barely managed to contain her already aroused breasts. She pulled the sweater off completely and tossed it to one side, shaking her head so her tousled hair concealed and revealed.

His quickened breathing told her she was on the right track, and her hands moved to her jeans. When she'd inched down the zipper she slipped her hands into the waistband and began sliding her jeans off her hips. She stopped suddenly before she'd done more than expose the lacy band of her undies, saying, "I forgot."

He groaned when she sat down on the chair by the bed, but he never looked away as she bent over and unzipped first one boot, then the other. She sat up and stretched to remove her boots, making sure he could see cleavage as she did so. Then she stood and shimmied out of her jeans, leaving them in an untidy pile on the floor.

Shane moved so quickly Carly didn't even have time to breathe before he'd plucked her from where she stood and dragged her back to the bed with him.

"Wait," she protested. "I'm not fin—"

"You're all done torturing me," he assured her, his voice husky with desire. He parted her legs with one of his, a hand stroking between her thighs, and she knew he could feel the dampness there caused by the striptease that had aroused her nearly as much as it had aroused him. He pushed the fabric aside and slipped two fingers into her. "So wet for me," he said with male satisfaction, his thumb seeking and finding the heart of her desire as he pressed deeper. "God, Carly, you have no idea what you do to me. How good you feel."

She moaned and arched, her breasts straining against the satin-and-lace bra that suddenly chafed her sensitized skin. She was already throbbing around his fingers, so close to completion she could scarcely think, much less speak, but she managed, "This isn't what I—oh, Shane!"

"Oh, Shane, yes?" he demanded, his thumb stilling.

She'd die if he stopped. That's all she could think of. "Yes," she moaned. *"Please!"*

"My pleasure," he whispered, kissing her belly button. Then his lips moved lower. He held the satin fabric aside for his tongue, which picked up where his thumb had left off, and Carly went crazy. She gasped and gasped again, arching into the slight roughness that teased and tormented until she couldn't take anymore. Until she sobbed at the unbearable pleasure. Until she cried his name.

Shane didn't know how he managed not to simply rip Carly's remaining scraps of clothing from her body. Nor did he know how he managed to find a condom in his frenzied haste. But he managed both. And when he had Carly pinned beneath him, when she welcomed him into her body with a catch in her breath and a tiny whimper deep in her throat, when her fingernails dug into his back urging him on, he knew this was the only place he wanted to be. Now and forever.

He didn't last long. He couldn't. Carly's seduction had pushed him to the edge of control. Loving her with his hand and then his mouth until she saw stars had unchained the wolf inside him. And now, feeling her so hot and tight around him, so slick as he plumbed her depths, was the last straw.

It wasn't quite as quick as their first time...but it was close. And when they were done, Carly was crying again. His heart clutched for a second, but then he knew he hadn't hurt her. There were a few things that moved Carly to tears...and this was one of them. The alpha male in him exulted—maybe he couldn't control the electrical pulses in his brain, but he could make Carly weep with pleasure.

He gathered her close and dragged the bedclothes over them. Then he crooned softly as he brushed his lips over the tears on her cheeks, bringing her down gently. Eventually her breathing slowed, and her hand moved, fingers idly crisscrossing the hair on his chest. Then she said with a trace of regret, "I wanted to seduce you."

He smiled and pulled her closer. "You did."

"I mean all the way."

"Can't get more all the way than what we just did… unless you're talking something kinky."

She laughed softly. "You are so bad." Then said, "Oh damn. Our breakfast is cold. Just like dinner."

"I told you, I seem to have a one-track mind where you're concerned. First priority is you…and a bed. Food runs a far-distant second."

She sighed softly, and he knew it was a good sigh. "That's nice. That's really, really nice. But…" She pulled away from him suddenly and darted from the bed, then yanked her sweater on over her head without bothering with a bra. "Where are my—oh, there they are," she said, glancing around. She picked up a tiny ball from the corner where Shane had thrown it in his haste, then apparently changed her mind. "I think I need new ones."

Yeah, she does, he thought, remembering how damp her bikini underwear had been when he'd caressed her while she was wearing them. And for some reason the wolf in him was very, very pleased with that knowledge. Inordinately proud. And pleased.

"Come on," she said, tossing Shane's sweater at his

head after she'd pulled on her jeans over clean undies. "Let's see if we can salvage that oatmeal."

The lights were off in Adams Hall in Old Town University, and though the wintry morning sun streamed through the stained-glass windows on one side, most of the two-tiered structure was still shrouded in eerie shadows. The sparse light didn't bother Marsh. He'd set up in worse.

Circumventing the security had been child's play for him, and once inside he'd gone immediately to the front, mounting the five stairs leading to the raised stage that would undoubtedly be used for the panel discussion. Neither he nor the man who'd provided the information knew exactly what the configuration of the panel would be, or where the senator would sit, so Marsh needed to plan for any contingency.

He snapped a few photos with his digital camera on its best low-light setting, mentally picturing where he might lie in wait. He'd already looked Adams Hall up online and had downloaded a half dozen pictures, so he knew it was possible a lectern might be placed somewhere on the stage, in front of the red carpet runner. If the speakers were standing to deliver their opening remarks, it was very likely they'd stand at a lectern, which would make his job that much easier. Either way, the layout of this hall was perfect for him—clear line of sight to the stage from practically anywhere, especially from the balcony. Six rows of yellow seats ascended from the balcony railing in the far back, with a wide aisle bisecting them; three rows lined the sides.

Marsh paced off the distances, making cryptic notations in the little book he carried. He used a code that would be damned difficult to crack—he wasn't stupid enough to create evidence against himself in the unlikely event he was ever arrested. Then he picked up the long, zippered case he'd brought with him, containing another AS50 sniper rifle, the same kind he'd used in his first attempt on the senator. He had other sniper rifles, but the AS50 was his favorite—it fit him like a glove.

He walked to the left side of the stage and down, then climbed up to the balcony, looking for a good place to stash his weapon for tomorrow. It wasn't as easy as he'd thought it would be. He knew from his research that the hall had more than seven hundred seats, but he had no idea how many people would attend tomorrow's panel discussion. And since this was being held on a college campus, who knew where the attendees would sit? College students were notorious for sitting in the back rows, so secreting his rifle under or in one of the seats there or in one of the window embrasures was problematic. He planned to arrive well before the starting time, but he needed to be able to retrieve the AS50 without being seen. And he had no idea what the janitorial schedule was. He couldn't leave his rifle where it might be found.

Then he found the perfect spot beneath the first tier of seats in the balcony. It took him a few minutes to pry the slats open without splintering the wood—and he commended himself for coming prepared with the tools he might need for most eventualities.

He unzipped the rifle case, and from long practice quickly assembled the pieces of the AS50 while still wearing his gloves. Then he fit it in the curve of his shoulder. He sighted down the scope, taking careful aim at the stage. No problem.

He loaded cartridges into the rifle from the box in the case and repeated the process, wanting every little edge he could have. A loaded rifle weighed more than an unloaded one, so he needed to be sure his aim was perfect.

"Click," he whispered to himself. The senator would never know what hit him.

He stashed the loaded rifle and the case in the hiding place he'd created, then fitted the wood slats back in place. When he was done, few people would have noticed the difference between the before and after. And anyone who'd never seen that spot before wouldn't have a clue that it hid anything.

Marsh glanced around, thinking Adams Hall looked more like a medieval church—with its arched ceiling, lavish use of wood, ornate paintings and stained-glass windows—than a lecture hall. His lips twisted in cynical amusement. Not a bad place to die...if you were going to die.

Chapter 19

The oatmeal was edible...barely. Shane added salt and milk to his bowl before popping it into the microwave. Carly added a teaspoon of sugar and—after scrounging in the cabinets—a dash of cinnamon to hers.

They sat at the table, eating and not saying much, until Carly raised her head and asked quietly, "Would you tell me what it's like when it happens?"

Shane didn't pretend not to understand. "I told you before, that first day, remember? I also described the symptoms for the interview last Sunday."

"I know. You feel cold all over, as if you've walked into a freezer. You don't black out—you have total recall of each episode. And you're able to carry on a conversation when it happens—I know that from my own experience. But that's not what I mean." She made a face of frustration. "I'm not talking about the *symptoms*. I want to know what's going on in your mind."

"Honestly? I'm not really thinking anything except 'Damn it, not again.'" He shook his head. "There's no warning. No odd feeling that a seizure's about to hit. And unless my arms and legs are visible, no one but me can tell I'm having an episode." He scraped up the last bite of oatmeal before adding, "I had one on the Senate floor on Wednesday morning. Right at the beginning of my speech on the pipeline bill."

"You did?" Her expression was half startled and half wondering. "I had no idea—I was in the gallery and I couldn't tell." Then her expression changed. "Why didn't you tell me?"

"What am I supposed to do? Announce to the world, 'The show's starting, folks. Senator Jones is having an epileptic seizure'?"

"Of course not." She gave him a long-suffering look. "But you could have told me later." She thought for a moment. "That was the night we came here, wasn't it?"

"Yeah."

Her voice was very quiet when she asked, "So why didn't you tell me?"

He had no easy answer. Why hadn't he told Carly? "You'd already witnessed one episode, the night of the reception at the Zakharian embassy," he said finally, stalling for time. "I didn't keep that from you."

"Not after I guessed. No, you didn't." After a long silence during which her gaze never left his face, she said, "You didn't tell me...because you're ashamed for me to know."

Sudden anger shook him. "That's a crock."

"Is it? Then why didn't you tell me?"

He stood so abruptly his chair scraped against the tile floor, a grating sound. He carried his bowl to the sink and ran water in it before turning to confront Carly. Only to find her bent over, her hands covering her face, her body shaking uncontrollably…and silently. Sobbing without making a sound.

"Carly!" He was on his knees in front of her in an instant. "Don't cry, Carly. God, don't. I can't bear it."

She raised a tear-wet face to his. "It's my fault." She sucked in her breath as tears continued to ooze out of her eyes and trickle down her cheeks. "There's something wrong with *me*. That's why you didn't tell me. That's why Jack didn't tell me about his depression. About his thoughts of suicide." She bit her lip and squeezed her eyes shut, obviously trying desperately to hold on to her emotions, then she sobbed again as if she couldn't help it. "That's why he's dead. Because of me."

"No, sweetheart, no," he soothed. "It's not your fault." The endearment slipped out and he didn't give a damn if she later made the connection. Because all he cared about in this instant was letting her know it *wasn't* her fault. Not what happened to Jack. And not what was happening to him.

He stood and scooped her into his arms, carrying her—still sobbing—into the living room. He settled into the recliner with her on his lap, his arms enfolding her. "Shush now, stop crying, sweetheart—you'll make yourself sick. Come on, Carly."

But it was as if she couldn't hear him. This wasn't like her tears of yesterday—unexpected, stress-induced but quickly over. This was as if she were locked in her own misery with nothing but self-recriminations tearing at her heart, as if the only words she could hear were *your fault, your fault, your fault*.

He cradled her head against his shoulder, stroking

her dark hair, making soothing, wordless sounds. Wishing he had the words to ease her pain. Wishing with all his might he could go back to eight years ago and make Jack's suicide not happen. Even though it would mean Carly would have married Jack and would have never been his, he would have done it in a heartbeat if it meant shielding her from this agony.

Eventually Carly cried herself out and lay quiescent in Shane's arms. He blotted her tears with his hanky, then gave it to her. When she was done he said, "Keep it," making her choke and laugh. Somehow, with her laughter, the words came to him. "You're right, sweetheart. It's not your fault, but you're right. I didn't tell you because I was ashamed."

He breathed deeply and drew a measure of comfort when Carly's hand moved of its own volition to stroke his arm in soothing fashion, the same thing he'd done to her a few moments ago. "It's not easy for me to admit weakness. My entire life has been about control. I was the oldest child. The toughest. The strongest influence on my siblings—even more than our parents in some ways. And yeah, Niall and I competed, but I always won." He brushed one knuckle against her now-dry cheek. "You were right. I always had to win."

He paused for a second. "Even when Wendy and our baby were murdered," he said, pain welling up at the memory, "I still managed to be in control—I tracked down their killers myself and turned the information over to the Belgian authorities. The terrorists chose to blow themselves up instead of being arrested, and that was okay with me because *I had still won.* Justice and vengeance were one and the same."

Carly spoke at last. "So when you were diagnosed with epilepsy..."

"Yeah. I couldn't accept it. I thought I had. I thought, 'Okay, I still have everything under control. The medication will handle the seizures and my life will return to normal.' Then you showed up in my hospital room, and because I was able to talk to you about it, I thought I was dealing with it. And doing the interview with you was more proof I was in control of my life—*I* was making the choice to go public."

"Then you had that seizure in my house." And from the note of understanding in her voice, he knew she'd connected the dots.

"Right. I had that seizure. Logically I knew it was too soon to expect the medication to work, but it bothered me because I couldn't control it. It bothered me even more because you were there to witness my weakness."

"Oh, Shane..." The hint of chiding in her voice made him smile, because this was more like the Carly he knew.

"I regained a little of my wounded pride the next night, when—"

"When you displayed incredible stamina." Her droll tone made him smile at first, then he laughed when she added, "I'm glad I could do my part helping you set a personal bedroom record."

"I wasn't shooting for a record, Ms. Edwards," he teased back, "but I'm always up for a challenge."

She pounded his arm with her closed fist, but lightly. "You are so bad."

He kissed her nose before continuing his story. "Then I had another seizure at the worst possible moment. Again, if logic was the only ball in play, I should have expected it—the doctors had told me the meds' time frame, and six days just weren't enough. But I was ashamed I still wasn't in control of my body, so I hid it from the world. And I especially wanted to hide it from you that night."

"Because you wanted me to see you as the white knight riding to my rescue, taking me where I'd be safe. Got it."

He winced. "Ouch."

"I don't mean it that way." She buried her face against his sweater, and the rest of her words were muffled.

"What did you say?"

She lifted her head. "I said I never needed a white knight before, but it sure felt nice having one when I did."

He couldn't look away from the bright intensity of her blue eyes. "Is that how you see me?"

"Sometimes."

"What am I when I'm not a white knight?"

"Well, sometimes you're a hot stud."

If he'd been drinking something, he would have choked. As it was, he spluttered with laughter. But something about the mischievous expression on her face stoked his male ego...which needed stoking after his earlier confession about what he saw as his weakness. "Thanks for the compliment... I think."

"It *is* a compliment...as if you needed one after all the times I...we..." Her cheeks were tinted with a hint of pink.

"So what am I when I'm not a white knight or a hot stud?" He was trying to keep it light, but God help him, he needed to know.

Her eyes softened. "You're a man I admire tremendously. A gentleman with a strict moral code, who believes passionately in right and wrong and who's willing to fight the good fight even when he knows he might not win...this time. A man who doesn't give up, though. Who never surrenders. Not perfect, but you try."

His heart swelled with love...the love Carly had professed she didn't want. He wanted to say something in response, but the only words that came to mind were the words he was forbidden to say. He brushed her hair gently away from her face, tucking it behind one ear. "Thank you," he said, clearing his throat as he finally found the words that hit the right light note. "That means a lot coming from you."

Her lips turned up in a faint smile, but her eyes were vulnerable when she asked, "So how do you see me?"

A darling, he wanted to say. *The only woman I want from now until eternity.* But he couldn't say those things. He could only think them. "Tiger shark," he said at last. "But that's a compliment—you never give up, either. You're smart. Very smart. And ethical. Stubborn as hell...but not too proud to admit your mistakes. A true lady." His voice dropped a notch. "With a body I can't stop thinking about."

The vulnerability in her eyes vanished, and she drawled in that soft Virginia accent she used when she wanted to tease him, "Well, at least you didn't list that last thing first."

"I'm going with you," Carly told Shane on Sunday, after lunch. "And that is that."

"Not in this lifetime," he responded, his jaw clenched so tight it ached.

"I'm not letting you make yourself a target without me."

He caught her arms with his hands and shook her. "This is *not* happening," he said harshly. "The only reason I'm making myself a target is to catch this guy before he can kill you. That means *you* stay *here*!"

Her face was as determined as he felt. "I know why you're doing this, and I'm not trying to stop you. I want to, but I won't. But you're not taking this risk without backup."

"I've got Niall. I don't need you."

Hurt flashed in and out of her eyes so quickly he thought he must have imagined it. Then her face turned stony. "Fine." Her lips barely moved. "You win again, Shane." She pulled free from his grasp and ran into the bedroom. Then he heard the unmistakable click of the door lock.

He stared at the locked door for a moment, pain clawing through him like a wild thing. Carly didn't understand. If anything happened to her, the sniper might as well put a bullet through him, as well, because his life would effectively be over.

Just tell her, an insidious little voice in the back of his skull whispered. *You may never have another chance.*

Shane moved to the door and placed his palm flat against it, as if he could touch Carly through the barrier. "No," he whispered, fighting the temptation. He couldn't tell Carly he loved her, then deliberately put himself in harm's way. *I'll be damned before I'll hurt her the way Jack did.* It wasn't the same situation—he wasn't committing suicide, leaving Carly to pick up the pieces of her shattered life alone—but it was close enough. If something went wrong, Carly wasn't going to have deal with the death of another man who'd professed to love her. *Not happening*, he told himself silently. *Not. Happening.*

There was a sharp rap at the front door, and Shane glanced at his watch. It was twelve-thirty. He and Niall had arranged to go to the university together, early, and his brother was nothing if not precisely on time.

The doors to Adams Hall weren't open to the public yet, but a locked door had never stopped Marsh. He retrieved his already-assembled AS50 well before one, but left the case inside. He wouldn't need it. With an economy of motion he moved into place in the corner of the balcony, the spot nearest to the staircase he'd decided would be perfect to accomplish this job *and* escape capture. One without the other would be meaningless to him.

He removed his raincoat and laid it to one side. The raincoat would conceal the rifle until he was ready to use it. He fit the rifle in the curve of his shoulder and sighted down the scope, taking careful aim at the lectern that—as he'd expected—had been set up near the front of the stage, off to one side. Also as he'd expected, from this vantage point he had a clear shot.

The rifle felt a little off, and with a tiny frown Marsh double-checked, but yes, it was still loaded. He was going to remove the cartridges to be sure, but the sound of footsteps on the stage made him quickly and surreptitiously move into the shadows as a man and woman walked out. He watched as the two people placed five name tents on the table, then arranged water glasses and what appeared to be pads of paper and writing utensils on the table in front of each chair.

"We'll put out fresh water right before we start," the woman said, her voice echoing in the empty hall as she and the man left.

Marsh waited for five minutes, until he was sure the couple wouldn't return. Then he sighted through the scope again, reading the name tents on the table. *Bingo!* There was the senator's name on the far right. Which meant he might not need to wait for him to speak at the lectern after all. He'd have to play it by ear, but if the opportunity arose, he'd take it.

He slung the rifle's strap over his shoulder, then put his raincoat back on. For the next few minutes he practiced shrugging the raincoat off, lifting the rifle and fitting it into his shoulder, all in one motion, then taking the shot. Again and again. Both at the table and at the lectern.

Precision was his goal. Precision, practice and careful planning, all of which he'd learned in the military. All of which was how he'd avoided prison all these years.

He rehearsed the next steps in his mind. *Drop the rifle as soon as the shot is taken. The crowd will be screaming, confused, rushing to get out before they become targets, too. Join the frantic melee on the staircase, one of the escaping crowd. Then out the door, using the crowd as a shield. Toss the gloves, but not in the nearest Dumpster, the one behind the student union. Then walk calmly to the parking lot. Retrieve your truck. Drive sedately off the campus, across the Potomac and safely home in Virginia.*

Marsh smiled to himself. He'd already emptied his bladder and had drunk nothing today so he wouldn't have to worry about that. He didn't worry about the rifle case, either. It was hidden, but if it was found, it would reveal exactly nothing to investigators. The same went for the rifle and the raincoat. The serial number hadn't been removed from the weapon, but that didn't matter. The serial number could never be traced back to him. And he'd purchased the raincoat four years ago at a Goodwill store. Untraceable.

He buttoned his raincoat over the rifle carefully, then glanced down, assuring himself there were no visible bulges that might alarm anyone who saw him.

He was ready.

The minute Carly stormed into the bedroom and locked the door in a fit of pique, she turned around and pressed her body against the door, face and palm, too, and she cried inside, *Oh, Shane, Shane!,* although she didn't shed a tear. She wanted so desperately to tell him how much she loved him, to beg him to *please* be careful—if anything happened to him the sniper might as well put a bullet through her, as well, because her life would essentially be over. But she couldn't do that. She couldn't do anything that might distract him when he walked into Adams Hall.

And she couldn't bear to sit home and wait passively while he risked his life for her. To keep her safe. Not just because he loved her—*and he does, he does!* her heart insisted—but because he was a protector down to his marrow. He would make himself a target for her even if he didn't love her, and that made her love him all the more.

The longer she stood there, the more determined she grew that Shane wasn't going to do this on his own. The hell with his brother—Niall couldn't have eyes everywhere. She was going, and that was that.

Through the bedroom door Carly heard a faint rap that sounded like a knock at the front door. Then she heard low-pitched male voices from the other room—she couldn't quite make out the words, but she knew it had to be the two brothers. She waited until the sound faded away, until she heard the tiny metallic click indicating the front door being secured behind the two men, ensuring her safety.

Then she unlocked the bedroom door.

Chapter 20

"You're strapped, right?" Niall asked Shane for the third time.

He couldn't keep the exasperation out of his voice. "How many times are you going to ask me that? Yes, I'm strapped. And before you ask, yes, I'm wearing a bullet-proof vest, too. Although that won't do me much good if he goes for a head shot." He glanced at his brother. "Is everything in place?"

"Yeah. Didn't even have to call in any favors." Niall turned the corner, then stated, "I didn't see Carly at my condo. She still with you?"

Possessiveness flashed to life. "Yes, and I'll thank you to keep your thoughts off her."

Niall chuckled softly, stopped his truck for a red light and looked over at Shane. Then the smile faded from his face and he said, "You're serious."

"As serious as a heart attack."

"I never thought… I mean, you've known her what? A week?"

"Ten days." *Ten glorious, incredible, indelible days.* Ten days etched in gold against the stark black and white his life had been for years.

"It doesn't sound like you. I mean, you and Wendy knew each other for years before you got married. Besides, it's fifteen years since Wendy…well…since she died. I figured you were never going to get over losing her, and…well…hell, you know what I mean."

Shane didn't say anything at first. "It knocked me off kilter," he finally admitted. "Especially how fast it all came down. Part of it's the situation—not that how I *feel* about Carly is due to someone trying to take me out—but the swift intensity…yeah."

The light changed to green and Niall shifted into gear. "You going to ask her to marry you when this is all over?"

The tightness in Shane's chest had nothing to do with what he *wanted*. Only with what he knew he could have. Carly cared—he knew that. That whole emotional distance thing had been a load of crap from the get-go. But whether she'd ever let herself care enough to fall in love with him the way she'd been in love with Jack? That was a whole nother thing.

And then there was his epilepsy. Even if she grew to love him anywhere close to how he loved her, could he ask her to marry him? Maybe if he didn't feel so helpless every time a chill struck without warning. Maybe if the seizures were under control. But that was a big maybe.

"Maybe that's a question I shouldn't have asked," Niall said quietly. "Sorry. It's none of my business."

"It's…complicated" was all Shane could think to say.

"You're not sure you love her enough for forever?"

"That's not it."

"Then what? You think she doesn't love you?" Niall kept his eyes on the road, but there was something in the set of his jaw that tipped Shane off that his brother refused to believe it. "I saw the way she looked at you Friday night, Essbee," he said, using the nickname from their childhood only he used, the initials of Shane's given names—S.B. "And I heard her say you weren't doing this." Niall darted a glance at him. "Seemed pretty obvious to me, and it didn't take any special black-ops skills to see it, either."

Shane desperately wanted it to be true, but... "It's not that easy."

His brother grunted, but Shane wasn't sure exactly what he meant by it. A long silence was broken by "She try to change your mind about today?"

"No," he said, remembering. "She didn't." He'd thought she was going to. When she'd shown up in Niall's office Friday night, he'd been sure she was going to force him to choose between her and his plan to catch the hit man. And he'd wondered ever since—if she cared for him the way he wanted her to—why she hadn't. She wouldn't have changed his mind, but...

"That's one brave woman."

"What do you mean?"

"Thought you were smarter than that, Essbee."

"Just spill it."

"Takes a brave woman to stand by and let someone she loves risk his life without trying to stop him. Like Mom. She loves us—and it would *kill* her to lose one of us—but she never tried to stop us from being 'one.'"

The reference to Edward Everett Hale's famous "I

am one" quotation about making a difference in the world streaked through Shane's consciousness like a lightning bolt. Their parents had thought the idea was so important the entire quotation hung above the fireplace at home—almost before Shane could read, he could recite it by heart. *I am only one, but I am one. I cannot do everything, but I can do something. And I will not let what I cannot do interfere with what I can do. And by the grace of God, I will.*

"You really think...?" He couldn't finish the question.

"Hell yeah."

Overlaid against his brother's emphatic agreement, he suddenly heard Carly saying, *I owe you another apology.* And when he'd asked why, she'd said, *I can't tell you... I'm too ashamed.*

Ashamed because she loved him and wanted to keep him safe, wanted him to sit back and let someone else take the risk, even if that was the coward's way? Ashamed because for a brief moment she'd wanted him to be less than the man he was? And when she'd realized what she was doing, she'd backpedaled and apologized?

Then the words she'd uttered just before he'd left today flashed into his mind. *I know why you're doing this, and I'm not trying to stop you. I want to, but I won't.*

Adrenaline surged through every part of his body at the realization. If Niall was right, then Carly didn't just care for him, she loved him enough to let him do without protest what he *had* to do...because he couldn't do less. Because he was "one."

Students filed noisily into Adams Hall, accompanied by faculty and the general public. If the weather had been better or worse, the crowd would have been smaller. A warm, sunny day would have driven most people to the parks to enjoy the extra-early gift of springtime weather. A snowy or rainy day would have kept many of them home with a good book or watching a basketball game on TV. But the weather—sunny and cold—was perfect for maximum attendance at the panel discussion on a topic that was polarizing, both on campus and with the voting public.

The cold outside meant Adams Hall, with its high, arched ceiling, was chilly inside. Chilly enough for many in the crowd to keep their coats or jackets on, at least until more people showed up and their combined body heat warmed up the large space. Marsh didn't smile, but he could have. He would not stand out in the crowd by keeping his raincoat on. It hid his deadly intentions.

And that was a good thing.

"Taxi!" Carly's voice was loud and shrill as she flagged down the first cab she spotted. She jumped in, glad to be out of the sharp wind.

"Where to, ma'am?" the driver said with a musical lilt to his voice that Carly pegged as probably Jamaican or Bahamian—but definitely from the Caribbean.

"Old Town University. Adams Hall." She referred to the piece of paper she pulled from her pocket, and read him the address.

The driver wrote the destination on his trip sheet, then depressed the meter's flag. "Do you mind if I turn on some music?" he asked as he pulled away from the curb.

"So long as it's not rap."

The driver laughed. "Oh no, ma'am." And soon the sounds of reggae filled the cab's interior.

I was right, Carly thought with a tiny smile. *Caribbean for sure.*

Almost immediately she tuned out the upbeat music, because her mind was focused on only two things—making sure Shane was safe, and making sure she didn't put him in more danger by becoming a target herself.

She closed her eyes and concentrated on that moment a week ago Saturday when Shane had been shot at and she'd chased after the sniper. She wasn't a stranger to gunfire, so while the shots had startled her, she hadn't been frozen with fear, either. She'd grabbed her smartphone and had done what she'd done her entire adult life—she'd gone after the story.

She visualized in her mind every move she'd made, every step she'd taken, right up until Shane had tackled her as the shot from the sniper's rifle whizzed harmlessly overhead. But in those seconds before, she'd seen the man's bearded face. Had captured him on video.

The tech guys at the network had done their best to blow up and enhance the images, but the end result really hadn't been sharp enough to see the details she remembered now. The deep-set eyes. The shape of his body. The way he pulled the rifle into his shoulder and took aim all in one smooth motion. Practiced. Professional.

She'd told all this to the Phoenix police, of course, and to the FBI. And she'd worked with a sketch artist. But the sketch artist couldn't possibly capture the way the man *moved*.

And suddenly Carly knew if she saw this man again, if she saw him running or taking aim, she would know him. The hat and the beard were probably disguises, so she couldn't let herself be fooled into looking for them.

No, she needed to search for those deep-set eyes. The stocky build. The smooth way he moved.

And she needed to do it without letting him see her.

Shane and his brother parted company once Niall had escorted him to the building adjacent to Adams Hall. As arranged, the five panel members debating whether or not climate change actually existed, and the cadre of university students from the debate club sponsoring this event, were assembling there an hour ahead of time. But Shane had arrived very early to allow Niall enough time to do his thing in Adams Hall.

He ran through his notes while he waited. He considered rehearsing his opening speech once more, then heard Carly's voice in the back of his mind saying at breakfast, *You've practiced your speech until you're word perfect. And frankly, I'm sick of hearing it. I've posed mock questions for you until you could answer questions on this topic in your sleep, and you have...if that mumbling I heard last night means anything.*

He'd laughed at her dry tone and her words this morning, but now he acknowledged she was right. That control thing he had going extended to just about everything in his life, including his need to be hyper prepared for any contingency.

It had been a mistake letting himself think of Carly, though, because now he couldn't get her out of his mind. He sat facing the door—you always faced the door unless you wanted to be taken unawares—but he wasn't really seeing it. He was seeing Carly as she'd looked the first time he'd made love to her. God, he hadn't even gotten his pants off. Hadn't even undressed her. He'd been a Hellfire missile locked on target, and he could still remember the explosion that had rocked his world.

Did she love him? That was the sixty-four-thousand-dollar question. Niall thought she did, and Shane knew his brother was rarely wrong. But there was always a chance she *didn't* love him. In which case he'd have to be a gentleman about it, even though that was the last thing he wanted to do. Despite the possessiveness that dug its talons into him whenever he thought about any other man touching Carly, he'd have to find a way to let her go.

The panel moderator made introductions all around, then ran through the agenda and the order of the opening speeches, which had been decided by lottery that morning. "You will be seated at a table stage right—that's the left side from the audience's perspective. I'll be standing at the lectern stage left. I'll introduce you in order to the audience with the short bios you provided. Please remain seated, but feel free to acknowledge any applause.

"After the initial introduction, when I call your name, please move to the lectern for your opening remarks. As was already communicated to you or your staff, you will each have up to six minutes. I'm afraid we must strictly adhere to this limitation in order to have time for the prepared questions and for the open-mic questions from the audience."

He then went on to explain how the prepared questions had been chosen from the dozens submitted by members of the debate club. "I'll pose the questions from the lectern, but to save time your answers should be delivered from the table—we have microphones set up at the table for this purpose," the moderator said to

Shane and the other four panelists. "We would like each of you to have an opportunity to answer every question, but in order to do that, we ask that you keep your answers to one minute or less. If you go over ninety seconds, I will politely interrupt and ask you to wrap up your comments. If you choose not to answer a particular question, just say 'pass' and I'll move on to the next panelist. Is all that clear?"

Shane glanced around, but all he saw were heads nodding, so he said for all of them, "Crystal clear."

"Are there any questions?" When none were forthcoming, the moderator said, "Thank you all in advance for participating. We're looking forward to a lively discussion." He smiled and held out a hand, indicating one of the debate club members who'd been introduced earlier. "Please follow Sandra Beckett. She'll take you where you need to go. I'll be there shortly."

Shane's eyes were watchfully alert as the panelists followed Sandra into Adams Hall through a door from outside that led directly onto the stage. Just because he and Niall had anticipated he'd be targeted on the stage didn't mean the hit man might not try something they hadn't planned on. But all was serene, and Shane brought up the rear of their little group, then closed the door behind him.

The panel took their assigned places at a long table covered with a red tablecloth—name tents made it easy to find who sat where. Microphones, pitchers of water, glasses, notepads and pens were all neatly arranged at each place. Shane noted they'd been seated in the order in which they would speak, with the first speaker at the far end of the table. Which meant Shane was closest to the lectern.

* * *

The cab stopped, and the driver said, "This is as close as I can get, ma'am."

Carly handed him the two bills she already had in her hand, saying, "No change. Thanks."

She slid out of the cab, buttoned her coat against the wind that was still blowing, and wrapped her scarf around the lower portion of her face. Then she pulled her hat brim lower, and joined the throng of people hurrying into Adams Hall.

As he took his seat on the stage, Shane sought out the four men on his staff he'd asked to be present this afternoon—Bobby, Hank, Miguel and Terry. They were all sitting together, third row back, right on the aisle. He smiled and nodded when he caught their eyes, although smiling was the last thing he wanted to do. One of them had sold him out. *Which one?*

Then he searched for his brother. At first he couldn't see him—Shane made two full passes over the balcony and was on the third circuit before he spotted Niall, dressed like a workman in faded jeans and a worn jacket, leaning casually against one of the pillars in the far back on the left side. At least, he appeared to be leaning casually to the uninformed eye. But Shane knew his brother. And he knew that air was misleading.

Shane let his gaze pass on by as if he'd never seen Niall, completing the circuit he'd begun. He did nothing to acknowledge he got the message his brother was sending him, but his heartbeat accelerated with a kick of adrenaline. All the pieces were falling into place.

Stragglers were still filing in and taking seats in the rows in the back, but a few came down the aisles to the front where one or two empty single seats could still be found. A trickle of disappointed people made their way up the front staircase on Shane's left and found places in the balcony.

Then the house lights dimmed.

Chapter 21

Saying excuse me, Carly sidled her way past two men and a woman—Old Town students by the looks of them. She didn't know why they were standing in the back—the hall was fairly full, but not standing room only—and she needed to get by them to mount the staircase.

She'd already scoped out the first floor, and the hit man wasn't there. At least…she was fairly confident he wasn't there. She couldn't be absolutely positive, but she didn't have any more time to waste because the third speaker had already taken the lectern. That meant in a few minutes, Shane would be standing there. Unprotected. And that was unacceptable.

Marsh was slouched in his chair—the only way he could sit unnoticed with the rifle strapped to his right shoulder. He glanced around to see if anyone was watching, and was reassured no one seemed to be paying any attention to him. Exactly what he wanted. Everyone seemed to be focused on the lawyer now at the lectern. One more speaker after this, and then it would be the senator's turn.

He could have taken the shot earlier. All five of the panelists had been lined up at the table like targets in a carnival booth when the initial introductions had been made. But too many people had still been moving around the balcony, searching for seats at the last minute, and the risk had been too great. Not so much that one of them could have gotten in the way of his shot, but that one or more of them might have seen him as he took aim. And he wanted no more witnesses he would have to kill.

Then, when each speaker had risen and crossed to the lectern for his or her opening remarks, the moderator had politely backed away to one side—*right* in Marsh's line of sight to the senator. Every frigging time. He'd cursed internally the first time it had happened, because he'd already unbuttoned his raincoat, preparatory to taking the shot. Then he'd berated himself for being too eager. *Patience*, he'd reminded himself. *Patience* was one of his bywords. Patience. Practice. Planning. Preparation. The senator would eventually take the lectern. And Marsh would be ready.

The twitch between Shane's shoulder blades was getting worse with each passing minute, and he gritted his teeth. *What's taking so long?* he fumed silently. He wanted this over, one way or the other. *Take the shot, damn it*, he told the sniper in his mind. *Take the damned shot!*

Then he saw a woman in a coat and hat that resembled Carly's rapidly climbing one of the staircases in the back, and his brain stuttered as his heartbeat quickened. *It looks like...no, it can't be...* The woman disappeared from view, and he told himself he was imagining things. She might *look* like Carly from a distance, but it couldn't be her. Carly was safe in Niall's condo.

Then the woman's head and shoulders appeared atop the balcony, and though her hat was pulled low and her scarf obscured the bottom half of her face, his heart recognized her even before his brain did. *Son of a bitch!* The anger and fear curling through him at the sight of Carly—here...at risk—far eclipsed anything he'd ever experienced with the seizures. His lack of control over the situation...his inability to do anything except pray the sniper didn't see her, didn't target her instead of him...

Shane had drawn his Beretta and was racing toward the wooden staircase at the front long before he realized what he was doing, his legs pumping like pistons as he ascended the stairs. The speaker stopped in midsentence and gawked. The crowd gasped and turned to watch in stupefaction. But Shane heard nothing. Saw nothing except Carly at the far end of the balcony, kitty-corner from him...too far away. One thought pounded through his consciousness. *Oh, God. Oh, God. Oh, God.* As if prayer could keep her safe until he could reach her.

Time slowed to a crawl, although it could only have been a few seconds. Movement at the back of the balcony on his left was followed immediately by Carly's cry of "No! No!" Then Carly's .22 was in her hands as she squared up and took aim at the corner of the balcony farthest from her. The crack of a rifle preceded another gunshot by a fraction of a second, so close together one appeared to be the echo of the other.

Screams split the air. Panicked bodies blocked Shane's view for a moment as most of the crowd frantically clawed its way toward the exits. He grasped the railing with his right hand and clutched his gun with his left as he pushed and shoved and stumbled over dozens of feet in his mad haste to reach Carly.

He neared the far end and made the turn around the curving balcony, then saw two men struggling for possession of a rifle. Bright blood stained the left arm of the shorter man. The other was Niall. Shane didn't consciously decide his brother didn't need his help incapacitating the sniper—he just knew. His gaze swung right, and despite the press of bodies jostling Carly as they surged toward the staircase, he could see her standing frozen, as if in a state of shock. He followed the crowd until he reached her side, then wrapped his arms tightly around her, shielding her with his body against the buffeting tide of humanity that threatened to sweep her away.

He dragged her—without resistance—to one side. He thrust his Beretta into his pants pocket, took Carly's .22 from her unresisting grasp and stashed that in his pocket, too, then pressed her head against his shoulder. She was saying something over and over, and he bent his head to hear her above the noise of the mob. "No," she whispered, her eyes wide and dark in the dim light as she clung to him, her body trembling uncontrollably. "No, no, no."

"It's okay," he told her roughly. "You're okay." He didn't know what else to say. Then he realized he'd used the exact same words she'd used toward him during his last episode. *"It's okay. You're okay."* The helpless words of someone who couldn't bear to be helpless.

All of a sudden a half dozen FBI agents—part of the contingent Niall had arranged to be there—swarmed them with their guns drawn. "You okay, Senator Jones?" one man barked at him. "You weren't hit?"

"No," he confirmed. "I'm fine." He angled his head toward the far corner of the balcony. "The shooter's up there. But I don't think he's a threat anymore."

He glanced over his shoulder and saw exactly what he'd expected to see. Niall had the sniper pinned to the wall, incapacitated, the man's right arm at a sharp angle behind his back. The left arm hung uselessly, the bloodstain there much larger now.

He turned back to Carly. "You got him," he said in a low voice, his heart squeezing at the aftereffects of the shooting still holding her in their cruel grip. *The shakes*, his brain processed, remembering the first time he'd shot someone, and the reaction that had immediately followed. "It's okay, sweetheart. I'm okay. You got him."

The hours following the shooting dragged endlessly. As they'd been after the first sniper attack, as they'd been following the discovery of the car bomb, Shane and Carly were separated. Shane repeated his story endless times, each time identical to the first. But in between he kept asking about Carly. "She's in shock," he insisted. "You can't question her when she's in shock. I don't need a lawyer, but she does."

The third time he said it—to the third team of interrogators—one of the FBI agents laughed, but not unkindly. "Don't worry, Senator Jones. She's fine. And her recounting of the incident is as precise and detailed as yours is."

"Is she under arrest? Because if she's under arrest, she's entitled to a lawyer before you—"

"Relax, sir. She's not under arrest. We have no intention of arresting her. Two of our agents in the balcony witnessed the entire thing from start to finish. Her story matches what they saw. It also matches your story. And your brother's."

"If she's not under arrest, how long are you going to keep us here?" He couldn't help the tone of command in his voice—he'd been a marine too long to break the habit.

The two FBI agents glanced at each other, then back at Shane, and the one who appeared to be the man in charge smiled briefly. "Not much longer. We're just waiting on the results of the ballistics and GSR tests," he said, referring to those done on the rifle and Carly's .22 as well as his own Beretta, and the gunshot residue tests on both shooters—Carly and the sniper—and him. His weapon hadn't been fired, and there were plenty of witnesses to back up his story, but the FBI had to go through its complete routine—too many trials had been lost because something *hadn't* been tested.

"Has the sniper said anything?"

"Not so far. He's standing mute, but he hasn't asked for a lawyer yet, which makes me hopeful. I think he's weighing his options."

"Have you identified him?"

Again the two FBI agents shared a look. "Marsh Anderson. Does the name ring a bell?" When Shane shook his head, the agent said, "Retired military. Navy SEAL. Chest full of medals, too."

Shane grimaced. "Damn."

"Yeah. This isn't going to go over well in the press."

The grimace morphed into a faint smile. "I happen to know a hell of an investigative reporter who can put the right spin on the story if you want. Especially seeing as how she's the one who took a rogue former Navy SEAL down."

Carly was still shaking inside, but she was sure her interrogators would never know it from the calm way she answered their questions. And no one—not even Shane—would ever know the desperate fear that had gripped her when the sniper had stood, shrugged off his raincoat and pulled his rifle up in one smooth move. And she'd known in an instant it was *him*—the man she'd seen in Phoenix. No hat. No beard. But she'd known.

And no one would ever know the despair that had swamped her when she'd thought she was a split second too late. When the sniper had taken aim at Shane and fired before she could pull the trigger.

But then Shane had reached her, alive and whole, wrapping his sheltering arms around her and she could breathe again—she hadn't been too late after all.

This time the man she loved hadn't died.

Shane, Carly and Niall were enjoying a little R & R in Niall's condo late that night. At first Carly had wanted to go home to her town house, but Shane had reminded her they still had clothes at his brother's place. "Besides," he told her, "just because the hit man has been caught, doesn't mean I'm entirely in the clear. Not until Tuesday's vote." Her immediate concerned reaction and insistence they return to the safety of Niall's home had been music to his ears—Carly cared. A lot.

Shane had made a pot of coffee for Carly, and she was curled up next to him on the sofa, sipping her favorite beverage. Every so often she rested her head against his shoulder, and every time she did that, his arm tightened around her. He would never forget those terror-filled moments this afternoon, when he thought he might not reach her in time.

In the recliner across from them, Niall stretched his arms above his head, then rolled his shoulders as if to remove the kinks, before leaning back and saying, "I'm not sure if I should tell you…"

Shane wasn't really paying attention to his brother. He was looking at Carly, at the gentle sweep of her dark hair, the delicate curve of her cheek. He was thinking about how soft and warm she felt beside him, the way her breasts rose and fell with her breathing. Quietly exulting that she was alive, which meant he could go on living, too. But he replied absently, "Tell us what?"

A tiny smile played over Niall's lips. "That all the heroics this afternoon weren't necessary."

Carly took another sip of her coffee. "What do you mean?"

"In addition to the FBI agents staking out Adams Hall, who I called in just as we planned, there were no real bullets in Marsh Anderson's sniper rifle."

"What?" Shane's attention was jerked away from Carly onto Niall, and he sat up straight, bringing Carly with him. "I heard the——"

"'Sound and fury,'" Niall said, quoting Shakespeare. "'Signifying nothing.'" He smiled lazily at Shane. "There was gunpowder in the cartridges, but no real bullets. You really think I'd let someone take a shot at you, Essbee?"

Carly glanced up at Shane, her eyebrows raised in a question. "Essbee?" she inquired, looking like a hound on the scent.

Or like a tiger shark smelling blood in the water, he thought humorously. "It's S.B. Short for Shane Breckenridge," he explained before Niall could. "And don't ask," he added when she opened her mouth.

"Okay, I won't."

That meek acquiescence might last all of a day, he told himself, holding back a chuckle with an effort. Carly was many things, but meek and acquiescent weren't among them.

Carly turned her gaze back on Niall. "What do you mean, there were no real bullets?"

"I searched Adams Hall last night," Niall replied. "I figured, professional like him, he'd want to stash his rifle there ahead of time, just in case there was some kind of metal detector or body search at today's event. Took me a couple of hours, but I finally found it."

"And?" Carly asked.

"And it was already assembled, ready to use. I removed the cartridges from the rifle, took 'em apart, removed the bullet tips—that's the projectile part of a rifle cartridge," he explained for Carly's benefit, "replaced them with fakes, put the cartridges back together, then reloaded them in the rifle. Did the same with the remaining cartridges in the box."

When Carly just stared at him, Niall said, "I was a *leeettle* concerned he might detect the slight weight difference—the fake bullets don't weigh quite the same as real ones—but he didn't. I couldn't use blanks," he explained patiently. "For sure he would have noticed."

"You mean I shot an unarmed man?" Her dismay was obvious.

Niall shook his head. "Not unarmed. He would have killed Shane in a heartbeat if he'd had his way. I just made sure he couldn't, that's all."

"But how did you know—" She caught herself before she finished the sentence. "You were a sniper in the marines," she said, nodding to herself. "That's how you knew what to do. That's how you knew what *he* would do." She was silent for a moment, and when Shane looked at her, he saw growing frustration on her face. "Why didn't you at least tell your brother?" she demanded of Niall. "I get that you weren't going to tell me, but why did you let him think—"

Silent laughter, which Shane tried to restrain but couldn't, convulsed him for a moment. Carly punched him on the arm—and not the light tap she'd given him once before, either. "What's so funny?"

"I should have known," he said, his eyes brimming over with humor as they met his brother's eyes. "Payback for being an idiot, right? For making myself a target?"

Niall just grinned. Carly glanced from Shane to Niall and back again. "Is this some stupid guy thing?" she asked pointedly. "Because I have to tell you, no woman would even *think* of pulling a stunt like that." She rounded on Niall. "Yes, and you're forty years old," she accused him, her eyes narrowing. "Not a kid. Don't guys *ever* grow up?"

Shane took Carly's coffee cup from her and placed it on the end table beside him. Then he cradled her face in his hands and kissed her. When he finally raised his lips from hers, her eyes were dazed, her cheeks flushed. But she still retained the ability to say, "And don't think you can distract me this way, Marine, because I—"

He kissed her again. And again. Until she melted into his embrace and kissed him back. Until he forgot where he was. Until he forgot his own name.

"Jeez," his brother said from somewhere far distant. "Get a room, would ya?"

Chapter 22

Not quite six weeks later

Carly hung up the phone with Shane, a slight, puzzled frown between her brows. This was the third time since his return from Arizona that he'd made an excuse not to see her, and she didn't know what to make of it.

Despite maintaining separate residences—Shane's political advisors had been adamant he couldn't publicly flaunt cohabitation with a woman not his wife, even in this day and age—they'd been practically living together for the past six weeks. They'd given each other keys and they hadn't slept a single night apart, which—given how much Shane had suffered when he found out which one of his staff was the traitor—had been a blessing for him. Not that he would admit it, of course. He'd acted as if he wasn't devastated...even though he was.

The day after the pipeline bill was narrowly defeated, Marsh Anderson—his arm still in a sling from where Carly had shot him—had taken a plea deal in exchange for naming names. Including those he referred to as the Agenda Men, and the name Shane had most wanted to know—the man who'd betrayed him.

But then Shane had fought believing it. Bobby? *Bobby?* He'd gone to high school with Bobby Vernon, he'd told Carly in a state of shock. Had given his friend a job over more qualified men when he'd first been elected to the House of Representatives because Bobby had worked hard on Shane's first election campaign and Shane was nothing if not loyal. And Bobby had gotten up to speed so quickly Shane hadn't had to think twice about keeping him on as deputy chief of staff when he'd moved to the Senate.

Carly had grieved for Shane, for the loss of his trusted staffer and friend. There were no words she could have said to him to cushion the blow, and Shane wasn't the kind of man who could talk out his grief. So all she could do was hold him. Love him. Be a constant, reassuring presence in his life.

She'd even turned down a story J.C. had offered her that would take her out of the country—and she'd only ever done that before for her sister, Tahra. That, more than anything, had convinced Carly she truly loved Shane. Totally. Completely. She loved her job…but it didn't need her the way Shane did.

So they'd spent every night together…until Shane had flown to Arizona a few days ago for a follow-up visit with his neurologist there. The Mayo Clinic had given Shane the name of a highly regarded neurologist in the DC area for emergencies, but apparently whatever was wrong with him required a trip out west.

Carly had wanted to go with Shane, but he'd declined her offer. She'd been hurt—she'd admitted as much to herself at the time—but then had reasoned he was entitled to his privacy…if he wanted to keep this private from her. Which, apparently, he did.

Shane had flown out Thursday evening and had flown back Friday afternoon. Friday night, he'd pleaded exhaustion. She'd offered him some TLC but he'd gently turned her down, and Carly hadn't pushed. Saturday he'd claimed Niall was in town briefly, and he wanted to devote the day and night to his brother—some one-on-one male bonding time. Again Carly hadn't protested, because if her sister Tahra had been visiting, she would have wanted to spend time alone with her without male distraction.

But today was Sunday. And Shane hadn't even bothered to come up with a lame excuse. He hadn't lied to her, she'd give him that. But all he'd said was "I can't, Carly" in a tone that brooked no argument. Then he'd disconnected, as if that was the end of it.

He's avoiding you, she acknowledged. Any other man and she would have gotten the message loud and clear—the cold-shoulder brush off. But Shane wasn't like that. If he didn't love her, he'd be a man about it and tell her to her face. So whatever the problem was, it didn't have anything to do with how he felt about her. Which only left one explanation.

For just a moment, burning anger and a sense of injustice took possession, and her lips thinned. What kind of woman did Shane think she was? Did he think she'd crumble at the first sign of trouble? And who the hell gave him the right to make unilateral decisions about them both that affected her?

But then she realized Shane had taken her words to heart when she'd told him all those weeks ago they had to keep an emotional distance. He saw her exactly as she'd told him she was—an emotional coward. A woman who couldn't—or wouldn't—be there for him when the chips were down.

He has *to know that's not true*, she protested silently. He *had* to know emotional distance had quickly gone south when they'd both accepted you couldn't overrule your heart with your head no matter how much you tried. But Shane was a protector. Would he sacrifice what he wanted, what would make him happy, if he thought Carly would be better off without him?

"In a heartbeat," she whispered to herself. "And that's exactly what he thinks he's doing—protecting me." A part of Carly was touched, but a bigger part just wanted to slap Shane upside the head and knock some sense into him.

If he thought she would let him just walk away to keep herself from being hurt again, he had another think coming. "They don't call me Tiger Shark for nothing, Shane," she muttered. She was already moving toward the front door closet, her purse in one hand, her car keys in the other. She grabbed a light spring jacket from the closet and had barely shrugged into it before she was out the door.

Shane was sitting in his family room, an unopened book in his lap, doing nothing except staring at the fire in the fireplace. The main reason he'd rented this older house in Virginia, instead of an upscale condo in DC like Niall, was because of the wood-burning fireplace, which reminded him of the one in his parents' home in Denver and the one in their family's cabin near Dillon Reservoir in the Rockies.

A real fire was a lot more work than a fake gas log because he had to haul the wood into the house and clean the ashes out of the grate, but it was worth it. Usually. Now the fire leaped and crackled, as usual, and the dry apple wood he paid extra for was doing its best to hold a conversation with him. But he wasn't really hearing the hiss and pop, just as he wasn't really seeing the flames. He was hearing Carly's voice in his ears, seeing her face in his mind.

Juxtaposed with his memories of Carly was the recent one of Dr. Rachel Mattingly, his neurologist at the Mayo Clinic. Whose voice and face were filled with gentle concern and regret as she said, "We've increased the dosage steadily and we've given it enough time. I think we have to admit this medication isn't going to work for you, and try something else."

Which meant a brand-spanking-new prescription bottle now resided on the counter in the master bathroom next to the old one that hadn't worked. He'd been taking the new medication since Friday evening, but they hadn't taken him off the old one, not cold turkey. "Ramp up and ramp down" is how Dr. Mattingly had described it. Steadily increasing the dosage on the new medication while steadily decreasing the dosage on the previous one. Another six weeks before he'd know if the new medication alone worked any better at controlling the seizures—and the "chilling" symptoms.

In the meantime the seizures could continue. Hell, if the new medication didn't work, they could go on indefinitely. And as the doctors had told him back when he'd first been diagnosed with epilepsy, while the seizures up until now hadn't caused any damage visible on his MRI, that could change. Uncontrolled, they could transform from tiny seizures to big ones, and they could migrate from one localized area in his temporal lobe to other areas in his brain. Causing damage. Irreversible damage.

His dreams had come crashing down around him. He couldn't fool himself into believing he had things under control any longer. He couldn't keep Carly dangling on a string, either. He couldn't make promises his brain might not allow him to keep. He loved her too much to ask her to tie herself to a man who could end up the way Jack had...or worse. Better to ease himself out of her life. Better to free her to find a man who didn't have a giant question mark hanging over his future.

Only...why the hell did it hurt so much? When he thought of Carly with another man, his heart ached and throbbed like a broken bone that refused to heal, denying him sleep.

But that wasn't the worst of it. The worst was being deprived of Carly's presence in his life. Not being able to reach out his hand and touch her. Just touch her. Not seeing her blue eyes lighting up with humor, or hearing that gurgle of laughter she couldn't suppress. Not expressing his love in the way he loved best—the way that made her sigh and moan and call his name in ecstasy. Not holding her as she slept, breathing in the scent of warm woman that was uniquely Carly. Not being with her, keeping her safe.

What else could he do, though? What the hell else could he do except set her free?

At least she was safe…for now. Marsh Anderson, who'd pled guilty, was in jail and would stay there for a good long while. And Bobby Vernon wasn't a threat to Carly, even though his trial was months if not a year or more away, and he was out on bail in the meantime.

Thinking of Bobby reminded Shane of how he'd finally accepted the betrayal. He'd made sure to be in the courtroom when his deputy chief of staff was arraigned. He'd tried to give Bobby the benefit of the doubt—Shane really believed in the "innocent until proven guilty" concept—even though the evidence was piling up against him. But Bobby had refused to meet Shane's eyes at the arraignment, and in that moment he'd known his onetime friend was guilty as hell.

He still didn't know for sure why Bobby had done it—you couldn't ask a man who'd yet to be convicted that question—but the extensive investigation had revealed the answer most likely was…money. The Agenda Men, as Marsh Anderson referred to them, had had too much at stake with the pipeline bill, and they'd offered too much money for Bobby to resist.

Betrayed for money, Shane thought sadly. He didn't know how he would have gotten through these past weeks without Carly's support and understanding. Without her quiet comfort in the still of the night when memories of the Bobby he'd known in high school kept Shane from sleeping.

But all that was at an end. There would be no more Carly to call him "Marine" in that teasing way she had. No more Carly to grumble and groan when he woke her in the predawn hours—until he convinced her sleepy, early-morning sex was the best way to start the day. No more Carly to keep all the demons in his life at bay.

No. More. Carly. Period.

The pealing of the doorbell and a rapping on the front door jerked Shane out of his bleak contemplation of the sacrifice he was being forced to make. Before he could answer it, he heard the unmistakable sound of a key in the lock. He reached for his Beretta...which wasn't there. He'd stopped wearing it after Marsh Anderson had been caught.

He jerked the door open, ready to physically confront whoever it was, then stared in surprise at the sight of Carly on his doorstep, her hand reaching for the doorknob. "What the hell are you doing here?" They weren't the words he'd intended to say the next time he saw her. But then, he hadn't been prepared for her, either.

Then he realized she was steaming angry.

"You...you...*man*!" she blazed, pushing him backward with the flat of her hand as she forced her way into his home. She slammed the door shut behind her, then confronted him again. "What is wrong with you?"

Despite himself he laughed. Carly could always make him laugh, even if laughter was the furthest thing from his mind. "You mean, other than being a man?"

"That's exactly what I mean." Then she shook her head. "No, not just that. That's part of it, of course, you stupid, stubborn man." She poked him in the chest. "Don't pretend you're trying to find a graceful way out of a relationship you no longer want. Don't pretend you're trying to let me down gently."

"Is that what I'm doing?"

She ignored his question and poked him again with her pointer finger, sharper this time. "Don't pretend you don't love me to distraction, either, because I'm not buying it."

He steeled himself, knowing he'd never have a better opportunity. "I don't love you."

"You *liar*," she hissed. "You *coward*."

No one had ever accused him of cowardice, and the word stung. "Coward?" he demanded. "I saved your—"

"Don't wave your hero credentials in front of me," she threw at him. "You *are* a coward. An emotional coward. The same way I was for all of about one day."

That froze him in his tracks for a moment, but he made a quick recovery. "Just because I don't love—"

She cut him off. "Don't even go there," she insisted. "You love me, but you're afraid. And *that* makes you stupid enough to try to *protect* me." She used *protect* as if it were an insult. She suddenly stopped, closed her eyes and held up her hands, palms out. Telling him to wait. Just wait. From the varied expressions flitting over her face, Shane could tell she was trying to get control of her emotions.

When she finally opened her eyes and spoke again, she was much calmer. "I'm not stupid, Shane. It didn't take me long to figure out why you're trying to push me away. What you're afraid of, deep down. You received some bad news from your doctor at the Mayo Clinic. Because of that, you'd rather sacrifice what we have than risk being a burden on the woman you love."

She'd cut right to the heart of the matter in her insightful way. "Carly, I…"

"'In sickness and in health,' Shane. Those traditional wedding vows we both take seriously." She swallowed hard. "If I told you I had cancer," she whispered, "and I only had six months to live, would you walk away?"

Appalled she could even ask the question, his anger flared and he shot back, "Of course not."

"Then why are you asking *me* to walk away?"

"I'm—" *Not* was what he'd intended to say, but then he realized she was right. He'd never considered it from her perspective. Protecting his woman was what a man did—his father had taught him that by deed as well as word. Protection was his *right*, not just his duty. It hadn't occurred to him a woman could feel the same way about her man. That she had the *right* to protect him should the worst occur.

The only thing in his mind had been shielding Carly from the possibility that the seizures could cause mental damage, and subsequently drive him to take his own life…or become a drain on hers. His pride wouldn't allow him to face the possibility of becoming dependent on her, dragging her down.

But just as he would still love and cherish Carly if something catastrophic happened to her, she would still love and cherish him if their situations were reversed. Whether she wanted to take that risk with him or not was her choice to make. Trying to take that choice away from her was an insult.

"I love you, Shane," she said quietly. "I know I told you I wanted emotional distance. You knew that wasn't really true or even possible because we were already beyond that point. But you pretended, because you wanted to give me everything I asked for. You wanted to make me happy." Her eyes glistened with unshed tears. "I want the same thing. I want to make you happy, want to give you everything you need, whether you ask for it or not.

"That's what love is, Shane. I can't ask you not to die. I can't ask you not to get sick. Those things *happen*, whether we want them to or not. But I *can* ask you to let me be there for you, 'for better, for worse…in sickness and in health.' Just as I can ask you to be there for me."

She moved closer, sliding her arms around his waist and resting her head on his shoulder. His arms wrapped around her, holding her tight. "Whatever the doctor told you, we'll face it together," she assured him quietly. "Whatever the eventual outcome, we'll have each other, and that's all that matters."

"You don't know," he began.

She raised her face to his. "So tell me."

He laid it all out for her. The probabilities and the possibilities—including the worst-case scenarios. "So you see," he explained, "this new medication might not work, either. There are other meds they can prescribe, but every one has serious side effects to worry about. And there are no guarantees *any* of the meds will work—small percentage odds on something like that, but…it's still a risk."

"You're looking ahead and seeing only the worst that could happen, when the odds are it won't."

"But what if it does?" He'd done nothing but agonize over this possibility since the moment he'd seen his doctor, and that pain was reflected in his voice. "You'd be stuck with a husband who might not even remember you." And the worst thing he could imagine—"Who might not even remember loving you."

"'Don't borrow trouble, because you can never pay it back.' My mom used to say that to me," Carly said with a tiny smile of remembrance. "I was in my teens before I understood what she meant."

"My mom uses that phrase, too. She's really big on aphorisms."

"She sounds like a woman after my own heart. I'd love to meet her."

Carly wasn't hinting—she rarely did that, Shane knew. She usually came right out and said what she meant—so he knew she was just expressing her true feelings. But he suddenly realized he'd been wanting to introduce Carly to his mother for weeks, and not just for the symbolism involved, although that was a big part of it. The biggest reason, though, was that he thought the two women would hit it off because they were so much alike—although Carly was a career woman and his mom had been a stay-at-home wife and mother. But they both shone like a beacon in the areas that truly mattered—courage, strength, determination. And love. When they loved, they loved wholeheartedly. They would risk everything for that.

But knowing all that still didn't make it any easier for him. He'd been a protector for too long to change now, and try though he might, he couldn't get the words out to ask Carly to marry him. Even though he wanted it fervently.

But Carly seemed to understand the gulf he couldn't cross. "I love you, Shane. You're worth the risk," she said softly, her true-blue eyes holding his eyes captive... the way she held his heart captive. "Will you marry me?"

A wave of emotions swept through him, topmost being gratitude and humility. Gratitude that Carly had asked the question he couldn't, and humility that he didn't deserve her. Then another emotion surged to the fore—determination. Determination that he wouldn't pass up the opportunity to make Carly happy on the off chance that someday he'd break her heart through no intent of his own.

"Yes," he whispered, forcing the word past the obstruction in his throat. He cleared his throat and repeated, firmly this time, "Yes. God, yes."

"Good," she replied with a decisive nod. "I was hoping I wouldn't have to hurt you to make you agree."

He laughed again, because the idea of Carly physically overpowering him tickled his funny bone. She wasn't a little bit of a thing, but she was no match for him, either, and they both knew it. But there was a touch of relief thrown in with the humor, because he knew without a doubt Carly wouldn't have taken no for an answer. That her determination was as strong as his own. That she would do whatever she had to in order to convince him they belonged together, even if it meant fighting dirty.

"I love you, Carly." The words seemed to say themselves. "I can't promise forever—you know I can't. But if you'll take a chance on me, I'll do my damnedest to make sure you never regret it."

Those tears he'd seen in her eyes earlier returned, but she blinked rapidly to hold them firmly in check. "There's only one promise I want from you," she said now. "And it doesn't have anything to do with forever."

"What?"

"If we ever have children, I want your promise there'll be no corporal punishment."

He squeezed his eyes shut for a moment because the thought of children with Carly touched something deep inside him. Something that had been locked away since his unborn son had died with his mother fifteen years ago. When Shane's eyes opened again, they were damp. "You have my word."

She let out the breath she was holding, and smiled at him. "No matter what happens, I'll never regret loving you," she said with rock-solid assurance. And he knew she meant it. Some women might not be able to make that promise and keep it, but not his Carly. She would love him through the good times and the bad, just as he would love her. And she would accept whatever happened with the same dauntless courage with which she faced the world.

A promise like that deserved a kiss, which he gave her. But one kiss turned into two, which turned into a whole slew of kisses that couldn't begin to express the overflowing love in Shane's heart. There were no words, either, to encompass something this overwhelming, but he tried. "Carly, I...You know...God knows...Oh hell."

She nipped at his bottom lip. "Oorah, Marine," she murmured. "Don't tell me, show me."

And he did. Tying his own record.

Epilogue

Almost nine years later

On an unusually frigid January day on Pennsylvania Avenue in Washington, DC, Carly Edwards Jones held the Bible for her husband to rest his left hand on as he raised his right one in the air. Then, in firm, ringing tones, he repeated the words recited by the Chief Justice of the Supreme Court. "I do solemnly swear..." *You should be focusing on the meaning of the oath Shane is taking,* Carly told herself sternly, but all she could think of in this moment was that she was witnessing history in the making. Never before in the modern era had the US—or any country in the world for that matter—voted to have a man take the helm when he was publicly known to have epilepsy. Epilepsy completely controlled by medication, but the stigma still resided in the minds of many.

Shane's election had been a minor miracle because

he'd run as the independent he was. Two things had con-
tributed mightily to this unexpected achievement: the
country was sick to death of partisan politics and had
turned to Shane's candidacy with a sense of relief; and
the mainstream media had trumpeted Shane's qualifi-
cations for the job—including his stellar career in the
Marine Corps, his reputation as an incorruptible senator as well as his acts of personal bravery—rather than
focus on the illness caused by one of those acts.

Carly knew her reputation as a highly regarded reporter was partially responsible for the mainstream media's favorable treatment of Shane—and was fiercely
glad. The country needed a man like him, and whatever worked, worked.

She'd been forced to take a leave of absence from her
job—something she and Shane had discussed at length
before he threw his hat in the ring for the US presidency
two years ago. But she didn't regret her decision. Just
as she would never regret her decision to marry Shane.

"...So help me God." The immense roar from the
crowd that followed the final words of Shane's oath
snapped Carly back to the here and now. Her eyes met
her husband's, and she knew from the intensity in his
expression he was caught up in the solemnity of the
moment. But she also knew—because she knew *him*—
that he was thinking of her, as well. That in his supreme
moment he was thanking God for her love and support
over the years. That he acknowledged he couldn't have
accomplished this without her.

Despite the hundreds of cameras aimed at Shane, he
smiled at Carly. The private smile that started in his
eyes and eventually spread over his entire face. And she
smiled back. "Oorah, Marine," she mouthed at him, and

Shane's smile deepened, knowing that television networks everywhere would scramble to find lip readers who could tell the world what she'd said. He didn't care. Because even if they knew *what* she'd said, they wouldn't know why. And they wouldn't know what it really meant.

You can do this.

How many times over the past not-quite nine years had Carly said that to him? How many times had despair tugged him one way, while her belief in him had tugged him the other? Then there were the other occasions, too, happier ones. He'd been petrified with Carly in the delivery room because he couldn't bear to see her in pain. He'd also been worried because she was in her late thirties when they had their first child.

But she'd gasped those same words at him, and somehow he'd found the courage to participate in the miracle of birth. To receive their babies into his hands. First their son, Shane, Jr. Then, two years later, their daughter, Charis, named after Carly's mother. Both children were in attendance here today, even though they were still too young to understand why.

Shane wanted to mouth back, "I love you," for everything he owed Carly. For everything she'd given him, especially her steadfast belief in him. For understanding the man he was…and the man he could be. But he knew that would never do. Not in this arena. Instead, he nodded slightly to acknowledge the message she'd sent, and mouthed one word back to her. "Oorah."

Which, in their private parlance, meant *I can do this…so long as I have you.*

Then he clasped Carly's hand in his, and they turned to acknowledge the cheers of the crowd. Together.

* * * * *

Don't miss the next thrilling installment in the
MAN ON A MISSION *miniseries!*
And don't forget the previous titles in the miniseries:

A FATHER'S DESPERATE RESCUE
LIAM'S WITNESS PROTECTION
ALEC'S ROYAL ASSIGNMENT
KING'S RANSOM
McKINNON'S ROYAL MISSION
CODY WALKER'S WOMAN

Available now from Harlequin Romantic Suspense!

REQUEST YOUR FREE BOOKS!
2 FREE NOVELS PLUS 2 FREE GIFTS!

⬢ HARLEQUIN®

ROMANTIC suspense

Sparked by danger, fueled by passion

YES! Please send me 2 FREE Harlequin® Romantic Suspense novels and my 2 FREE gifts (gifts are worth about $10). After receiving them, if I don't wish to receive any more books, I can return the shipping statement marked "cancel." If I don't cancel, I will receive 4 brand-new novels every month and be billed just $4.74 per book in the U.S. or $5.49 per book in Canada. That's a savings of at least 12% off the cover price! It's quite a bargain! Shipping and handling is just 50¢ per book in the U.S. and 75¢ per book in Canada.* I understand that accepting the 2 free books and gifts places me under no obligation to buy anything. I can always return a shipment and cancel at any time. Even if I never buy another book, the two free books and gifts are mine to keep forever.

240/340 HDN GH3P

Name	(PLEASE PRINT)	
Address		Apt. #
City	State/Prov.	Zip/Postal Code

Signature (if under 18, a parent or guardian must sign)

Mail to the **Reader Service:**
IN U.S.A.: P.O. Box 1867, Buffalo, NY 14240-1867
IN CANADA: P.O. Box 609, Fort Erie, Ontario L2A 5X3

Want to try two free books from another line?
Call 1-800-873-8635 or visit www.ReaderService.com.

* Terms and prices subject to change without notice. Prices do not include applicable taxes. Sales tax applicable in N.Y. Canadian residents will be charged applicable taxes. Offer not valid in Quebec. This offer is limited to one order per household. Not valid for current subscribers to Harlequin Romantic Suspense books. All orders subject to credit approval. Credit or debit balances in a customer's account(s) may be offset by any other outstanding balance owed by or to the customer. Please allow 4 to 6 weeks for delivery. Offer available while quantities last.

Your Privacy—The Reader Service is committed to protecting your privacy. Our Privacy Policy is available online at www.ReaderService.com or upon request from the Reader Service.

We make a portion of our mailing list available to reputable third parties that offer products we believe may interest you. If you prefer that we not exchange your name with third parties, or if you wish to clarify or modify your communication preferences, please visit us at www.ReaderService.com/consumerschoice or write to us at Reader Service Preference Service, P.O. Box 9062, Buffalo, NY 14240-9062. Include your complete name and address.

HRS15

Fully dressed, they crossed the stable area with no one
but the horses to see their progress. Up the back road to
the quiet and dark house, they climbed the stairs to the
back patio, skirting the pool to her suite of rooms. "How
did you know which room was mine the other day?"

"I didn't. I took my chances. I knew you were housed
in the left wing. I'm just lucky I didn't knock on Fowler's
door."

She laughed at that, finding it extremely funny. "You
would have had some 'splaining to do," she said, wiping
her eyes.

They stopped outside the door. "I had a good time,
Jake. I will admit rubbing ointment into your shoulders
was just a ruse to get inside to talk to you."

Hooking his thumbs in the front pockets of his jeans,
Jake watched her, his expression light. "Sassy and
underhanded."

"Guilty." The longing on her face made his heart trip a little.

"Come here, sweetheart," he whispered.

She didn't hesitate and went right into his arms. He shifted, widening his stance, when she slipped her arms around his waist and turned her face against him. Resting his jaw against her head, he began slowly massaging the small of her back. Alanna tightened her arms around him and Jake could detect a light quivering in her, as though she had been braced for pain that hadn't materialized. Shifting his hold, he cradled her head firmly against him and brushed a gentling kiss against her temple, his expression unsettled.

He didn't know what in hell was going to happen to them. And if he'd realized anything during the past few days, it was that he wasn't sure what kind of future they had, if any. He suspected when she found out about why he was there and who he really was, that would be it.

Was he a fool to hope for a different outcome?

Don't miss
HIGH-STAKES COLTON by Karen Anders,
available September 2016 wherever
Harlequin® Romantic Suspense
books and ebooks are sold.

www.Harlequin.com

HRSEXP0816

Turn your love of reading into rewards you'll love with

Harlequin My Rewards

**Join for FREE today at
www.HarlequinMyRewards.com**

Earn **FREE BOOKS** of your choice.

Experience **EXCLUSIVE OFFERS** and contests.

Enjoy **BOOK RECOMMENDATIONS**
selected just for you.

PLUS! Sign up now
and get **500** points
right away!

MYR16R